THE SUPPLICANT

THE SUPPLICANT

LUCINDA BETTS

APHRODISIA

KENSINGTON BOOKS

http://www.kensingtonbooks.com

For JLP, who excels in publicity.
For WTT, who knows how to appease the gods.
For SKK, who wields a mean red pen.

1

In the cool shade of the adobe wall, the knife blade in Sureya's hand glittered madly, dangerously. For a heartbeat she thought she heard the impossible, her little brother's gurgling coo. Careful of the thorns, she looked up from the blood-red roses expecting to see one of her charges.

Instead, she gasped. A second sun burned on the horizon—a lava-red heart surrounded by a halo of deep blue. Two icy white tails trailed behind, long and bright against the summer sky.

A strange sensation pervaded her senses. Between her thighs a rhythmic pulsing began, matched by the throbbing of the heart in the sky. She became aware of the length of her neck, the weight of her breasts, the curve of her lips.

A catty voice from the cherry tree in the distance caught her attention. "Oh, no," it said. Had one of the children climbed the tree?

Looking across the courtyard, she saw no child. Her employer, Risham, was plucking the last fat cherries of the season.

He cupped several in his hand, looking like he was holding something precious. Even in her confusion, her nipples hardened with desire. He was supposed to be in town, with his wife.

"Risham," she called.

With a dark look, he strode toward her. He looked purposeful and strong. Knowing she shouldn't, Sureya admired his lithe movements, his fine features.

"Risham," she breathed as he moved into her space. The musky scent of him swirled around her, luring her toward him. Wordlessly, he cupped her cheek in his hand, his eyes locked on hers. She recognized desire. He burned with it, just as she did. "What are you—"

But he raised his sun-soaked fingers to her lips, and brought the warm, succulent fruit to her mouth. The sweet juice kissed her. The moment ripened in her mind. She could turn away now. She could leave Risham to his wife and children.

Instead, she opened her mouth, accepting his gift.

His finger brushed against her lip as she took the cherry, sending electric jolts through her. The tangy sweetness spread over her tongue, delighting her senses. Putting his hand on the curve of her waist, he pulled her toward him. Closing her eyes, she yielded to his touch.

"Oh, no," she heard again from the branches across the courtyard. The voice sounded husky, almost feline.

She opened her eyes and found Risham gone. Had he even been there? Alarm flooded through her. What was happening? And where were her charges?

"Nika!" she called. "Dayy! Lulal!"

Across the courtyard, gray feathers fluttered among the leafy branches. A catbird struggled in its nest, shoving something around with its beak. "This just won't do," the bird called to her, and then it meowed.

Sureya blinked, and the new sun shifted in the sky again, lurching its fiery heart closer to the horizon.

Standing in the cool shade of the fat adobe wall, Sureya's nipples hardened, almost painfully. Her breasts were tight, longing for something to loosen them—a hand, lips, fingertips. Anything would be better than this unfamiliar longing.

"Nika! Dayy! Lulal!" she called.

"These won't do at all," the bird said in its catty voice. It tossed its eggs—glossy and blue—out of its nest and into the air.

Sureya gasped, wanting to catch the eggs, wanting to return them to the feathery safety of their nest. She ran, hands outstretched, knowing she wasn't close enough to help.

But as the eggs fell, they hatched. Naked chicks squeaked indignation at their early flight. Midair, they flowered into frothy blossoms and floated softly to the ground.

The chicks, Sureya thought as a bloom caressed her cheek. Fighting a growing panic, she looked around the courtyard for the children in her care, the children of her heart.

They stood right before her.

But the yard, filled with the happy screams and laughter of older children just moments ago, was eerily silent. Nika and Dayy eyed the sky, oblivious of the catbird in the cherry tree, to chicks that turned into flowers.

Ignoring the throbbing between her thighs, hoping the sensation would go away, Sureya watched the red heart pound on the horizon.

"It's beautiful," Dayy said.

"But so strange," Nika added.

The children were enthralled. Watching the new sun, awe etched in their plump expressions, they stood rapt. Only the youngest child still chattered at her side, happily, thoughtlessly.

The throbbing between Sureya's thighs matched the pulsing on the horizon beat for beat. Sureya sighed, getting a hold of her strange emotions.

She set aside the basket of roses she and the youngest child were cutting. Over the thick peach adobe wall, fields of artichokes and grapes spread before her, just as expected. No talking birds. But the brawny peasants had stopped their work to stare at the horizon, pale-skinned hands on their white foreheads to better see the new sun.

Little Lulal grabbed Sureya's skirt and tugged. Sureya ripped her gaze away from the new sun and looked down, amazed even now at how much the girl's eyes looked like her father's. Her skin was as dark as her father's, so beautiful. So unlike her own. Affection for the girl surged through Sureya's heart.

She ignored the liquid silk flowing between her legs. She ignored her aching nipples, the way she felt suddenly aware of the fullness of her lips.

"Why's everyone quiet all of a sudden, Miss Sureya?" Lulal asked. Sureya realized the little girl couldn't see above the wall. She picked up her beloved charge and balanced the girl on her hip. Lulal clung to Sureya's side like she belonged there.

"Now you can see it," Sureya said, pointing to the bizarre sky. The warm comfort of Lulal's body soothed her jangling nerves. The child smelled like her father.

"What is it?" Lulal asked. "The sky looks so weird."

"I don't know, little girl. It's probably nothing."

But the plaza bells started ringing wildly, off kilter and chaotically, as if to contradict her calming words. Someone in town was yanking on the tower ropes, randomly and hard.

Hard.

Hard hands. Hard mouths. Hard bodies pounding into hers. What was happening?

For a frantic moment, Sureya wondered whether she should run, take the children and go someplace safe. The mountains, maybe. But how would the children's parents find them? She couldn't leave without Risham—without his shiny brown hair and his deep, lambent eyes. She'd miss the burning look he sometimes gave her across the dinner table, while he sat next to his wife and their children.

And how could she outrun the sky?

"Let's go inside," Sureya said to the older children over the resonating clanging. Her charges looked at her blankly, and Sureya realized they couldn't hear her over the cacophony.

"Into the house!" she shouted, pointing to the door with her empty hand. The two older children ran inside, their hands over their ears, screaming. Nika was crying, her face pink in anger and fear. Sureya cursed the bells. The new sun was frightening enough without their riotous racket.

Sureya's upper thighs slid together as she fled into the house. An image—a woman's dark hair and skin, crimson nails—danced through her mind. The woman carried a scent of sun-ripe mulberries, a dangerous aura of sensuality.

The thick adobe walls of the house muffled sound and cooled the hot summer air, but her small charges were staring at her with terror-struck eyes.

"Shh, my little girl," she said, petting Nika's forehead. "Don't fret so. It's a little nothing."

"What is it?" asked Dayy, worry etched on his eleven-year-old face. "What is it, exactly?" He raised his voice slightly to overcome the pealing bells.

Sureya ignored the question. She ignored the swollen pearl between her thighs. Still carrying Lulal, she closed the door behind them with her foot. Then she walked around the house and shuttered the windows.

What would Risham do, if he were here with his children?

Sureya knew the answer—he'd pretend everything was normal. He'd make things customary with his calm attitude.

"Now," she said in a steady voice as she closed the last shutter, "we'll be able to hear each other." Maybe it would shut out some of the afternoon's evil, too.

"But what *is* it?" Dayy asked again.

Sureya put Lulal down on the floor and stroked her head. "Lulal, my love, why don't you go with Nika and ask Cook to prepare tea and cakes for us?"

"Yay!" Lulal chirped. She grabbed her sister's hand and dragged her toward Cook's lair. Trailing behind her little sister, Nika shot a look at her nanny. Sureya read reluctance to leave the safety of her nanny's side.

"But what—" the boy said again.

"Dayy!" Sureya said. "I heard your question, and I don't know the answer."

"But you always know the answer," the boy said, his green eyes shining in dismay. He looked more like his mother than the other children did, and Sureya had to remind herself that she had nothing for which to feel guilty.

Except . . . she'd eaten a summer cherry from sun-soaked fingers. And the catbird had fed her eggs to the wind.

Images of a woman's dark hand sliding over her white breast skated through her mind: long, tapered nails over her hardened nipple. The area between her thighs ached for—for something she couldn't name.

What was wrong with her?

"Miss Sureya!" the boy said.

"I'm sorry, Dayy," she said, shaking herself from her inappropriate thoughts. "I don't know what that thing is in the sky, and I just wish those bells would stop ringing—"

Just then, the bells fell silent.

"How'd you do that?" Dayy asked.

Sureya laughed, sounding nervous to herself. "I didn't do it!" She wiped her damp palms on her skirt and said, "The priests probably stopped the village madman from pulling the ropes."

"Do you think they know about the new sun—the priests, I mean? What will they do?"

"Dayy, my love, I just don't know. The holy fathers probably have to make a sacrifice or two and say a whole bunch of prayers. Then it'll probably leave."

"But it's a new sun," the boy said. "How can anyone make the sun leave?"

The girls burst into the room before she could answer, and Sureya breathed a sigh of relief.

"Look! Cook gave us honey!" Lulal said. Nika hurried back to the dining room with a kitchen servant in tow. The sweet scent of almond cakes filled the room, warm and delicious. The servant set out a pot of honeyed *khal* and plates for the rolls.

"Thank you, Weset," Sureya said to the servant, and to the children, she said, "Sit, please."

Sureya placed the last roll on Dayy's plate just as the door swung open, wafting hot, dusty air over them. "Risham!" Sureya said, resisting the urge to throw herself into his strong, safe arms. "Daddy!" the children shouted.

His gaze flew over the children sitting around the table eating almond cakes. "Thank the One God, the children are safe!" Finally, he looked at his nanny. "Thank you, Sureya." He sounded surprisingly relieved.

Sureya blinked. His fingers dripped with what looked like cherry juice. Had there been a real danger?

But when his eyes locked on hers, she felt a different hazard. Her knees tingled and her stomach fluttered. "You're welcome," she said.

"What's happening, father?" Dayy asked.

"And where's Momma?" Nika asked.

The front door opened again, this time smacking the adobe wall behind it with a loud crack.

"Momma!" Lulal cried, rushing from the table and flinging herself into her mother's arms. Nika did the same. Even in the chaos, Sureya caught Dayy's look. He dearly wanted to find comfort in his mother's arms, but he didn't want to look like a baby. Sureya stepped behind him and surreptitiously put her hand on his shoulder.

Fajal closed the door and paused to pet her girls. Sureya watched the woman close her eyes as she ran her brown fingers over the silky hair of her children.

Sureya squashed a jagged pang of jealousy. Of course the children loved their mother. They might also love Sureya in their own way, but she would always be hired help. She would always be white.

Watching the mother's fingers as they stroked her children's heads, Sureya wondered whether it were Fajal's hand she'd imagined skimming under her chemise, hardening her nipples. What would it feel like if Fajal actually touched her like that?

But somehow the thought didn't seem . . . accurate. Fajal didn't smell like mulberries. The scent of ginger wafted around her employer.

Sureya shook her head. Why was she thinking such absurd and disturbing things?

She snuck a gaze at Risham and found him looking at her. Was that burning intensity she saw, or was it her heated imagination? His fingertips were stained a cherry red, and her mouth watered for sun-soaked summer fruit.

Silly girl, she chided herself, ignoring her wobbly knees. *Stupid girl.* She would always be in the peasant class. Her skin color ensured it. Risham belonged to his wife, and no amount of longing would bring him to her.

Sureya shook her head. She'd never do anything to hurt this family. They were all she had. The bloody barbarians had orphaned her; only Risham's and Fajal's kindness redeemed her.

Fajal untangled herself from her brood and straightened. Then she walked over to the heavy door and locked it, making butterflies flutter through Sureya's stomach. Why would the door need locking in the afternoon?

Then Fajal looked right at her, as if the older woman could

read all the longing Sureya felt, as if Fajal could sense the strange magic pulsing through her thighs and breasts and lips and fingers.

"Children," Fajal said, "I want you to play by yourselves quietly for a few moments—in the cellar."

"But Momma!" Lulal objected. "It's dark down there. And stinky."

"Sureya will light a lantern for you—no, two lanterns. Grab your paints and your books if you want them, Nika, and yes, Lulal, you may bring your stuffed pony. Be quick."

Why did Fajal want them hidden in the dark amongst the roots and apples? Squashing her growing alarm, she turned to usher the children to the cellar.

"Sureya," Fajal added.

"Yes, ma'am?"

"Please return to the study immediately after you get them settled."

"Yes, ma'am."

"You'd better hurry," her mistress added in her smoky voice. "I want to talk to you."

2

With a feeling of unease, the king of Marotiri inhaled deeply. Scraps of ancient song wafted over the wall in the breeze. Voices kept time with swinging scythes, and peasants worked calmly under the warm sun, singing stories filled with longing, with ache.

Wondering if the feeling was contagious, Kalief looked over the rooftop parapet to the fields sprawling before him. Sheep grazed placidly on the hilltop. Barley, tomatoes, and grapes filled the flatlands. Everywhere he looked he saw an abundance of food. He saw safety and prosperity.

He saw it, but he didn't feel it.

"Sire!" His castellan burst onto the parapet.

"What is it?"

"The barbarians, sire! They've attacked Xoreztown!"

"By the Above, they're getting bold. Ready my warhorse," he ordered, turning toward the door.

"He's ready, sire. The soldiers are waiting for you."

Running now, Kalief shouted over his shoulder, "Teron?"

"He's there, too, sire."

"Inform Abbess Anhara!" he shouted to his castellan as he pounded down the stairs toward the stable. Reaching the base of the tower, he flung open the stable door and shouted, "Teron!"

"Here!" His second was mounted, his huge gray pawing the ground impatiently. One hundred mounted soldiers waited on Teron's cue in silence.

"What do we have?" he asked Teron, vaulting atop his horse.

"The standard company—fifteen longbows, fifteen short-bows, seventy swordsmen."

"Magic users?"

"No, sire," Teron answered. "Do you want the Abbess Anhara or her nuns?"

Kalief grabbed his reins, and his horse leapt forward toward the stable door, eager to run. "No," he answered Teron. "She knows where we're going. Let's run."

As one, Teron and the other soldiers followed him, and the pounding of the hooves behind him shook the ground. The sound sent an undeniable surge of power through him. He wanted to annihilate the barbarians.

But as they approached Xoreztown, Kalief saw smoke pouring from within the walls. The acrid odor burned his nostrils. The village would be lost. "The One's balls," Kalief swore.

He ached to bury his sword in throat after barbarian throat, in gut after gut. Battle lust licking through his veins, Kalief kicked his stallion, but his outrider galloped past him. It was the man's job to draw out any enemy, and his horse was the swiftest among the king's herd. Kalief should have let him pass.

But bloodlust had replaced sense. Kalief urged his stallion into a faster gallop. He was tired of letting others take his risks.

With bone-jarring effort, his horse approached the outrider's. Kalief shot a grin to the young soldier, who stared at him with astonishment.

"Yeehaa!" he shouted to his horse, but the stallion's muscle-bound form was bred for combat, not speed, and the outrider's horse began to pass them.

Then the outrider's horse exploded from beneath him. Crouched over his stallion's neck, Kalief saw hooves churn through the air as the brave horse tried to gallop even as its legs twisted over each other amid blood and foam. An arrow protruded through the horse's neck, and another through his rider's chest. The outrider, just a boy, still wore an astonished expression.

Having more sense than he himself, Kalief's men surrounded him, protecting him from enemy arrows. Locking his gaze on Xoreztown's front gate, Kalief once again urged his horse.

As he and his men neared the gate, barbarians on their scrappy dun ponies poured into the surrounding sand and fields. Yanking his sword from his scabbard, Kalief targeted a bearded barbarian and kicked to spur his horse.

His horse knew exactly what to do, and Kalief released the reins to swing. "Heyah!" he bellowed, lopping off a barbarian's arm at the shoulder. He jerked his sword back and locked another barbarian into his gaze. His stallion rushed toward the pony, and Kalief swung again with another mighty yell. His opponent's bearded head flew to the ground.

All around him Kalief heard the sounds of his soldiers chopping body parts from the barbarians, who seemed to buzz around his men like angry bees. As his horse locked onto a third man, Kalief raised his sword. Blood dripped from it to his unarmored thigh. Hope surged through him—maybe this time, they'd win the battle. With a vicious battle cry, he swung for the man's neck, but the barbarian's rangy pony ducked away at the last moment.

As Kalief's horse lunged left, compensating for the shifted balance from the futile swing, he heard. "Keyyyyieee!" Kalief didn't understand the word cried in the ancient language.

But the meaning became clear as the barbarians each turned their ponies west and began to flee as one.

"Follow them!" Kalief cried to his own men. His horse needed no urging. Wheeling on its hind legs, it sprang toward the barbarian herd.

As the sand-colored ponies ran, their dark dorsal stripes confused Kalief's eye. His archers seemed to have a similar problem. Arrows flew too long or too short, too far wide. One hit a pony's hindquarter, but it glanced off harmlessly.

And then the enemy horses disappeared altogether into the sand. Kalief stared at his men, wondering if the entire battle was a figment of his imagination.

"I hate when they do that," Teron said, heaving from exertion. "What black wizardry do they use?"

"Maybe Anhara can tell us," Kalief answered. "But they're getting bold, and that worries me."

"And close," his second said. "They're getting close. Shall I give the order to ride back to Xoreztown, see what's left of the folk?"

Kalief nodded, and they walked back in silence, men and horse alike catching their breath.

Devastation. That's what Kalief saw upon entering the Xoreztown gate. Every building had been set aflame, but not before the people of the town had nailed a barbarian to the gate. His eyes had been burned out.

"Barbarian skin's unnatural," he heard one young soldier say to another. "It's not dark like it should be, but it isn't white like a slave's either."

"Amber skinned," his friend replied. "That's what my mother calls it."

"People of Xoreztown!" Kalief called in a loud voice. "It's safe to come out!"

"The barbarians are gone!" Teron added after conferring with another outrider.

But no one came forward.

Every building Kalief examined was destroyed, and his horse stepped around the body of a man with a barbarian arrow through his chest. A well-made bed and chest of drawers lay half out of a house. The sheets of the bed were soaked in what looked like blood. Kalief peered into the doorway and saw a woman with her head hacked from her body, her skirt ripped and legs spread.

"They've burned the town larder, sire," Teron noted. "There's no food."

"But the people," Kalief said. "Where are they?"

"Sire!" a soldier called. "Over here! In the infirmary!" Terror laced the man's voice.

When his horse turned the corner toward the soldier's voice, Kalief saw another solider puking into the dust, hanging onto his horse for support.

Hundreds of Xoreztown folk had been shot here. They lay crumpled upon each other in a gruesome heap. Men, children, women were filled with arrows. Blackened blood oozed from throats and eyes and chests. So many people lay piled atop each other that Kalief couldn't tell where one ended and another began.

"Sire," Teron said. "Look at this."

Kalief nudged his horse toward the infirmary door. "What is it?"

"All the vaccines are gone, sire. But most of the other medical equipment is still here."

As king, Kalief's duty included protecting the people of his land, peasant and nobility alike. This thought burned through his mind as he paced the heights of his gray parapet. He was a failure.

His stomach constricted while his mind raced in circles for a solution. He'd been searching for an answer for months, maybe a year. And he'd come up with nothing. His soldiers couldn't catch the barbarians, couldn't stop them. Not even Anhara with her scrying bowl could see how they faded into the sand.

And the barbarians were striking increasingly closer.

Kalief needed to try something different, something unexpected.

"What are you thinking about, my lord?" Her voice was light and sweet. It should have been the perfect antidote to the black morass in which he found himself.

Kalief only shook his head in reply.

"My lord?" she asked again.

Kalief noted that her eyebrows were perfectly arched, two thin crescents, a shade darker than her auburn hair. Lady Teanne lightly ran her fingers over his hand, tracing the length of it, to ensure that his thoughts ran in her direction.

"About the land," he finally said to his fiancée. "I'm thinking about my people and the villages and the land."

"My serious king," she said, taking his dark hand in hers. The pink of her gown perfectly offset the dark color of her skin. She held his hand above her head and spun so that her frothy skirt flared out around her calves.

Lady Teanne had gorgeous calves, but Kalief just shrugged his agreement.

Irrepressible, Teanne laughed. She spun again, letting the sunlight glint off the metallic buckles of her shoes.

"Look at this beautiful day," she commanded, leaning her breasts against his arms. "The fields are full. The sun's bright, and you have a young, willing fiancée." She danced around him in graceful little steps. "I'm right here in your arms."

Despite himself, he felt a smile start.

"See?" she said, tossing her head back in a movement he knew was meant to show off her elegant throat. It worked. Her throat was kissable. "You smile."

"You're indeed lovely, my Lady Teanne."

She nodded at the compliment, a playful look in her blue eyes, so shockingly pale against her dark complexion. "I can get you to do more than smile, you know," she said. Her husky voice suggested smoky taverns and hot mouths, clever fingers and yielding bodies.

When she moved in close to him and surreptitiously caressed his cock, she grinned at his look of surprise. He was as hard as the gray walls around them.

"Success!" she cried.

Hungering for more than play, he pulled her toward him roughly, lips and tongue seeking hers. He wouldn't call Lady Teanne's kisses maidenly, but that suited him fine. One taste of her, and all else would be forgotten.

At least for a few moments, he could overlook the horrors he'd seen, ignore the horrors he didn't know how to prevent.

The gentle caress of her lips against his took a new flavor, became hungrier, and she had his full attention.

Kalief groaned in pleasure when his lady wrapped her hand around the back of his neck and pulled him tighter, forbade him to leave.

He let her twine her tongue around his. She led the dance and he followed, glad for her strength and the healing in her touch. She pressed against him, her hardened nipples gliding across the breadth of his chest.

Finally Kalief tried to take the matter into his own hands. He slid his palms up from her waist, but Teanne was still in charge. Without breaking the kiss, she twisted so he had no choice but to caress her breast.

And he felt like she'd come from the Above. If only he could climb inside of her, deeply and completely. If only he could become her. Then the cries of orphaned and mutilated children would leave his mind. His eyes would no longer see charred fields and razed buildings.

Her world held no room for such atrocities.

Teanne's perfect breasts nearly spilled from the low-cut gown. Without removing her dress, his tongue found a nipple, his lips easily capturing it. She pressed toward him, sending a jolt of desire jagging through him.

As dark as he felt, she wanted him.

Then Lady Teanne broke away, took a step back and smoothed down her skirt. "My lord," she said, suddenly demure. "I know we aren't yet wed, but our betrothal's solid . . ." She paused, then looked at him from under her lashes. "If it pleases you, my lord . . ." Lady Teanne slowly lifted her skirt, first showing ankles, then calves, then—by the One God in the Above—she showed her well-honed thighs. They gleamed in the sun.

"It pleases me very much," Kalief said in a voice he hardly recognized. He stepped toward her, intent on finishing what she'd started.

With a teasing glint in her eye, Lady Teanne stepped back toward the wall, and Kalief gasped.

A yellow serpent slithered toward his betrothed.

And then it was gone.

"What?" asked Lady Teanne.

Kalief simply shook his head. Was he losing his mind?

She looked over her shoulder for the source of Kalief's distress and gasped herself. "What's that thing in the sky?"

Kalief blinked. How'd he missed the fiery ball adding light to the already blazing sun? Then he knew. "The Supplicant," he muttered, feeling hope pulse through his heart for the first time in months, maybe years.

"What did you call it?" she asked.

But he could only stare in silence.

"It's like . . ." Teanne fumbled for words. "It's like the burning eye of the One God peering down on us." She straightened her skirt, perhaps not wanting to be found behaving in such a wanton manner under the One God's eye.

Kalief shook his head. "It's a comet."

"Comet? I've never heard that word."

"The priests believe it's a harbinger."

"Of what?"

"War. Pestilence. Plague." *The Supplicant*, he thought, but he couldn't bring himself to say the words again.

The land hadn't seen a Supplicant in generations. Scripture told that when the One God's eye inspected them and found them wanting, a Supplicant had come of age.

And she could save them.

Despite the augmented sun beating its warmth down upon them, Lady Teanne wrapped her arms around herself, shivering.

A hissing, slithering sound came from the parapet. The yellow snake had returned, gliding across the gray slate parapets in a way Kalief had never seen a snake slip. It molded its form against the square brick blocks, fitting within the parapet's sharp angles.

The snake smiled at Kalief and said, "She's here."

"Who's here?"

"What are you talking about?" Teanne asked, following Kalief's eyes but apparently seeing nothing.

Kalief ignored his fiancée and stared at the serpent. It had sprouted feathers, feathers that shifted colors like the inside of abalone shells. First the feathers were white, then orange, then pink as a sunset. The snake lifted an eyebrow at Kalief and winked. "She thinks you've lost your mind."

"Who?" Kalief asked, feeling like an owl.

Then he grew aware of Teanne's voice. It sounded muffled, like myriad doors separated her from him. He breathed a sigh of relief.

"Let me show you something." The words fell from the feathered serpent's mouth like raindrops in the desert. Like the sand, Kalief ached for them, craved the growth they would bring.

"Show me," he breathed, wondering if he'd gone mad. Teanne's voice was silent now, and the sky had deepened to an unreal indigo.

"I think I will," the serpent said.

The clouds, the trees, his castle—all were obscured by the violent indigo of a stormy sky.

But a woman with fine, milky skin appeared before him, in an unfamiliar temple. He'd never seen skin so white. Some of the lords in his court plundered the service class for women so pale, but not him. Chocolate-colored Teanne made his mouth water.

"Cogitate less, observe more," the coatl hissed.

Kalief saw feathered and winged snakes carved into the stone above the woman's head, into the divan on which she lay.

He knew of no people, no land, who worshipped the feathered serpent, but still . . . this place felt holy. Godly power reverberated throughout her temple, originating from the woman.

A diadem made of entwined snakes held back her shocking hair—hair so strange in color that he didn't have a name for it. It was the color of spilled blood or oak leaves in autumn.

Scripture said the Supplicant had hair of flame.

The priestess—whoever heard of a priestess, especially a Supplicant priestess?—turned her gray eyes toward him, appraising him coolly. No matter he was king of all Marotiri, and she was no older than he. No matter that her skin was white and his was the color of the highest-ranking nobility: this snake goddess assessed him.

Despite everything, she somehow managed to outrank him.

"You may approach," she said. The woman with the white skin did not call him sire.

Too curious to insist on protocol, he walked toward her.

"What is your heart's wish?" she asked. "What's brought you to me?"

Kalief stumbled for an answer. He thought she'd come to him.

But then a voice fell from his mouth. "It's my son, Supplicant. He's in the throes of the pox. Black pustules cover him, and a fever burns through him like a fire through tinder."

And Kalief felt exactly like he had a beloved son in the throes of volepox. Despite the fact he had no son, had never seen volepox.

"And you wish to save him?" she asked.

Kalief nodded, his hair still damp from a recent bath. "I wish him healthy and happy." He wore nothing but a silk toga.

The Supplicant held a graceful hand toward him, inviting him to approach. The moment her skin touched his, his cock hardened. He looked down and gasped. His skin was as pale as a slave's! He'd become a peasant!

Then he realized what he was seeing, what he was somehow experiencing. The Supplicant was taking a common man to bed so that she could save his son.

This was not acceptable. She could not fuck a common man and then fuck a noble.

"Stop!" he cried, but the Supplicant gently took him in her arms, as if his words didn't exist in her realm.

Her cool palms ran the length of his arms, filling him with an unreal desire. She could save his son from volepox! Her gray eyes, wide and beautiful, weren't dilated. She'd not been drugged as required by Scripture.

This shocking woman took a peasant to her bed willingly, gracefully. And without the sacred drug.

Her lips slid over his, electrifying him with pleasure. Not even Teanne's skilled touch affected him as deeply as the pure chemistry of this woman. He slid his hand around the back of her head, savoring the silky texture of her hair between his fingers. Then he pulled her to him roughly.

He closed his eyes so he didn't have to see the white skin of the man whose body he somehow inhabited.

The mind of the servant bubbled through to Kalief's consciousness. Awe that someone as powerful as the Supplicant would suffer his touch filled him.

But she yielded to him completely, forbidding him to doubt his right to touch her. Her mouth opened to his. Her breasts arched toward his opened palm. Almost reverently, he ran a thumb over her nipple.

She arched toward him, inviting him to suck, to nip. Normally he savored this part of lovemaking, the foreplay, the teasing touches. But the man whose body he inhabited had a different idea, and Kalief wasn't strong enough to override it.

She helped him guide his cock inside her hot folds, and he thrust. He plunged into her, hard and fast. He slammed into her core with ferocious abandonment. Each thrust brought an image of the beloved's son to his mind, as well as a peasant woman with broad white features. The man he inhabited felt a strong sense of betrayal in fucking the Supplicant.

But the white-skinned woman appeared to have no such compunction. She bucked against him, pleasure obvious from her rolled-back eyes, her hardened nipples.

And then she came, the hot clamping of her cunt over his cock.

Tears ran down the peasant's face after he came, the Supplicant's arms wrapped comfortingly around him. She held him for another minute, then he slid to his knees and said the ceremonial words with which Kalief was so familiar, words pounded into him by learned monks since his schooling began all those years ago.

"One God in the Above," he began. "Please hear my prayer. I have granted You a gift—the passion of Your Supplicant. Please grant my prayer."

The peasant held back sobs. Kalief shook with the effort. He wanted to see his son playing stickball with the other boys. He wanted to see his handsome face free of pustules, feel his brow free of fever.

"Please bless my son with health and happiness," Kalief said through the peasant's mouth. "Save him from the pox and all its effects."

"Wait!" Kalief tried to shout. "You can't use 'and' or 'or' in your prayers—Scripture says. And the Supplicant can't grant the wishes of peasants. The Supplicant belongs to the great lords and ladies of the land!"

But his objections went unheard, falling powerlessly into the ether.

Velvet smoke filled the air, and the vision melted away, leaving Kalief floundering for some hook to reality.

The serpent fluffed its feathers and ran its fangs through the small plumes on its breast.

Kalief could only stare at it in wonder. "Are you a demon?" the man finally asked the snake.

If snakes could laugh, this one did. And it shook its head. "You better see to your fiancée," the creature said. "She's unconscious on the floor."

Kalief, remembering Lady Teanne, began to look for her.

The snake took wing in the summer breeze. "Open your mind, King Kalief, and all will be yours. And beware! I don't think your Lady Teanne will appreciate sharing you with the woman about to enter your life."

Kalief knew a warning when he heard one.

"I saw a vision," Kalief said to Abbess Anhara. "The new Supplicant is dangerous."

Anhara raised an inky eyebrow by the slightest increment. "Dangerous." Her voice was flat. "Perhaps it's simply that you find female sexuality dangerous?"

"Can you scry her?" Kalief asked, ignoring her snide comment.

"Scry her?"

"Everyone is going to be after her," Kalief said. "You have to find her first."

"Me?" Although Kalief thought she should be shocked by his suggestion, the stillness that surrounded her masked any surprise.

"The priests will want her. So will the barbarians. Surely even your nuns want her."

"We want a peaceful and prosperous land," Anhara corrected gently.

"That doesn't exactly contradict what I said."

"What's stopping you from retrieving the girl yourself?" Anhara asked.

"She's a whore! A king can't be seen fetching a whore." The abbess's eyes slid away from his, and he could tell he'd annoyed her. Annoying his cousin wasn't difficult. During their childhood, it had been his daily goal, his hourly objective.

"She's not a whore," the abbess said. "She's working as a nanny for a very respectable family, who adores her by the way."

"How do you know that?"

"How do I know anything, Kalief?"

"Fine, cousin," Kalief said. The less he knew about women's magic, the happier he was. "But the Supplicant's destined to be a whore—all Supplicants are. It's as the One God decreed."

Without moving her body, Abbess Anhara looked across the room, away from him. Her eyes were directed at a huge tapestry depicting a cerulean dragon flying protectively over a field of working peasants and growing hops. It was a common motif throughout the castle, throughout the land, but Kalief knew she saw none of the beauty.

"Your priests will make her into a whore," Anhara corrected quietly. "And so will your lords and ladies. You yourself will convince her to yield her maidenhood and then shun her from all society. You'll keep her drugged so that she's always willing to do your sexual bidding. The drug will slowly drive her mad, and she'll be unable to tell reality from fantasy."

"Is this what your female magic tells you?"

Anhara sighed. "No, Kalief, it's the logical outcome of your expected actions."

"Like I have a choice." Kalief slammed his fists against the desk in exasperation. "Scripture tells us exactly what we must do to her."

"Don't quote Scripture to me, *sire*." Behind closed doors, Anhara and he were equals. "I've been studying the Book of the One God my entire life, as you well know."

"Then you know I'm right."

"Yes," she said, closing her eyes for a long moment. "*You* are right." When she looked at him, she locked that steely gaze on him. "But the book isn't. I don't care if the One God himself wrote the words—treating a woman the way Scripture demands isn't right."

"What can I do, cousin? Buck thousands of years of tradition?"

"That Scripture's as outdated as your feel of woman's magic."

"Anhara," Kalief said, holding up his hands. He couldn't win this argument. "Please. Go fetch the whore for me."

She gave him a dark look.

"The girl then," he corrected. "Please. Fetch her for me."

An elegant shoulder shrugged while her body remained motionless. "I suspected you'd want me to retrieve her when the comet first appeared, cousin." Her stillness of body bespoke a stillness of mind, something he himself had never mastered. "I've been sending her messages that she's wanted. She'll recognize me when she sees me."

Relief flooded his muscles. "You amaze me, Anhara. You've made it so much easier to retrieve her."

Anhara gave the slightest shake of her head. One dark ringlet moved across her shoulder. "It might not be as easy as all that."

"What do you mean?" Kalief asked.

"I've not been the only one watching all the fire-haired girls in the land."

Kalief turned toward her, the taut muscles in his shoulders rippling with tension. "Who else knows about her?"

Anhara gave him that wry look. "She's been living in her village for more than twenty years. With hair as red and skin as white as hers, she's no secret."

"Can you scry her now?"

"With you here?"

"I don't fear all things feminine, Anhara."

She shook her head, telling him the choice was his with the succinct movement. "Over here," she said, indicating the silver bowl balanced atop the marble pedestal. It didn't look imbued with magic, but Kalief braced himself.

Taking a satchel from a shelf, Anhara pinched a small amount of dust into her palm. She closed her eyes a moment, then blew it into the liquid in the bowl.

Kalief looked down. "But I don't see anything. Are you sure this—"

Her wry glance told him to shut up, so he stared silently into the silvery liquid. A hazy image began to form. A gracile woman was snuggling a stuffed horse into the crook of a small child's arm. "Look!" Kalief said. He couldn't help himself.

Anhara shook her head at him, a small smile on her face. "It's amazing magic, I agree."

"Is that her?"

"I believe so."

Her red hair came into focus. So did her white skin as she lit a lantern. In the bowl's liquid, the girl looked tall, willowy even. Her breasts were big, just as he'd seen in his vision.

Next to him, he felt Anhara stiffen. "What is it?" he asked.

"Look." She nodded toward the water. The image had shifted.

Kalief spied a barbarian now, shrouded in bushes. He stood as still as an animal. "Is he . . ." Kalief didn't know what made him think this. "Is he watching the Supplicant?"

"Likely," Anhara agreed. "I usually see only the people I scry, but sometimes the water shows me related facts."

"By the Above," Kalief said. "Who's that?" Three men on donkeys rode on a sand-covered road. He couldn't quite make out their features, but the slump of their shoulders made them seem tired.

"Priests," she said.

"They're not mine." Kalief looked as the image focused. Heavy bronze *yats* hung from their necks. "By the Above," he said with disgust. "They're from the *Nirak* sect."

"Lovely," Anhara said with deep sarcasm. "Maybe they'll kidnap this Supplicant as they did the last. And we haven't seen the village priests. Perhaps they've told the family with whom she lives that their precious nanny is a Supplicant?"

"And you're in here arguing with me?" Kalief yelled, nearly spilling the scrying bowl. "Anhara, go get her. Keep her safe. That's an order."

"I'll fetch her, cousin, but you'd better have an army waiting for me near the Farfallinin Caldera."

"I'll be with them myself."

Anhara swept toward the door without acknowledging him. At the door, she turned and said, "You see this woman as a way to save your country—"

"And *your* country."

Anhara closed her eyes and nodded slightly in agreement before she said, "But this Supplicant may also provide a means to save yourself."

3

With the children safely tucked away in the cellar, Sureya knocked on the study door, heart in her throat. She knew Fajal sensed the desire for her husband coursing through Sureya's veins. She sensed it and disapproved.

Sureya didn't fault her mistress, but that didn't stop her distress. Sureya knew she was about to be fired. Fired and expelled from her family—her only family since the barbarians slaughtered her parents, her tiny brother.

A feeling of loathing swamped her. Even in her sorrow, her nipples ached. Unsuitably. The pearl between her thighs pulsed. She peered out the window at the fiery heart that added its light to the sun's. The ache, the pulse between her thighs— they matched the beat of the throbbing in the sky.

But these were private distractions, never to be acted upon. She needed to tell Fajal that this strange desire had never happened before; it would never affect her care of the children. She would never touch Risham.

But then phantom tastes of warm cherries assaulted her tongue. She could feel the texture of his fingers across her lip.

She deserved to be fired.

Swallowing hard, she blinked back tears and knocked a little louder. She couldn't bear to leave the children. Or Risham. Or even Fajal.

"Come in, Sureya," Fajal said in a voice that sounded as still as the quiet before a storm.

Fajal and Risham were sitting on their ancestral rug, thick orange fringe poking out beneath their bare feet. Each held a squat crystal glass, and the scent of the *satra* filled the air.

She'd never seen her employers on their ancestral rug, although since they had three children, they must have used it at least three times. Had the strange new sun affected them as well? Perhaps every living thing was now filled with the urge to mate?

"Are the children tucked into the cellar?" their mother asked.

"They're playing 'find the vole' with Weset. Everyone's happy—there're all sorts of new hiding places down there."

"They love you," said Risham.

Sureya looked at her pale feet modestly, although she knew what he said was true.

"Please," said Risham, holding out his hand to Sureya. "Join us."

On the ancestral rug? What could this mean? Could she say no? Should she?

Sureya nervously took Risham's warm, strong hand in her own, thrilling at the electricity coursing through her. She sat next to him without looking at Fajal. Her illicit pleasure must be apparent.

After emptying her glass, Risham's wife poured a measure of *satra* into a third crystal glass and handed it to Sureya.

"Thank you, ma'am."

"No more of that, Sureya. You've been with us too long. Call me Fajal. Please." The *satra* had given Fajal's eyes a strange glitter.

Or maybe that was Sureya's imagination. "Yes, ma'am," she said.

"Sureya!"

She looked at the glass in her hand, aware that a glass as nice as this belonged in a brown hand. The fine crystal did not belong in her unrefined white fingers.

The warmth of Risham's thigh didn't belong pressed against hers, either.

The world shimmered, and suddenly Sureya knew. A woman's thigh belonged pressed against hers. Sureya felt like she could almost see the face with whom these eerie emotions were associated. She could almost smell . . . expensive perfume, a feminine musk. Did she see . . . red silk? Yes. The woman wore red silk.

"My name is Fajal, Sureya. Please, say it."

"Yes . . . Fajal."

"We need to speak to you," her mistress said.

"Have I—done something wrong?" Her nipples throbbed. Her mouth hungered for cherries. Of course she'd done something wrong.

"No, of course not. You're the best nanny any family could hope for. The children adore you. In fact—" Fajal paused for a moment, perhaps seeking the right words. "Risham, help me here," Fajal said to her husband.

Confused, Sureya watched Fajal down another measure of *satra*. Then Risham said, "The church is saying that the new sun on the horizon is actually the One God's eye, that he's watching and judging us." His normally husky voice was laced with nervousness. "The priests are saying it portents change."

"Like war?" Sureya asked. She'd thought the new sun was a natural phenomenon, like a cyclone or a thunderstorm. That the fiery mass had something to do with the One God hadn't occurred to her.

"Like war," Risham agreed.

"They say it's an eye?" asked Sureya.

"They do."

Sureya paused for a moment. The thing in the sky burned, the way her heart burned for the forbidden man sitting next to her, pressing against her. Like her core ached for the woman just out of reach in her mind. "It looks more like a heart to me," she said.

Sureya watched Fajal give her husband a concerned look, and squashed her confusion. She didn't understand any of these undercurrents.

"Eye or heart—none of this is important right now," Fajal interjected. "The priests are looking for something called a Supplicant. They say the sun signifies the existence of one. That's why we've hidden the children—I would rather chew off my foot than wish that on anyone I love." Fajal poured another drink back between her delicate lips. "The priests don't describe a good life for the poor woman," she said.

"Which brings us to our point," said Risham, who also emptied his *satra*.

"We'd like to save you if we can."

"Save me?"

"From the priests."

"Why do I need rescuing from the priests?"

"You have no parents to protect you. What if you're the new Supplicant? What if they even think you're the new Supplicant?" demanded Fajal.

"The priests in town just told me what the testing involves," Risham added. "We don't want that to happen to you. We can protect Lulal and Nika, but we can't protect you—not yet."

"But I don't understand," Sureya said. "Aren't Supplicants just stories to scare young maidens? Are you telling me they're real?"

"The priests think they're real—that's all that's truly important. With your pale skin . . ." began Risham, but he couldn't finish the sentence.

"With your white skin," said Fajal with resolve, "those nasty priests will take advantage of you, treat you like you're less than human. We don't want that for you."

"So, Sureya . . ." Risham said, shooting a look at his wife. "Fajal and I have a question for you."

Risham took Sureya's small hand in his big one and brought it slowly to his lips, his eyes locked on hers. "Sureya May, I would be greatly honored if you would marry me."

Sureya felt a spurt of flame ignite at her knuckles and spread up her arm, across her chest, into her neck and cheeks. She could not speak. For a long moment, she could not think or move. How they honored one as lowly as she!

But then sense struck. Ignoring the delightful surge of desire throbbing between her thighs, she looked at Fajal. How did the woman feel about a second wife, a second wife with the palest skin?

Next to Sureya, Risham's wife—Risham's first wife—closed her eyes and nodded at her. The younger woman suddenly understood the measures of *satra* Fajal had been drinking. Sureya finally emptied her own tumbler.

And then another thought occurred to Sureya. If she married Risham, would her sin be absolved? Could she forgive herself for taking the luscious fruit from Risham's hand? If Fajal knew, would she forgive her?

"I can officiate the ceremony," Fajal said, and her voice cracked. "And I suggest that we do it now, if you're at all interested. The priests may be here soon. They're looking for virgins, which you undoubtedly are."

Sureya found it hard to think, even to answer. Risham hadn't released her hand, and he was running his fingertips over her palm.

The sensation he caused overrode the throbbing and pulsating that had attacked her upon the arrival of the new sun.

Risham turned her hand over, slowly brought her vulnerable palm to his lips, and kissed the center of it. His warm lips kissed a line to her inner wrists, and Sureya felt the *satra* go right to her head. No, it was his kisses turning her inside out. How she'd dreamed of them.

Risham's warm eyes were locked on hers, his intention clear. He wanted her. Sureya swallowed. She'd been imagining his arms around her for so long. She could have him! She could be loved! She could belong.

His lips felt hotter as they traveled up the vulnerable length of her inner arm. Sureya felt her eyes roll back in pleasure. She almost breathed her acquiescence. The word "yes" nearly escaped her lips.

But as her mouth moved to shape the word, Fajal slid graceful fingertips along the length of Sureya's collarbone. With a sensual slither, the woman pushed the full length of Sureya's hair out of the way, baring her shoulder. When Fajal ran her soft lips over Sureya's collarbone and neck, a shiver ran through her. Delicious.

Fajal leaned forward and kissed the nape of Sureya's neck while Risham's lips slowly kissed her soft inner elbow.

"What are you doing?" she demanded, coming to her wits.

"Saving you," whispered Fajal, wrapping her tongue around Sureya's clavicle. "We love you."

"Even before the priests went on their Supplicant hunt," Risham added, "I was going to propose on your twenty-fourth birthday."

"In two weeks," added Fajal, moving her tongue and lips closer to the edge of Sureya's bodice.

"Fajal and I both agreed you'd be old enough then to know your own mind—to know whether you truly wanted to be a second wife."

"Of course I want!" Sureya hadn't realized. Risham loved her! Despite her skin, so did Fajal. She could share Risham's bed, feel his arms around her as she'd dreamed.

"Say yes," Fajal said, lightly tracing a fingertip over the lace bodice above Sureya's breasts. Her nipples hardened. Her thighs ached.

"Please, say yes," added Risham, nibbling now on the softest flesh inside Sureya's arm.

"But—" Before today—before this strange new sun rose in the summer sky—she'd never imagined marrying anyone. Certainly not a woman, not even Fajal, with her almond-shaped eyes and long, thick eyelashes. Certainly not anyone of the noble class, not even Risham, whom she had admired since coming of age. Sureya never realized her fantasies about Risham, if they were to be realized, would include Fajal.

"But what?" asked Risham as Fajal ran her fingers through Sureya's long hair.

"You never imagined that women could lie together?" Fajal asked. "You never imagined we loved you?"

Sureya felt her face flush. She hadn't, and the idea was shocking.

"Drink this," said her mistress, handing her the crystal tumbler, newly refilled. The strong liquor burned her throat, her eyes. The *satra* immediately raced to her head.

"It's good, isn't it?" said Risham

It was. It was nearly as good as Risham's full brown lips caressing her inner arm.

Fajal's fingertips, Risham's lips, and the *satra* begged her to succumb to the pleasure. Risham removed Sureya's shoe as if she were a queen of the stars, slowly pulling each lace, letting his fingertips slide over the curve of her foot.

Fajal let her fingers glide over the lace of Sureya's bodice, stopping only when she reached the row of tiny, padded buttons. As each button cleared its hole, Fajal placed a kiss on that spot until Sureya's head spun with pleasure. Then Fajal put more *satra* to Sureya's lips.

Before she could marshal any strength to object, her breasts were bared. She'd never been naked in front of anyone. Never had she felt so aware of how milky and pink she was, even as her nipples waited for Fajal's hot tongue and Risham's admiring gaze.

Through the haze of *satra* Sureya looked down, pebbled nipples erect. Modesty and embarrassment burned through her, like a fire though the grasslands.

Risham ran his hot lips over the curve of her calf. He worked his way slowly to her thigh. And the thought struck her—he wanted her. Could she bear to let him go farther? Could she bear to say no?

Sureya moaned, thrilled with the pleasure brought by these wild new sensations.

With her eyes locked on Sureya's erect nipples, Fajal said, voice husky, "You are so beautiful."

Risham's shoulder-length hair hung in thick straight sheaths that were nearly black next to Fajal's kinky brown locks, and Risham's skin seemed nearly honeyed next to Fajal's darker hue.

"Your breasts, Sureya," Risham said in a smoky whisper. His pronunciation had a hint of the exotic, a carryover of his city upbringing. "You're so elegant."

The *satra* coursing through her blood caught the word 'elegant' and sent it to her head, to her nipples, to the apex of her thighs.

For the first time in her life, Sureya felt worthy of desire. Powerful with it. Beautiful enough to capture the attention of even the One God.

Sureya slid her hands across her breasts and stomach, over her waist. Fajal and Risham watched, captivated, and their lambent eyes electrified her. Sureya basked in her newborn power.

What was she doing? Sureya came to her senses and grabbed for her dress.

"You don't want to do that," Risham breathed again, as his hands slid over her thighs. His wife gently took Sureya's dress and tossed it out of reach.

"May I," Fajal asked, "touch you?" She ran her fingers over her own nipples, showing Sureya exactly what she had in mind. "Or would you rather touch me?"

The *satra* mist shrouded her senses, but Sureya could still see. She admired Fajal's breast, high and small, even while Risham gently pushed Sureya back to the ancestral rug. Fajal followed his lead. "Relax, Sureya," Fajal ordered her.

"I don't want to relax. I want—"

"Shh," Fajal said calmly. "We know what you want. We can help you. Shh."

"But, I—"

Fajal's lips descended on hers, silencing her words. The exhilarating sensation of Fajal's lips against hers left her weak and quivering. And when Fajal's tongue raced over hers, electrified nerves jumped to attention.

The heat between her legs, the silky river, wanted instant satisfaction, but Risham and Fajal together set a slower pace.

"Do you want this?" asked Fajal.

"Will you marry me—marry us?" asked Risham. His hot kisses swarmed over that tender spot behind her knee, teasing her inner thigh with the promise of unbelievable pleasure. "Please?"

She answered with one simple word. "Yes."

"We'll make you happy forever," breathed Risham.

"Hold her wrists, Risham," Fajal commanded, and her husband obeyed.

"Fajal—" Sureya tried to ask, but Risham's kisses were traveling up her inner thigh. "Why? Why hold my wrists?"

No answer. None with words. Risham poured oil into his

palm and rubbed his hands together, his eyes locked on hers. The scent of warm cedar. The jagged pleasure of Fajal's mouth over her nipples.

An animal noise escaped her throat.

Fajal pushed Sureya's oiled breasts together, making Sureya arch her back, begging for more. With her head gently spinning, she welcomed Risham's kiss while squirming under Fajal's touch, seeking a satisfaction she couldn't describe.

Risham's dark head bobbed, and she again thrust her breasts up, welcoming her lover's—her husband's—hot kisses.

And she wanted more.

She shifted her legs apart. "Please," she murmured. "Please."

"These things mustn't be rushed," Risham said, his voice husky with desire.

"I know what you want," Fajal replied with a need that shocked Sureya. "You want this." With her words she slid a finger between Sureya's thighs. Fajal's finger—no, Risham's— glided over her pearl, and Sureya writhed in pleasure.

Through the *satra* haze, Sureya heard a crashing from the entryway down the hall. She tried to sit, but Fajal sucked hard on her nipple, making her gasp with pleasure. Risham positioned himself above her, the length of him throbbing hugely. "Do you want to marry me, Sureya?" he asked, his eyes locked onto hers.

"I do, my love."

While Fajal licked her nipple, Risham sheathed his tip gently inside Sureya. "It'll hurt for just a second—"

Two priests burst through the door, shouting, "Cease! Heretics, you'll burn! Stop this instant!"

4

His long gray beard flying, a black-robed priest grabbed Sureya cruelly by her arm and jerked her from under Risham, whose bare behind, so beautiful just moments ago, now looked vulnerable.

"What're you doing?" screeched Fajal, holding her hand beseechingly toward the priest looming over her. "Don't hurt me! Please. Don't hurt my husband!"

The bearded priest answered by shoving Fajal away with his scuffed boot. "Whore," he rasped.

Sureya didn't know whether he referred to Fajal or herself.

Two younger, clean-shaven priests, white collars gleaming in the eerie afternoon light, pulled Sureya to her feet. She looked to the blond priest, thinking that their shared caste might make him more amenable, but he just stared at her bared breasts.

Sureya jerked her arms away from the priests. She bent to retrieve her dress, shrugged it on, and buttoned it with a cold deliberateness that belied her assaulted modesty, her quaking nerves.

"Risham and Fajal Astra de Calanda," the gray-bearded priest said. "You are under arrest for heresy and the vile corruption of a Supplicant. You shall both be burned at the stake in the morning. Your farm will be donated to the king, and your children shall be sold into slavery for a period of no less than seven years."

"No!" Fajal and Risham both shouted. Sureya couldn't tell where one voice ended and another began. It wasn't until her throat began to ache that she realized that she, too, was screaming. Hot tears ran down her face. The children of her heart! Lulal, Nika, and Dayy could not be sold into slavery!

One of the priests at her side, the blonde, restrained Risham, who, naked, had begun punching the gray-bearded priest. Despite the fact that the *satra* made his blows ineffectual, the ancient gray-beard didn't look like he could withstand the abuse.

"You will burn!" the old priest shouted between gnarled, yellow teeth. Drops of spittle flew.

"No!" Fajal began shouting with renewed strength. "My children!"

Beautiful Risham and Fajal could not die while tied to the priest's stake. She'd do anything to save them. She couldn't lose another family. Not to priests, not to barbarians.

Sureya put a soft look in her eyes—the *satra* helped—and turned toward the clean-shaven priest. She leaned right into his space, until his eyes were locked on her lips, which felt puffy and swollen from Fajal's kisses.

When the priest leaned in for a taste of his own, Sureya kneed him in the groin with all of her might. Something crunched right to her bone. The man crumpled to the floor, groaning, his hands covering his genital area.

Amid the shouting, no one else in the room seemed to notice that one of the three priests was writhing on the floor. Sureya hoped the children in the cellar couldn't hear this, or if they did, she hoped Weset had the wherewithal to keep them hidden.

The *satra* gave her a calmness, an ability to see through the chaos to the heart of the matter. The children could not be sold. Fajal and Risham could not burn.

The young blond priest held Risham by his waist, but her almost-husband had his arms free, and he flailed incompetently at the gray-bearded priest. Fajal slapped and bit the young man, who tried to fend her off while protecting his superior.

Sureya stepped next to the old priest, who still dodged Risham's ineffectual blows while shouting about pyres and slaves.

With a preternatural clarity she lightly took his beard in her hand. As if in a dream, his rheumy eyes turned toward her. Red veins amid a sea of mucusy yellow. His irises must once have been blue, but now they were green with age and ill health. Sureya brought her hair-filled hand so close to his face that she felt the heat of his skin while the old man remained speechless.

The old priest opened his mouth to say something, and Sureya yanked—she pulled the hair in her hand with all of her strength. She pulled so hard it jarred her shoulder. She felt skin tear from muscle, and he screamed like a child. Then she did it again.

Like one of Lulal's dolls, the man fell to her feet in a howling heap, face on the floor. She looked at him, and she stepped on the old man's neck.

Lying cowed on the floor, under her foot, she realized that this nasty priest was smaller than Dayy. She knew, if she stepped down with all of her weight, she'd kill him. The difference between his life and his death was the difference of a shift in her position. She held his life in her foot.

The room fell silent. Fajal now had a knife, probably from the desk, and she held it to the throat of the blond priest. The clean-shaven priest lay unconscious on the floor, hands still clasped around his genitals. She saw blood trickling from beneath his cassock.

Risham's wife observed the priest at Sureya's feet. "Kill him," Fajal urged.

"We can run to the mountains and be married there," said Risham, who'd done little to protect the women or himself.

"We'll take the children and run," his first wife—his only wife—added.

Sureya looked down at the worm of a priest, considering.

Before she could accept or refuse their invitation, footsteps clipped down the hall, too deliberate to be the children or the servant. The scent of some exotic fragrance entered the room heartbeats before the figure to whom it belonged.

That fragrance snagged something from her memory.

The memory. It skated gently through her mind again, pushing away all thoughts, just for a moment. Skin, the color of *khal* with cream. Long fingernails. Jewel-encrusted rings and a sprinkling of tinkling bangles. In her mind, that dark hand unbuttoned Sureya's blouse and cupped a white breast. Lips the color of mulberries—

With an ethereal grace Sureya had never seen in a person, a woman floated into the room. Her hair hung in tight, shiny ringlets, as black as a summer night. Her brows were elegantly arched, and her eyelids sparkled with gold dust.

Something deep in Sureya's core called to this woman. When she closed her eyes and breathed, she sensed tendrils of magic pouring from this woman and coiling around her heart.

"I sent a spell to introduce us, Sureya. That's what you sense."

"Oh." Sureya blinked. "A spell."

The woman looked at Sureya's foot on the priest's neck, and she winked. "I know Father Graybeard's a loathsome creature, but it'd probably be better for everyone if you didn't kill him." A smile danced over the woman's lips.

"But the children," Sureya said. "He's going to make slaves of the children, and he's going to burn their parents."

"These men will do no such thing," the creature replied with a steadiness that gave Sureya heart. "Isn't that right, brother?"

The dark-haired priest with the knife at his throat said, "But they were defiling the Supplicant, turning her toward their own purposes! They deserve the flames of hell."

"Why is everyone talking about a Supplicant?" Sureya demanded, suddenly angry.

With a graceful turn of her hand, the crimson-clad woman caressed Sureya's cheek. "My dove, it's likely you're the Supplicant."

"The Supplicant," Sureya said. "There's no such thing."

The woman's fingers lightly traced Sureya's collarbone. "But you're wrong, my dove. Scripture is filled with descriptions of her, and her abilities. I've studied her throughout my lifetime."

"Then you should be the new one!" Sureya said. "Not me."

"This isn't the place to talk about it. Release the old father, and we'll seek safety."

The blond priest snatched the knife from Fajal and lunged at Sureya. With his arm around her neck, he jerked her off the old priest and pricked her throat until blood welled to the surface.

"She's a whore!" shouted the crazed man. "She's already been defiled!"

The old man on the ground rolled to his back and groaned. "She must burn," he croaked. "With this entire family." He rasped a breath. "The children, too." His breathing grew more labored. "Heresy," he said. "And witchcraft."

"Witchcraft." The beautiful woman laughed, a small, refined sound.

Her lips, Sureya noted, were exactly the shade of mulberries.

"Fool," the woman said. "All priests are fools." Her robe rustled as she glided over to Risham. She reached out her hand, and Sureya noticed long, tapered nails. The beautiful woman delicately lifted Risham's flaccid penis and said to the blond priest, "Do you see blood?"

"No," said the priest after a moment. "But it's hard to see with his dark skin. He penetrated the girl! I saw it."

"Sureya, dove, I apologize for this, but could you please lift your skirt? Show the pig you inner thigh."

She felt her face flush, and she looked away.

"I've already seen more than your thigh, girl," the priest growled.

With clenched fingers, Sureya lifted her skirt. She felt the penis of the blond priest harden. He grunted, but he couldn't see from behind her. Keeping a painful hold of her hair, he whirled her around.

"See?" said the crimson-clad woman. "There's no blood on her thighs."

"I know a surer way to check," said the priest. And he shoved calloused fingers inside her. She cried in horror and pain, but his fingers stopped before they fully penetrated.

"She might be a virgin, but she's still a whore," the priest said, shoving her away. "Just like you are."

"I've had quite enough of you and your kind. Your father needs medical attention, as does your fellow brother. I suggest you get them out of here quickly, before the Astra de Calandas decide to take matters into their own hands."

"I'm taking the whore," said the blond priest. "We came here to get her, and that's just what we'll do."

The elegant woman gave a tinkling laugh and said, "No, my dear brother. The sisterhood won't allow the Supplicant to fall into your hands. She's mine."

"She's ours!" shouted Risham. "She's lived with us for years and agreed to become my second wife."

"Mr. Astra de Calanda, if she still wants you, I'll leave her with you. The choice is always hers."

"Sureya," Risham said, falling to his knees at her feet. "Stay. Be my wife."

Sureya blinked. She'd never imagined her adored employer, the man with whom she'd thought herself in love for so long, in this position. She'd never dreamed someone of his social class would be on his knees for her.

Fajal added, "You know we love you as much as the children do. We want you to join our family. We risked everything to save you today—that's how much we love you."

"Risked everything?" Sureya asked.

"We risked the wrath of the priests just to save you from them."

They were her family. They took her in after she'd lost everyone she'd ever loved. They took her in and loved her.

Sureya turned to the elegant woman and asked, "May I know your name, please?"

"Supplicant! Don't trust the whore!" the old priest said, his voice rasped from his chest. His dark skin was almost as gray as his beard. "Come with us! We'll save your soul."

"Oh, she's coming with us," the blond brother reassured the old priest. To make his point, he jerked Sureya's hair until she cried.

Without thinking, Sureya closed her fist and slammed it back, hitting the priest square on the nose. Hard. With a cry, he released her hair, and she smelled the blood that must have been streaming down his face.

Freed, she swept past Risham and stepped over the old man.

"What's your name?" Sureya asked the elegant woman.

"I'm Anhara," she said, talking Sureya's hand in hers. Anhara handed her a small vial. "Drink the contents. Your employers have given you *dawa*, a ritual aphrodisiac, to make their offer of marriage more appealing."

"But—" Sureya thought of the years she'd spent imagining Risham's arms around her. "They wouldn't have used that. They didn't need it." She would have gone willingly, so very willingly. "You didn't, did you?" she asked Risham, but he wouldn't meet her eyes.

"I believe they wanted to be certain you wouldn't refuse their marriage offer," Anhara replied.

"It was for your own good," Fajal cried. "You don't know what this woman's going to turn you into!"

"Still," Sureya said. "I would've liked the choice." She took the small bottle, which was cool in her hand. "And this is the antidote?"

"Yes," Anhara said. "Now, your choice, please."

"There's no choice. My heart's taken."

"Don't trust the whore!" said the old man, again.

"I'm tired of your tirade, old man," Anhara said to him. "According to the history books, your order captured the last Supplicant, and what did you do with her? What do you have to show?"

"You know nothing, whore." He coughed weakly. "Nothing." The old man took a shallow breath and turned his face toward Sureya. "Supplicant, you're still an innocent. Come with us and you'll stay that way. We'll save your soul."

Sureya looked at the three priests. One held his face as blood streamed from his nose. Another lay unconscious on the floor, his hands around his genitals. The third was likely dying, by her hand. These men had threatened to burn and sell and torment those she loved.

If these men could save her soul, she thought she'd rather burn in the One God's Hell.

She drained the bitter liquid in the vial. "I'll stay with my family, Anhara. I love them. I love the children. I want to see mine playing in the courtyard."

"The choice is always yours, but you must come with me now."

She shook her head. "I'm not leaving. I'm staying here. This is where I belong."

"Then I apologize for what I'm about to do."

"What?"

Anhara took a small pouch from her belt and pinched a bit of the substance into her palm. Anhara turned to face Sureya and blew the dust into her face. "You will come with me."

"I'll come with you," Sureya repeated, dully.

"Witchcraft!" hissed a priest.

Anhara turned toward the priests and blew dust toward them. "You will not harm this family." Pocketing the satchel, Anhara turned toward the door without looking behind her.

"Sureya!" Risham called.

"Stay, Sureya!" Fajal said.

But she followed Anhara wordlessly out the door.

"Out of the frying pan and into the fire," said the ancient priest.

5

Sureya's heart was tied to Risham and every step she took away from him unraveled her. "We need to hurry," Anhara urged her.

"Why?" Even as her feet followed Anhara's, her mind objected.

Anhara looked at the crazy sky, then said, "I think we have a half-day's lead before the barbarians attack."

Fear zipped through her. "We need to warn Risham! The children aren't safe!" Despite the intervening years, she could still see the slit throats of her baby brother, her mother, and her father, killed by barbarian knife.

"The barbarians aren't interested in this family," Anhara explained. "They want you."

A sharp nicker caught her attention as she followed Anhara through the gate. Two desert-bred horses were tied to the horse post, gold bridles flashing in the strange light of the new sun. She could save the children with these horses!

"Do these horses belong to you or the priests?" Sureya asked, walking toward them. Lulal could ride with her on one of them. Nika and Dayy could ride the other.

"The priests couldn't afford these." The dark bay whickered as Anhara approached and mounted it with a fluid vault. "Do you know how to ride?"

"A little bit." *Well enough to get the children out of here.* "Anhara, let me take the children away from here on the horses. You can walk with Risham and Fajal to safety, use your magic or something. Just don't let the barbarians get the children!"

"The children are safe, little dove, but you're not." Anhara pointed to the blood bay next to hers. Its coat was as red as Sureya's hair. "Firefly is yours. Get on him now."

Sureya's feet were forced to obey. Her toes found the stirrup. "I can't leave them, Anhara. I love them."

"I apologize for the spell—it really is for your own good. Let's start putting distance behind us, and I'll see if I can explain."

Sureya climbed into the saddle, but her full-length gray skirt was bunched around her hips, exposing her calves and most of her thighs. "I'm not dressed for this. Dayy has some trousers I can borrow. I can get them from the house." *And the children, too. Even tiny Lulal.*

With a small movement, Anhara shook her head. "Those vile priests distracted me. I forgot to give you your supplies." With a deft hand, she reached inside the bag behind her saddle and retrieved a green silk package. "It's a desert outfit. Just change your clothing here. Be quick."

Sureya slid off her horse, and Anhara tossed her the clothing. Hiding her embarrassment, she shook out the emerald silk and found stunning pantaloons and a cropped top, barely larger than her brassiere. The waist of the bottoms was embroidered in gold, like the bridles. "It's so . . ." The young woman searched for a word.

"Immodest?"

"Yes."

"It's a disguise, my dove. Wearing these clothes and riding Firefly, you'll look like a desert concubine. Even barbarians think twice before harassing desert folk."

Sureya glanced around the surrounding area, somehow feeling the weight of barbarian eyes upon her. Fear lent her speed. Leaving on her skirt, Sureya pulled the pantaloons to her waist. Still feeling very self-conscious, she turned her back to Anhara and unbuttoned her blouse. Just as she shrugged out of it, the wind picked up. Through her brassiere, her nipples stood out.

"Look how beautiful your nipples are when they're erect," Anhara said.

Discomfited, Sureya quickly pulled the billowing green blouse over her head. The new shirt bared her shoulders, but full jade-colored poufs covered her upper arms. Green embroidery, just a shade darker than the silk, outlined her breasts, and gold trim edged the plunging neckline. Most unsettling, her entire midriff—from well below her navel to just shy of her breasts—was bare. A deep vee pointed right to that spot between her thighs.

"No wonder desert women are so good with their knives—they'd have to be to get away with dressing like this."

"Mount your horse," Anhara said, looking around. Did she sense barbarians too?

"But my skin," Sureya said, climbing onto Firefly. "It's so white. I don't look like a concubine—of the desert or anywhere else." Sureya turned to the woman and pleaded. "We could take the children with us—I'll take the two small ones. You take the boy."

"We don't have time," Anhara said curtly. "There's a knife and a head scarf. Make sure you wrap the scarf so your flame-colored hair can't be seen. That's more dangerous than your skin." Anhara watched Sureya fumble with the belt and said, "The dagger goes into that loop on your left hip."

Sureya slid the sheathed blade into the loop. "Does everything look right?"

"Yes." But Anhara's voice was tight, distracted. Some secret part of her heart craved approval from this glamorous woman. But why would Anhara admire the likes of her? Sureya looked in the direction of the other woman's gaze.

A large wall of dust rose across the horizon.

"What is it?"

"Riders," Anhara said in the same tight voice. "We're going to ride like the wind. Remember to trust Firefly. Hold on to his mane if you feel unsteady, but leave his mouth alone."

"Are they barbarians? Let me go get the children!" Sureya tried to dismount, but the spell held her tight.

"No, Sureya! Let's fly!"

Just then, a huge blond man with amber skin appeared at the gate—a man Sureya had never seen before, but she knew what he was. He wore bone beads in his hair, and his beard glittered in the odd sunlight. The feral gleam in his eye matched the wicked blade in his hand.

Sureya froze, like a rabbit caught in the gaze of a wolf.

"Run, Sureya!" Anhara leaned across her horse and made a kissing sound, her heels jabbing her horse's flanks.

Anhara's horse exploded across the sandy plain, away from the riders. Dirt and pebbles shot from under its hooves and hit Firefly's face and chest.

Firefly shook his head and pawed the ground, obviously eager to run, but waiting for Sureya's signal.

"Kick, Sureya!" Anhara shouted over her shoulder, into the wind. But Sureya fought the urge to obey with every fiber of her being. She had to save the children!

As she fought to dismount, the barbarian sauntered toward her, and Anhara circled back. Anhara galloped behind her, and with her length of rein, smacked Firefly hard on his rump. He fled.

"Wait!" shouted Sureya, grabbing the horse's black mane. "I can't!—"

"Let's go!" Anhara shouted over the pounding of hooves and whistling wind. "Run, Firefly!" she said. Then she gave a bone-piercing whistle.

The horse leapt forward, and Sureya scrambled to keep her seat, grabbing his long mane with icy fingers. Firefly was flying like a Minion was on his tail.

Sureya risked a glance behind her, and saw the barbarian, legs spread, dagger glinting in the crazy suns. His mouth moved, but Sureya heard nothing over the hooves and wind.

She was safe. But Risham and the children . . .

Her mount settled into his ground-eating stride. Sureya couldn't control the horse, she knew, but riding him was like riding an arrow shot from a huge crossbow. Firefly's power surged between her thighs.

Finally, her hands loosened their hold on the mane, and blood began to flow to her fingers. They passed the outskirts of town, and then a rocky outcrop, which Sureya had never seen before. League after league passed beneath pounding hooves.

Clutching Firefly's mane again, she hazarded a glance behind her. A great wall of dust, taller than any building Sureya had ever seen, loomed behind them on the horizon.

Anhara and her horse swerved to the east, and Firefly followed, less than a length behind. Through eyes tearing from wind, Sureya saw Anhara's crimson robe floating behind her, just above her mount's flowing black tail.

The pair galloped around a rocky outcrop that towered into the sky from the flat, dusty plains. Anhara reined her horse to a halt, and Firefly slid to a stop without her bidding.

"Here," Anhara said. Tossing a glance at the approaching wall of sand, Anhara quickly reined her horse toward the towering outcrop. "There's an oasis in this volcanic monadnock." Her voice was breathless from the ride.

"Monadnock?" Sureya panted, "I've never heard that word."

"Maybe you know it as an inselberg?"

Sureya shook her head, not caring. Fear made her knees shake. She imagined Fajal and Risham in pools of blood. The barbarians wouldn't spare the children either. They hadn't spared her little brother all those years ago.

"Those men would've killed you too, Sureya," Anhara said, as if reading her mind. "You have to forget it for now, have faith that everything will work out."

"Faith," Sureya breathed. "I have faith that we're being chased, and I don't know why or by whom."

"Just follow me. Watch Turu's tail, and Firefly will know where to go." Hooves clambered across the red volcanic rock.

Sureya clutched Firefly's mane as he struggled over the rocks, and just when she was about to ask Anhara if she should dismount to ease Firefly's burden, the rocks parted.

Sureya gasped at the sheer beauty around her as Anhara dismounted. On all sides, towering walls of volcanic cliffs surrounded them, majestic and otherworldly. In the center was a field of green—lush, thick grass and date trees. "What is this place?" Sureya asked, eyeing a sapphire pond.

"It's a caldera. In fact, it's called Farfallinin Caldera."

"From a volcano?"

"Yes, and an oasis sprang up here. The bowl-shaped hollow caught rainwater and grass grew."

"Are we safe here? Can they find us?"

"Probably. The men will see our tracks end at the outcropping and they'll investigate, but they can't hurt us here—it's a holy place. The One God prohibits violence within his calderas." Anhara looked at the two suns in the sky, now both on the horizon. "Besides, our soldiers should be nearby now. My cousin's supposed to meet us here. He'll keep us safe."

Sureya stopped and looked at Anhara, whose scarlet veil fluttered in the light breeze. "I don't understand anything. I woke this morning safe in my world. I had three children to take care of. I had the respect of their parents." *One of whom I loved.* "When I woke this morning, I knew what to do. Now . . ." Sureya pushed her green silk from her face. "Now I don't know anything."

Anhara approached her, Turu's reins in her hand. "Sureya," she said, in a voice meant to soothe. Sureya stood a little taller than the other woman, who reached to stroke her cheek with elegant gentleness. As Anhara's fingertips caressed her jaw, Sureya admired her perfectly arched black eyebrows. The lids of her sloe eyes were covered in gold dust, unmarred by their ride across the desert. And her lips were the color of mulberries, moist and shiny.

Before her brief encounter with Fajal, Sureya had never imagined kissing a woman.

But now . . . now the images that had been haunting her since she'd first seen the One God's heart pounding in the sky crashed back through her mind. Sureya's mouth watered for the taste of plump mulberries, warm from the sun.

"I think," Anhara said, locking her gaze on hers, "that you know something, that you feel answers coursing in your veins." Anhara stepped even closer so that her lips almost touched Sureya's. "I think," Anhara breathed, "the hand of the One God lies heavily upon you."

"Do you mean . . ." Sureya blushed with frustration, but Anhara waited patiently. "Do you mean these feelings? Do they have something to do with this?"

"You need to be tested to be sure, but yes. Even without the *dawa*, I think you feel the burning need of the Supplicant."

Suddenly Sureya saw her mother's body lying limp in the sand, her lifeblood seeping from her slashed throat. She saw her little brother and father, dead. She could hear barbarian laughter even from her hiding place. Sureya didn't care at all about Supplicants. She wanted to go home.

"Sureya—" Anhara began.

She tried to hold her temper, but control wasn't possible. "I need to know the family I love is safe, not held at knifepoint!" she shouted. "Not slaughtered by barbarians!"

"Shh, little dove." Anhara's voice was unruffled. "I'll explain what I can. There're hobbles in your saddlebag. Why don't you unsaddle and let Firefly eat?"

"I want answers now, Anhara."

"Your horse is hot and hungry. Let's get settled for the night and I'll answer all of your questions. I promise."

Sureya had no choice but to nod, and Anhara led her horse off to a glade by the pond.

Using skills that struck Sureya at odds with her polished quietness, Anhara pitched one small tent. The stillness of her movements remained constant, even as she unsaddled Turu. Anhara unpacked dried dates and jerky. She also unpacked a flask.

"Drink some," Anhara said to Sureya, handing it to her. "And let's sit here for a minute." She'd tossed a light blanket over the cushiony grass. "It's not drugged."

"Did Risham and Fajal really give me an aphrodisiac?"

"They did. Your eyes were completely dilated, and I suspect you were behaving in an . . . uncharacteristic manner."

Sureya thought of the way she'd let Fajal touch her, the way Risham had kissed her thighs and arms. Feeling stupid for being duped, Sureya was glad the fading light hid her embarrassment.

"So," Anhara said, as if unaware of her discomfort. "You have a lot of questions. What would you like to know first?" Anhara drank deeply from the flask, then lay on the blanket, waiting.

Sureya took a long draw from the flask herself, expecting water.

The fire she tasted instead made her hack and choke. "By the

Above," she said. "*Satra*." But the oaken taste slid down her throat much more smoothly than any *satra* she'd ever tasted before.

Sureya's muscles relaxed. She lay down on the blanket, aware of Anhara's warmth. The natural sun was almost set, and a peach color infused the sky. "Well," she said, finally, "What's a Supplicant, and why does everyone but me know it's me?"

Anhara pointed toward the new sun, its ruby light just visible over the caldera's wall. "What would you call that thing in the sky?"

"I thought I was asking the questions."

"Bear with me—everyone in town, even the priests, are calling it 'the One God's Eye.' What do you think about that?"

An unfamiliar longing suddenly filled Sureya. She wished for Risham's strong arms wrapped around her, his hungry gaze raking across her silk-clad curves. Even if he didn't approve of this outfit, Sureya knew he would appreciate it—appreciate her body in it. He didn't care about the color of her skin. She craved his palm running the length of her bare stomach.

In his arms, she'd be home.

"If the new sun isn't a natural phenomenon," Sureya said at last, "then I'd guess it wasn't an eye staring down in judgment— I'd say it was a heart, burning with love and desire and ... hope."

"*And where others see despair, she shall see promise,*" Anhara quoted. "That's one of the ways Scripture says the Supplicant can be identified."

"I can't be the only person who sees a heart." But her head was pounding as she denied the evidence.

Anhara ignored her. "In which year were you born?"

"The Year of Ivies."

"The Year of Ivies," said Anhara, still staring at the heavens. "Ivy clings to surfaces, needs supporting structures to reach great heights. But it can kill the things to which it clings, and even if you cut it back, it grows again. Some ivies are deadly to the touch."

"I wasn't the only person born that year, Anhara." Two small facts—very general facts—didn't mean she was the Supplicant.

"Scripture says, '*Her hair shall be red like the berries of her birth year.*'"

Sureya took another drink from her flask. No flames from the *satra* this time, just heat—delicious, warm, relaxing heat. "I'm sure I'm not the only redhead born in the Year of Ivies."

But was she?

"How many other people have you met with hair the color of the One God's Eye?" Anhara challenged.

Sureya had met none. She'd gone her entire life without meeting a single redhead. Not that she traveled much, but still. "But that doesn't mean—"

"When the One God's Eye appeared in the sky today, across the land priests examined Scripture. Every flame-headed girl across the land is being interrogated tonight. I should hope that the priests limit themselves to girls born in the Year of Ivies, but I suspect they won't."

"So," Sureya asked, "there are other people with red hair?"

"Yes, but few."

One of the horses softly whinnied on the other side of the pond. Sureya said, "I might very well not be the Supplicant, then."

"You can't fight your fate, little dove."

Sureya only grunted her response.

"Do you know what a Supplicant is, Sureya?"

"She's a myth."

Anhara said coolly, "What do you know about the myth?"

"Vague details. The One God answers her prayers." With a loud huff, Sureya threw up her hands. "That's the thing, Anhara. I can't say any of my prayers have been answered." Certainly when her parents had lain dead, her little brother massa-cred, the One God had remained silent. While she'd hidden, lis-tening to barbarians rape her mother, no god had answered her prayers.

Anhara rolled to her side and trailed her fingertips lightly over Sureya's bared midriff. Anhara's touch was just as sensual as the images in her mind she'd been fighting since the appear-ance of the new sun. And with the *satra* coursing through her veins . . .

Sureya didn't modestly pull away, although she knew that even yesterday she would have. Instead, she hummed in plea-sure. "No one's ever touched me like this."

"Of course they haven't. You're a good girl." Anhara ca-ressed the grooves of her ribs, just beneath her breasts, and Sureya hummed again, squirming.

"You have a great power in you, Sureya. And I can help you unleash it. I can guide you, and the others who seek to use your powers, for you cannot use that power alone."

Sureya closed her eyes and took a deep breath. In the dis-tance a horse stomped, and frogs gave peeping calls into the fading light.

Then Anhara's fingers traced the gold-gilt edge of her vee-cut pantaloons, and Sureya caught her breath. The vee plunged from the curves of her hips down to just above her pubic hair, and as Anhara's cool fingertips traced the edging, Sureya's nip-ples pebbled beneath the green silk, and the sensitive spot be-tween her thighs ached.

"What're you doing?" Sureya managed to ask, her voice choked with desire.

"Shh, my dove. Lie back and enjoy it."

And when Anhara's warm lips traveled the same line her fin-gers had traced, Sureya found it easy to surrender. The day's horrors and shocks melted away like frost under the morning sun.

"Does that feel good?" Anhara asked, flicking her tongue just under the gilt edge by her hip.

Words failed. With a long stretch, hands above her head, she arched herself toward Anhara. A strange taste of power surged through her. Molten silk slid between her thighs. In her mind's eye, the new sun pounded in rhythm with her pulse.

"I'll take that as a 'yes,'" Anhara said, with a tinkling laugh.

"Mhm-hmm," Sureya said. "It's good."

Anhara retrieved a small container from her bag. When she unscrewed the lid, the scent of almond butter teased Sureya's nose. "I'm going to give you a massage, my dove," she said, gracefully working the almond cream between her palms.

"Mhm-hmm."

Anhara's hand slid lingeringly over Sureya's stomach, her hips, her navel. Then Anhara moved higher, coating Sureya's shoulders and arms with the warm almond butter. Relaxing under her touch, something deep and primal opened.

When Anhara began to push the tiny emerald buttons of her flimsy blouse through their holes, Sureya didn't object. She didn't even think of objecting. Even as she looked down and saw her breasts shining in the light of the full moon—and the One God's Heart—Sureya didn't want to object. Her nipples pebbled in the cool evening air, and she longed for . . . something. For something she didn't know how to describe.

Anhara leaned down, kissing her cheek and then her chin, teasing her with the press of her lips. With half-closed eyes, Sureya parted her lips, inviting Anhara's attention. But Anhara kissed around her opened mouth, smiling when Sureya turned her head to meet her.

"I can teach you a new game, one with an amazing consequence particular to only you," Anhara said.

Just thinking about the possibility left her nipples tingling, waiting for Anhara's attention.

Anhara moved her oiled hands, molding Sureya's large

breasts, running her fingernails lightly over her nipples. The friction sent a sizzling crack of electricity through her. Writhing from the sensation, Sureya felt her very core soften and yield. That silken river flowed between her thighs. She parted her legs to reduce the throbbing, but the texture of her silk pantaloons against her thighs did little to soothe.

"My dove, you're very beautiful. Every man who meets you will want to please you. And every woman, too."

Sureya blushed at Anhara's words, under her touch, but she couldn't deny her increasing desire. Not even embarrassment at the compliment could still the storm brewing within her.

Then Anhara slid a finger just under the edge of Sureya's pantaloons. Her smooth fingertip glided over the bone of her hip, dancing just above her pubic line. Rubbing one hand lightly over her nipple, Anhara's hand swept over Sureya's mound, careful not to touch too much.

Anhara was teasing her, driving her to distraction.

And then the other woman's finger caressed Sureya's nerve-filled pearl. Her breath hitched in surprise and pleasure. The throb between her thighs intensified, hovered right on the line of exquisite pleasure.

Sureya bucked, seeking release from this excruciating torture, but Anhara pulled back, leaving Sureya writhing in frustration.

"Do you know what you want?" Anhara asked.

"Yes—" Sureya begged. "I want . . ." She grabbed Anhara's hand and shoved it between her thighs. Anhara smiled, but she only rested her hand on Sureya's mound. Her clever fingers remained unsatisfying.

Anhara leaned forward, kissing Sureya's lips gently, firmly. She flicked her tongue just inside Sureya's mouth, tracing the line of her lips.

Pleasantly dizzy from the *satra*, she conceded to Anhara's knowledge, to her kiss, then opened herself to it. Anhara's tongue skillfully twined around hers, teasing and promising. A groan of pleasure escaped her.

Anhara's lips burned a path from Sureya's lips down her neck to her breast. First, tiny kisses covered each breast, leaving Suryea breathless. She'd never imagined that a woman's touch could feel so . . . erotic. She thought it should feel wrong, immoral somehow. But it didn't. When Anhara softly sucked a nipple, it felt as natural as breathing, and much more delightful. With quiet grace, Anhara applied the gentlest pressure, as light as a butterfly landing on a petal, and Sureya blossomed under it.

Sureya lay back, giving Anhara everything she wanted. She arched her back, willing Anhara to do more, to satisfy her.

And Anhara did not disappoint. Instead, she seemed to read Sureya's mind. Sureya's breast ached for more, and Anhara increased her suction, grazing her nipple with careful teeth. Sureya pressed toward her new friend, moaning, and Anhara ran her thumb over the other nipple, pressing harder as she circled.

Delight swept over each inch of her skin, leaving her feeling as malleable as clay. Anhara nudged her thighs, and Sureya opened them. Anhara asked for Sureya's mouth, her lips, and Sureya gave them.

When Anhara sat up and pulled the emerald silk from Sureya's hips, leaving her bare skin gleaming under the light of the full moon, Sureya didn't object. She felt as natural as her surroundings. The russet hue of her pubic hair shone like fire under the stars.

Naked, vulnerable, Sureya felt as powerful as the earth beneath them. She locked her eyes on Anhara and smiled. "Lie back and relax, my dove," her friend said through lidded eyes. But Sureya was already tranquil, anticipating the inevitable heat of her friend's touch.

Anhara's languid fingertip traced the edge of Sureya's collarbone, then trailed between her breasts and over her belly. She traced the low line of her pubic hair, sending delicious shivers of anticipation through Sureya.

When Anhara's fingers lightly slid over Sureya's inner thigh, liquid fire lit through Sureya's blood. *Open your legs*, the fingers demanded, and Sureya wanted nothing more than to obey.

"By the One, you're beautiful," breathed Anhara. And Sureya believed her, but still, as the other woman dipped her face toward her pearl, she squirmed. Could she really let Anhara do this?

Her worry lasted heartbeats. Writhing under the talented tongue of the other woman, she thrilled on the power of being so desired. But the longing for fulfillment couldn't continue. She needed immediate resolution.

She pushed her pelvis toward Anhara in hopes that she would ease her hunger, that she would lick and suckle between her thighs, that she would fill her—that she would end this beautiful yearning.

Lying on her stomach between Sureya's spread legs, Anhara spread her with deft fingertips. Sureya felt Anhara's hot breath as she nuzzled her face into her. Lightly at first, Anhara trailed her tongue up and down, swirling around the tip of Sureya's pearl.

The torment of her tongue sent Sureya's head spiraling in pleasure. Each time Anhara neared her throbbing pearl, she thought she'd explode from the pleasure of near release.

"By the Above," Sureya moaned, grasping the silk blanket beneath her in tight fingers. "Please. I need—" But she didn't know what she needed.

Anhara did.

Anhara nudged her pearl with the tip of her experienced tongue. Sureya jerked in response to the searing lash of delight that burst over her. With one hand, Anhara pushed Sureya's stomach toward the ground, keeping her immobile while she continued her skilled ministrations.

Between butterfly-light strokes of her tongue, Anhara sucked. Then, while she licked, Anhara slid her thumb heavily over Sureya's pearl, gliding just barely inside her opening.

Squeezing her eyes shut against the sudden rush of pleasure, Sureya screamed as her friend found just the right spot. She didn't care what Anhara thought. She didn't care if her voice bounced off the inselberg's walls.

Anhara sucked hard as the orgasm began to wrack Sureya's body. White blinding light flashed behind her eyes, and she couldn't catch her breath. Without thought, she grabbed Anhara's head, pulling her hair to release the exhilarating hold she had on her.

But Anhara wouldn't relent. Her expert fingers removed Sureya's from her hair, and Anhara continued to suck Sureya's pearl, softly at first, and then much more insistently.

Another powerful orgasm pounded through her. Every muscle in her body was tightened in throbbing ecstasy. If Anhara didn't stop her sucking, flicking, gliding, Sureya felt certain she would go insane. But the sizzling flicks of delight unrelentingly swarmed her body until she could think of nothing but the sensations battering her.

Finally, Anhara stopped, resting her thumb against Sureya's pearl, keeping it still.

For several moments, Sureya was unable to move, unable to take any but the most shallow breaths. Slowly, she opened her eyes. The stars above were nearly spinning.

Then the world steadied, and she blinked and smiled at Anhara, whose mulberry lips glistened with her juices.

"Sureya?" Anhara breathed.

"Mmmm."

"Congratulations on your first orgasm. Let me be the first to introduce you to your powers."

A pebble clicked down a rocky cliff, and a horse whinnied. Sureya froze. All the horror of the day, held at bay by these delights of the flesh, flashed through her mind, driving all sensuous thoughts from her head.

Her emotions—freed by the potent orgasm, by the *satra*—ran high, and tears dripped down her face. The barbarians were in the house she'd come to think of as home. Would she really never see the daughter of her heart again? Would she never hear her laugh?

Sureya sobbed. "My mother? My brother and father? Can I see them again?"

Anhara looked at her a moment, contemplating, then she nodded. "When we get home I have ways to help you."

"Thank you."

Anhara nodded, then fell to her knees and said, "One God in the Above, please hear my prayer. I have granted You a gift—the passion of Your Supplicant. Please grant my prayer."

She watched Anhara's lips move. It looked like Anhara was humbly beseeching the One God's ear with a private plea. Sureya would see her mother's loving smile, hear her brother's funny laugh, see the strong curve of her father's hand . . .

"No!" A male voice bellowed. A figure rushed from behind the boulders and scrub bushes. With all of his might, he launched himself at Sureya. "You can't bring back the dead!"

6

The man—the one from the bushes—he must have killed her. She must be dead. Sureya couldn't breathe, and her world made no sense.

Then she heaved a painful breath, and realized what was happening. Something huge lay on top of her. She wasn't dead. Not yet. The massive man had trapped her beneath his chest. She was pinned like an insect on display. Then Sureya gasped again, peering over his well-muscled—and brown—shoulder.

The noble color of his skin shocked her for only a heartbeat because the caldera held a bigger surprise. Somehow, thousands of butterflies had filled it. Sureya blinked, not sure she believed her eyes. But the fluttering wings—like the man atop her—remained solid and real. She saw some butterflies had wings the size of dinner plates. Others were the size of her thumbnail.

She tried to push him off, only dimly aware of the feel of her naked breasts against his massive chest. She couldn't look away from the spectacle in the sky.

Iridescent blues and greens flickered in the starlight. Yellows shimmered between gold and orange. A fuchsia butterfly landed on the man's *khal*-colored shoulder, just above Sureya's nose, and she saw the intricate indigo pattern, the complicated structure of its antennae.

The man above her shifted, and it fully registered that she was naked—completely naked. His muscular thighs pressed hard against her naked hips. Her nipples rubbed against the cloth of his shirt. She shoved against him, fighting a growing panic.

"Did you enjoy the show, cousin?" asked Anhara coolly, lying on her stomach next to them.

Hearing the words, Sureya felt her face burn. This terrible man had watched as Anhara brought her to ecstasy? This horrible man was Anhara's cousin? How could that be?

"You fools," he said, in a voice as thick as fog. "You can't bring back the dead."

"She misses her mother, her family," Anhara answered. In her mind's eye, Sureya could see the woman's brow arch with the words.

"You've no idea what you've done." Even though the moon hid his face in shadows, Sureya saw the man's scowl.

"But—" Sureya tried to say, pushing against him again. He was so much bigger than she. It was like pushing against a granite wall—futile. *But the butterflies*, she wanted to say.

"But what, you unnatural *zewah*?" he asked, finally looking at her face.

Locking eyes with him, Sureya gasped. The man was as breathtaking as the wings floating around them. Dark haired and dark eyed, the angular planes of his face gave him a dangerous look, or maybe it was the menacing snarl on his lips. He was gorgeous.

Sureya quit pushing, painfully aware of her bare stomach against his chest.

"But look," Anhara answered for her. Keeping that elegant

stillness she stood and pointed around the oasis while Sureya caught her breath. "We've filled the oasis with messengers of peace—not blood and death and war."

"Not the undead," Sureya managed to croak. She'd never wanted to bring her family back from the dead. She'd imagined a vision of them. She'd heard that the abbesses could scry visions of the past.

The dark-haired man finally looked down at Sureya. She could feel his cock harden as he examined her, which made her feel weak and helpless. Obviously discomfited, he rolled off. Had he just now realized she was naked, that she was white?

"But I heard you pray to see your family," he said.

"You know nothing, Kalief. We aren't men, fighting the world at every turn. Now get away from that poor girl before you hurt her."

The man—Kalief—stood. "Is she the Supplicant?"

"You're looking at the proof around you." Again Anhara elegantly gestured at the insects while Sureya shrugged into her clothing. Still on her back, she wrapped the blanket around her for good measure, wishing for her staid dress instead of the provocative desert clothes.

Kalief turned away from Anhara and eyed Sureya critically. Suddenly he whipped off her blanket, spun her onto her stomach, and yanked her pantaloons to her thighs.

"What are you doing?" Sureya cried. Anhara's cry of outrage echoed her own.

"Look," he commanded, running a hot, rough thumb over the curve of her ass. "She's got the One God's mark. Just as described by Scripture."

"A perfect butterfly birthmark," Anhara breathed. "I had no idea."

Sureya jerked away from both of them, glaring as she stood and pulled up her pantaloons. "What's going on? Tell me now!"

"You haven't told her?" Kalief asked Anhara.

"I showed her."

"Showed me what?"

"After you've had an orgasm, my dove," Anhara replied, "the one who made you come can ask the One God for a favor, and if her—or his—heart is humble, the One God will answer."

Kalief looked around the caldera in awe. "You prayed for . . . butterflies?"

"You know nothing, Kalief."

From high atop the cliffs the man watched, bow notched and ready. He sent a wordless prayer, thanking the Mother Who Loves Silence for the bright moon. The light let him see the people below.

But uncertainty unsettled the watcher's calm. The king below couldn't dedicate the flame-haired girl here, could he? The watcher believed the Humans-Who-Weren't-People needed the basilica and the Penetrator to prepare the girl for her new life.

He held his long bow aimed. He couldn't take the chance. If the dark-haired king made any move to annul the Supplicant's power—to penetrate her—he'd kill him.

The Mother Who Loves Silence prohibited violence in this spot, in this caldera. She would surely strike him dead if he loosed an arrow.

But the sacrifice would be necessary. He'd die with a clear conscience. His people needed the Supplicant, and he wouldn't let anything—not even his life—stand in his way.

Despite his fatigue, Kalief stood guard while the women— his cousin and the whore—climbed into their tent. He'd stand guard all night long and ride hard tomorrow, ensuring they reached the basilica quickly.

He knew some soldiers would have difficulty keeping a lone watch, especially in the safety of this oasis, protected as it was by the One God and surrounded by fifty of his best men.

But his standards were higher.

Unlike his father before him, who took advantage of every luxury offered, Kalief practiced hard discipline. And he expected it from his men. Whatever he demanded of them, he demanded three-fold of himself.

The slight breeze shifted, bringing a foreign scent—something disturbing. Something barbaric.

Something barbaric.

Identifying the scent made the hackles rise on the back of his neck. His enemies were watching. They'd been watching the whore in her home—he'd seen that in Anhara's scrying bowl. Were his men safe now? Was the whore?

Portraying a casualness he didn't feel, Kalief walked toward a dark shadow cast by a cliff wall. Any watcher would have difficulty seeing him there. He stood for a long moment, listening, looking.

Into the quiet of the night, he sounded the nasal, buzzy *pee-yah* of the nighthawk. And then he waited.

A heartbeat later, the call was returned from the eastern side of the caldera. And several heartbeats after that, a nighthawk call sounded from the northern side. Two or three actual birds added their noise to the night.

His men were safe.

Kalief breathed a little easier. His enemies might be watching, but they weren't taking action—not yet.

Standing deep in shadow, Kalief observed the quiet oasis. Butterflies floated on the breeze, looking like they'd always been in the caldera.

The whore—the Supplicant, he corrected himself—had the mark of the One God's peace on her ass, which was as beautiful as the butterflies fluttering in the moonlight. Kalief found it hard to believe that the safety of Marotiri—his land—depended on a creature as fragile, as weak-minded, as she.

The Supplicant.

By the One God, she was beautiful. That flame-red hair, and the matching spots scattered over the bridge of her nose ... And had he ever thought that milky skin was beneath him?

She exactly matched the woman in the warning vision sent by the feathered serpent. If he didn't protect her, she'd end up in some foreign land sleeping with every peasant who had a wish. That wouldn't do.

Kalief had borders to keep safe. He had crops to grow. He had villagers to protect. One small boy with the pox was certainly a heartbreak for the family—Kalief remembered the anguish from the vision. But a peasant's unhappiness was less important when weighed against the needs of the land. The whore, not even a white-skinned whore, could not be allowed to spread her legs for the common and noble people alike. He needed to save her for the nobility.

From the small tent, a peal of laughter rang out, interrupting his thoughts. Anhara was explaining all the whore needed to know about her new life, and apparently, it wasn't striking her as all bad.

Well, why would it? The Supplicant's nature was to crave sex. His coatl vision made that clear. So did Scripture.

Then Kalief heard a different sound—a mewling, a panting. It made him instantly hard. He could all-too-easily imagine the Supplicant's sensual pink lips parted, her eyes dilated in desire, her red hair spread around her pale face like a halo. By the One, the Supplicant was losing no time in practicing her new power, her new talents.

And his cousin had claimed the woman wasn't a whore ... Anhara had a lot of nerve claiming *he* knew nothing. She was the naïve one here.

Then the cries in the tent grew more urgent—and his cock grew harder.

For what would the two witches beseech the One God this

time? A herd of cavorting unicorns? A rainbow to follow them all the way to the basilica?

As the sound of their passion reached a crescendo, Kalief struggled with the urge to palm his cock. He was throbbing. He craved the Supplicant's full lips wrapped around him, sliding and sucking. He didn't have long to wait, but still . . . he wanted her now. He didn't care if she didn't yet know how to properly service a man. He'd be happy to teach her.

And then the Supplicant came. He was certain every man in the cliffs heard it. Now he couldn't help himself. He slid his hand over his cock, grabbing hard and high enough to spread the drops of liquid over his entire shaft. He imagined her writhing beneath him, calling his name. He imagined sucking her breast, tasting her kiss.

Up, he slid, then back. He was close, so close. Once more and—

And then he fell asleep.

Kalief awoke to the rich smell of *khal*. He opened his eyes and yawned. In that disoriented moment, he wondered where he was. Through bleary eyes, he saw the comet. It menaced the sky still, burned the horizon. In that glimpse, Kalief remembered.

Then he sat up, startled.

Those *zewah*! He had a pillow beneath his head, a blanket over his chest, and someone had removed his boots.

All without him waking. Impossible. That he should have slept was impossible.

And then he remembered—his cousin and the whore enjoying each others' bodies, making wishes.

Damn.

Then he remembered something more insidious: the scent of a barbarian in the night breeze.

Ignoring the sharp sting of goat-head thorns on his feet, Kalief marched to the women.

"Do you know what you've done?" he demanded.

"Let everyone within five leagues of here get a good night's sleep?" Sureya asked. When had the little servant girl become so flippant?

"That's exactly what you did," he said. "Do you know what could've happened? There's a barbarian in the cliffs!"

"Umm," said Sureya. "He would've gotten a good night's sleep, too?"

And self-assured. Where had this girl come from? "He could've come down and kidnapped you."

"While . . . sleepwalking?" Kalief thought he liked the demure version of the whore better.

And only then did he realize what the women had done. They hadn't just wished him to sleep—they'd wished everyone in the caldera to sleep.

"*Zewah. Erup xes,*" he muttered in the ancient language.

"I knew you'd need your rest for today's journey," Anhara said, turning to tack up her tiny horse. "And our Supplicant is still a little shy, Kalief. She didn't want you to hear everything." A wicked grin lit her mulberry lips. "Not . . . all night long."

Like lightning through a summer night, jealousy zinged through him. He wished he'd been the one to make the redhead writhe in pleasure throughout the night.

Stifling a groan, he turned away. It was going to be a long day.

Stretching to work the painful kink from his neck, the man in the cliffs shook his head in disgust. As if the volcanic rock behind him was the softest pillow, he'd fallen asleep while on watch—something he hadn't done since he'd been a boy wet behind the ears.

Bleary eyed, he groped for his spyglass. He found it, the

brass plating still chilled from the night air. Luckily, it hadn't rolled off the ledge, smashing into unusable parts and alerting everyone to his presence.

The man in the cliffs glassed the surrounding ledges. A number of the king's lackeys tucked away in the crevices and grottos were yawning and stretching. Most looked embarrassed or dismayed.

He paid no attention to the new sun riding the horizon. The comet was here to stay until She Who Loves Silence was satisfied that the Supplicant was in good hands.

The man in the cliffs saw that the king with the women seemed as angry as a Minion—stiff-legged with anger and red in the face. The women, however, looked unbothered by his wrath.

They appeared unsurprised too.

A silent guffaw escaped the man in the cliffs, and he shook his head, this time in laughter. The women had made all the men sleep—him, the lackeys, the barbarian king below. Probably so they could enjoy a quiet night to themselves.

The man in the cliffs knew about longing for quiet nights alone.

Now he grinned, satisfied. Not only had he enjoyed an unexpectedly good night's sleep—but the women had banished all doubt within him. He knew for certain—the woman with the flame-red hair was the Supplicant.

He planned to take her for his own.

7

Kalief and his second in command rode out of the inselberg before the rest of the soldiers. The morning air felt chilly through his light armor. Kalief was used to the heat brought on by heavier protection.

In silence, both men scanned the horizon with their spyglasses. Their horses were as quiet as the desert morning. Deep sand muffled the fall of their hooves.

"So what're we looking for?" Teron asked in a hushed voice. Kalief was grateful that his friend dropped his formal title in private.

"I smelled barbarian stink last night," Kalief answered. "Was it just one or a damned army?"

Teron grunted before he said, "Don't want to be ambushed with the Supplicant, that's for sure." He reined his horse a few degrees north.

"Exactly." Kalief turned the glass west and looked for rising dust.

"See anything?" Teron asked.

Kalief inspected the horizon a moment. "No. You?"

"No."

Kalief let his hand drop and rubbed his eyes. "I don't know if finding nothing makes me feel better or worse."

"I hate to ask, but are you sure you smelled a barbarian?"

"If my second in command can't question me, no one can. I won't live like that."

"I know." Teron scanned the horizon again.

"But to answer your question, the stink made the hairs on my neck stand up. It made me want to kill someone."

"Sounds like barbarian smell," Teron agreed. "So what do you want to do?"

"Let's lead the party south."

"South?" his friend asked.

"Yes."

Teron dropped his spyglass. "You mean to backtrack east once we get clear of barbarian territory?"

"It might confuse whoever's watching us."

"Might confuse me," Teron joked.

"No chance of that."

"Seriously, confusion would be good." Teron put his spyglass into his saddlebag. "But maybe we can do better than that. Maybe we can flush him out."

"You have something in mind?" Kalief asked. He packed his own spyglass.

Teron pointed his horse back toward the inselberg. "After you lead the group out, I stay behind. See if I find our tail."

"No," Kalief said, nudging his stallion forward. "Not you."

"But—"

He held up his hand. "I can't let you take the chance." Seeing his friend was about to object, Kalief said, "If something happens to me, you've got to get that woman to the safety of the castle. We're lost without her."

With an expression of suppressed humor, Teron nodded. "That's probably true. We need her."

"What're you laughing about?"

"You," Teron answered.

"What is it?"

Teron chuckled. "I've seen the way you are around her. You can't even say her name."

"Whose name?"

Teron laughed. "That's exactly my point."

Kalief scowled and turned his horse back toward the camp. "So who do we have with us who's good for tracking barbarians?"

"Ondras," Teron said without hesitation. "He's got desert blood."

"Let him get left behind, then."

Teron nodded with a smirk. Kalief tried to ignore the laughter.

She was a means to an ends, that was all.

Risham. That was the first thought that struck her when she woke. Not strange skies or Anhara's touch. Not Anhara's handsome, brooding cousin. Her first thought was of Risham.

His warm, strong arms offered stability. His home was loving and happy, and it had been that way since he and his wife first took her in.

She wanted to go back.

No, she thought, rubbing her eyes. It was more than that. She didn't want to go back—she needed to go back. She needed to know the children were safe. She needed to see Risham's smile. And now—she stretched long and languorously—she knew exactly how to please Fajal. Anhara had seen to that.

Anhara and her cousin would forbid her return if she asked. But that didn't mean she couldn't take matters into her own hands. She just had to avoid suspicion, avoid Anhara's spellcasting dust.

Forcing a smile to her face, she left the tent.

* * *

Despite the precautions he'd taken, a sense of unease pervaded Kalief's senses. Something wasn't right.

As a safeguard, he kept Anhara and the Supplicant between him and Teron. Soldiers rode in front of and behind them. They shifted constantly, unpredictably, making a plan of attack difficult for the barbarians.

Kalief should have felt safe.

But those hairs on the back of his neck were telling him something, something bad. He glanced at his friend, wondering whether he felt it too. Teron shot him a grim look in return. Kalief slid his hand back behind his saddle until he palmed the pommel of his sword. Its cool weight reassured him.

"What is it?" Anhara asked.

"Noth—" he began. But a wicked yell filled his ears, and the whore bolted away. Her voice filled his ears as her desert-bred animal ran through the sand like it was on a racetrack.

"She's running home!" Anhara cried. "To her family!"

Without thought, he aimed his stallion toward the whore. He'd catch her in two strides.

"Wait!" Teron called to him.

Kalief slid his horse to a halt and looked at his friend. An outrider was approaching, fast and intent. His chestnut horse was leathered in foamy white sweat.

Kalief shot a glance to the runaway whore.

"I'll get her, sire!" Teron shouted, bolting into the distance.

Kalief turned toward the outrider. "What is it, man?"

"A group of barbarians, sire," he panted. "Two *nalps* ahead."

The whore was riding right toward them. "How many?" Kalief asked.

"Fifty, sir. Same as us," said the soldier. "Only—" The soldier shot him an uneasy glance.

"What is it, boy?" Teron growled.

"They have captives, sir."

"Who do they have?" asked Kalief through clenched teeth. They couldn't have the Supplicant, not yet.

"A man and a woman. Three children." The young soldier said the last in almost a whisper, adjusting the helm on his head. "The oldest child is maybe twelve, a boy. The youngest is a girl of maybe three. The middle child is also a girl."

"Sureya's family!" Anhara gasped. "I promised her the'd be safe, Kalief. They're her only family. If she sees this . . ."

Sureya kicked Firefly into a mad gallop, heading toward home. Knowing soldiers would be after her, she crouched along the horse's neck, willing speed into his legs, willing arrows to fly above her, around her.

She ran. Suns set and rose hundreds of times in the span of time she fled. She didn't care. She concentrated on the beat of Firefly's hooves beneath her, the churning of his breath.

When she finally looked up, she knew she'd succeeded. She was home! Slowing Firefly to an easy canter, she admired the people of her heart. They waited for her—Fajal, Nika, and Dayy stood together, clutching hands. Risham held Lulal in his arms.

And then Sureya realized the children were crying—their ankles and wrists were tied. The family was bound together by tears and ropes. Fajal's right eye was swollen shut, and Risham's long hair had been hacked off. All three children looked stricken, shocked.

"What's—" But then Sureya saw the barbarian atop his shaggy pony.

Fear froze her. For a moment, she was six years old again, helpless. Defenseless. Her family would be slaughtered before her while she mutely watched in horror.

But then she realized she had a dagger and a fast horse. This time she could save them!

She reached for the knife at her hip. Using all her strength, she threw it at the barbarian, wishing him dead with every bit of her heart.

The dagger flew! She watched it close the distance between her horse and his. She willed the blade to bury itself in his eye, his throat, or his heart.

Instead, the handle bounced harmlessly off the man's foot, and the blade fell into the sand.

She had his full attention now. Cold fear gave way to frantic heat.

"Run, Risham!" she cried as the barbarian began to chase her. Surely Firefly was faster than the barbarian pony. She grabbed his mane and leaned forward, digging her heels into his sides. Firefly answered with breathtaking speed.

The horse could fly! As his legs pounded beneath her, Sureya knew no one could catch her. No one.

And then the legs beneath her were gone. The world cartwheeled. Dazed, she wondered why she was looking at the sky. Firefly grunted beside her and struggled to his feet.

She saw a bristly rope twisted between his legs, and deep rope burns ran the length of his cannon bones. He'd been lassoed. She cried in dismay as he shook his head and snorted.

"*Zehwah.*" The barbarian stood before her, grinning. Heart in her throat, she turned and ran.

But the sand snagged her feet, grabbed her ankles. The sand sucked her to the ground. The barbarian was on her in a heartbeat, twisting her arms painfully behind her back, pawing her breasts, poking between her thighs.

Screaming, she kicked at him, tried to sink her teeth into him. She wouldn't let him massacre her, wouldn't let him slit her throat.

She wouldn't end up like her mother.

*   *   *

Kalief waited for Teron to return with the whore. His bay horse pawed the ground, picking up on his impatience.

"I think I see something, sire," Teron's second said. The young soldier was as impatient as Kalief himself.

"What?" he barked. He willed the answer to be "the Supplicant."

"Someone's riding toward us." The man looked a moment longer. "It's Ondras, sire. The man we sent to track the barbarians." Teron's second paused for a moment before adding, "Ondras is riding a barbarian horse, and he seems to have a captive riding in front of him."

"Is it that woman?"

"I—" The man paused. "I can't tell."

Kalief whipped out his own spyglass and looked. The captive was a barbarian. Ondras's captive guided the horse while the soldier held a knife to his throat. Kalief blinked. Why didn't the barbarian just jab Ondras in the gut and escape?

But when he looked more closely, Kalief could see that Ondras held the barbarian's arm twisted hard behind him. They were near enough now that Kalief no longer needed the spyglass.

"Sire," Ondras said a moment later, reining his horse toward Kalief. He bowed his head awkwardly to his king while maintaining his grip on his captive.

"Well done, Ondras," Kalief said. "You've captured our spy." Kalief examined the spy for a moment. The man's bead-filled blond beard covered his nose and his mouth.

Kalief pointed to Erac, a burly soldier who typically watched Kalief's back. Understanding the wordless order, Erac vaulted from his horse with the strength of the dragon after which he'd been named. He yanked the barbarian from his scrubby pony and quickly tied his hands and feet. "What would you have me do with him, sire?" Erac asked.

"Tie him to his pony, and take the reins. Tether his horse to yours. Check he has no knives."

"Yes, sire," Erac said, his fingers quick with the ropes despite his brawny form.

"Sire?" Anhara said. He heard the barely controlled anger beneath the question. She managed a *What the Minion's sphincter do you think you're doing* with one overly polite word.

Kalief held up his hand in response. *Wait.*

But she wouldn't. "What are you doing, cousin?" she asked.

"Maybe the barbarians don't know what they have. We're going to barter a trade," Kalief said. "Erac, come with me, and bring that prisoner."

Sureya whimpered as the barbarian yanked her toward him. With his tongue outstretched, he leaned into her face. One paw kneaded her breast. She shrank away from the stench of his breath. Then he licked her neck, long and wet.

She screamed and tried to knee him in the groin, but he just laughed and pulled her hair so hard she saw stars. He wrapped his hand in the length of her hair and dragged her to her feet. Then he started walking, dragging her backward. Resisting it hurt. She fought to keep up with him, stumbling awkwardly after him.

"Sureya!" she heard, a chirping voice filled with hope. It was Lulal! But she couldn't see the child—the barbarian still held her backward.

A foreign tongue snarled something, and she heard the crack of a hand hitting skin. The child whimpered weakly.

"Lulal!" she cried, lurching toward the voice. But the barbarian laughed and jerked her hair, sending pain ricocheting across her scalp and down her neck. The barbarian slapped her then, hard, making her teeth clack as his open palm smacked her face.

She stood stunned as the barbarian tied her ankles to those of Kalief's second who had also been captured. She watched several other barbarians lead Risham and his children away. All three children were crying. Fajal shot her an angry glare through her good eye. "Leave them alone!" Sureya cried to her captors. "They're nothing to you!"

The barbarian ignored her outcry this time, painfully continuing to tighten the ropes so that her hands and feet tingled.

"Risham!" she yelled after her captor finished tightening. "Lulal!" But they were gone.

"You took the bait, you stupid girl," Teron muttered to her after the barbarian left.

Embarrassment and guilt washed over her. She should've ridden back to Kalief and pled for his intervention. He had an entire army. He could've saved her loved ones.

"They're my only family," she said, hating the smallness of her voice.

"Those barbarians know that!" Teron spat quietly. "They've been watching you for years. They know exactly how you feel about them."

"I couldn't just—" she began. "I couldn't just let them—" Tears rolled down her cheeks, but her arms were tied so tightly to Teron's that she couldn't wipe them away. "Do you know what barbarians do to children?" she threw back. "Maybe you just don't care!"

"I don't think you understand," Teron replied. "Your cunt holds the land's salvation." He spat into the sand. "And you've given it to our enemy."

Sureya cringed at his anger, at the thought of being violated by the barbarians. "Risham and Fajal took me in after the barbarians slaughtered my blood family. They loved me! I couldn't—"

"Your stupidity threatens the best leader our land has seen in centuries," Teron interrupted. "Do you think the king of

Marotiri is just going to ride away from here? Let you fall into barbarian hands?"

"What king?" Sureya was baffled.

"King Kalief, you ignorant girl."

"Kalief's the king?"

"And now he's going to ride in here like a hero to save your neck—no, your cunt!" he hissed.

"I'm so thirsty, Teron," Sureya said, comforted by his warmth despite herself. The natural sun had sunk to the horizon.

"Keep your misery to yourself, girl," he growled. "It's only been a couple of hours."

"But I'm seeing a mirage." She blinked in disbelief as she watched Kalief approach. He wasn't alone. A barbarian escort held a drawn bow aimed at him. "Kalief's riding toward us," she said to Teron.

"Fuck," the soldier said. "That's no mirage—I hear horses." He couldn't see since he was tied to her back. "I told you he'd rescue you."

"Us," she corrected. "He's rescuing us. But a barbarian's holding a bow, drawn and pointed at him."

He sighed, "That's not good. What else do you see?"

She looked. Kalief and his horse outclassed the hairy barbarian on his scrappy horse. His profile, the set of his shoulders, everything about him was regal, even the way his muscled stallion held its head.

"He looks mighty," she said. "Undefeatable."

"He's stalwart, yes," Teron replied. Did Sureya hear his voice crack with amusement? "But he's just one man—one man riding in light armor into a battalion of the fiercest warriors we've ever met."

"Oh." She would have cringed if the ropes allowed it.

"Do you know," Teron began, trying to turn toward her, "that we've never won a battle against these men?"

"But I thought—"

"Everyone does," he replied. "We've made them run. We've made them hide. But we've never defeated them." She felt him work his fingers against the ropes. "We don't know the first thing about this enemy. We lack even a common language."

"He's coming toward us, Teron," she said, but Kalief announced his own presence.

"Supplicant," Kalief said, a crazed laugh ringing out across the sand. "Teron." Ignoring his bearded escort, the king bowed to them.

"Sire?" Teron asked, his voice thick with caution. "What happened?"

"They've challenged me to armed combat, judicial combat." Kalief laughed, and she though he sounded maniacal. "One-on-one with their second-in-command."

Sureya felt blood drain from her face and Teron stiffenned behind her.

"Sire!" Teron said. "I cannot allow it."

"You can't stop it, my friend." Kalief was unperturbed. "I can risk either myself alone, or all of you *and* myself."

"What're the stakes?" Teron croaked, craning his neck to see Kalief.

"Your freedom, should I win." She watched him run his hand through his dark hair. "My life—and yours, and the land's—should I lose."

"My family—" Sureya began, but Teron interrupted her.

"But the challenge, sire," Teron asked. "Why did they issue a judicial challenge?"

"Apparently, they had no choice."

"No choice?" Teron asked. "I don't understand."

"Using Ondras was good advice, Teron. He caught our barbarian, and the captive speaks our language."

"But no barbarian speaks our tongue," Teron answered.

"This one does."

"What'd he say?"

"An old priest with a long gray beard did it," Kalief answered. "He sold us out. The priest gave the family away to the barbarians."

"No!" Sureya said. "Anhara promised they'd be safe!" She knew who that priest was—in Fajal's office, he'd threatened her, threatened those she loved. She herself had yanked the priest to the ground by his beard. She'd stepped on his neck and thought about killing him. Anhara had stopped her.

She should have killed him.

"Well," Kalief said, that crazy smile still on his face. "The barbarians say the family belongs to them, and our law agrees. By asking for the family back, we've slandered them as liars. They issued the judicial challenge, and if we don't accept, the barbarians will slit the throats of each family member." He paused, looking at his second-in-command, then said, "They'll start with the youngest child."

Sureya kept her voice calm, though she felt like screaming. "I caused their deaths as truly as if I loosed an arrow though their hearts myself."

Kalief leapt from his horse and bowed low to the ground, his head nearly touching the sand. Again Teron rumbled his objection, and she couldn't blame him. Nobility—the king himself—didn't bow to the likes of her.

"My lady," Kalief said. "I couldn't allow that to happen. I've accepted the challenge."

"No!" Teron growled. "Sire, don't!"

The barbarian escort rode closer to them. "Enough," he said in a guttural accent. "Now fear they will breathe. Go you now must."

To Sureya, everyone looked ghoulish, especially the barbarians. The moon was up, and the fading sun threw long shadows across the high clouds and under the onlookers' eyes.

"What do you see?" Teron asked. She knew facing the wrong way irritated him. He constantly worried the ropes, hurting her wrists and ankles, but she didn't dare complain.

"One of the barbarians seems ready for combat," she said.

"What's he look like?" He jerked the rope. Was it loosening?

"I think he's taller than the other barbarians."

"He'll have a longer reach then."

She saw that the warrior wore a cold snarl, and his eyes glittered, but she didn't see any reason to mention that to the soldier behind her.

"What's he wearing?" Teron asked.

"A vest," she said. "I think it's suede."

"Not much protection against Kalief's sword," Teron noted, and she agreed. But the vest showed off his thick biceps, which rippled in the moonlight. The barbarian warrior exuded a palpable capability of his own. He stood, legs apart, thick with muscles. His nostrils flared, and the light desert breeze rippled his hair and beard. Was this barbarian the one who'd massacred her mother, her father, and her tiny brother?

"Kalief's got his sword, doesn't he? The one with garnets in the pommel?"

"Yes," she answered. "And he's got a dagger in his left hand."

"His off hand," Teron corrected.

The dagger looked wicked, but Kalief looked cool. The wind didn't touch his thick, dark hair, pulled back as it was in a tight club.

Someone blew a horn. It made a deep, resonating bellow, and the hairs on the back of Sureya's neck stood erect. "What's that mean?" she asked.

"The combatants enter the arena now."

Teron was correct. Kalief and the barbarian entered the agreed-upon area and stood off, basked in the queer light. Kalief nodded at the barbarian, who merely snarled in response. The men crossed the tips of their sword blades, their daggers poised behind them in their left hands.

"The barbarian hulks over Kalief." The observation made Sureya's heart leap to her throat. "Surely, his reach is longer than Kalief's."

"Don't worry yet, lass."

As one of the barbarians began the long countdown in their rasping language, Kalief's sword glittered wickedly, somehow reflecting only the moonlight. The barbarian's narrow blade glowed red. Sureya didn't know if the color came from the blade's metal or from the creepy sun that refused to set in the late twilight sky.

"What strange weapon is the barbarian using?" Sureya asked.

"You have to tell me what it looks like before I can answer that question," Teron said caustically.

"It's longer than Kalief's, and narrower. It curves but doesn't taper until the very tip."

"That's a shamshir, my lady, a slashing weapon. It's sharp on both sides, and if that barbarian can use it like a hook, he'll slice an arm right off a torso."

"Oh." Kalief's arm. Kalief's torso.

"But thrusting that weapon with any precision's impossible." Teron worked at the ropes a bit more. They were definitely loosening. "At least for any swordsman I've met."

"Do you think he'll win, Teron?"

"Kalief can beat any of our men."

Relief flooded her, and then she said, "But against—"

"We've won with numbers rather than skill. We don't know their techniques, their strengths and weaknesses."

Suddenly Teron freed himself from her, just as the foreigners' counting stopped. Sureya froze.

Everyone froze.

The barbarian and Kalief stood motionless for a moment. Neither blinked. Sureya could see their eyes locked together, perhaps assessing each other. Teron stepped quietly to her side. All eyes were on the combatants.

Then the barbarian swung his dagger from behind and sliced viscously at Kalief, the King of Marotiri. The move was so quick that Sureya nearly missed it, but the soldier next to her gasped, then swore. "Can't parry that kind of speed," Teron said.

"And in a man so large," she said.

But Kalief had no difficulty stepping neatly out of the way. Then he lunged with his sword, a move easily parried by the barbarian.

Metal clanged on metal for heartbeats, for days. Man attacked man, thrust after thrust. Swords tangled and daggers swiped. She couldn't follow who attacked, who parried, who fell back. The men were a blur before her. Sureya stood rigid, willing her body to remain invisible.

She willed her loose bonds to remain invisible.

Blades glittering in the fading light, neither man gave ground. Neither man fell back. Sureya searched their faces, looking for clues to who was winning. Sweat ran down both faces, disappearing into the barbarian's beard, trickling beneath Kalief's leather armor.

As far as she could tell, neither was winning.

Swords tangled again, and again daggers shot out for a killing thrust. She saw a dagger meet leather chest armor and slide off. Whose dagger? Whose armor? She couldn't tell.

"By the One God's dripping asshole," Teron muttered. "That was close."

Kalief's armor, then. The barbarian's strange, curved sword.

Suddenly Sureya could see, could comprehend. The barbarian was falling back under the unrelenting strength of Kalief's thrusting and swiping sword.

"Watch out," Teron muttered, as if the king could hear him. "It could be a trap." Sureya realized then that the bond of friendship ran between Kalief and Teron.

Drawing on reserves of strength Sureya could barely imagine, Kalief clanged his sword again and again against the barbarian's, who seemed to be slowing, tiring. Was Kalief taking advantage of it, or was he running out of energy?

She clutched Teron's forearm, wanting to draw on his strength, wanting to lend her strength to Kalief.

But then the barbarian slashed with his dagger, hard. He whipped his hand back, but the dagger stayed, embedded in the leather armor.

While slicing his sword toward the barbarian, Kalief looked down at the implement. With his off hand, he plucked the offending dagger from his side and threw it far into a sand dune—without missing a beat in the thrust-and-parrying. Sureya heard the blade hiss through the air and thud into the sand.

Now the barbarian was partially disarmed.

But then—just as the barbarian lunged at Kalief with his glittering shamshir—Sureya saw blood trickling from Kalief's side, from under the armor.

"Teron," she said without taking her eyes from the men. "Do you see that?"

She felt the soldier slowly nod.

The tempo of swordplay picked up. Before now, the clanging had been so regular that Sureya could have danced the waltz to it. But now, now the metal scraped and slid rather than clanged. The irregular screeching sent shivers from her teeth to her toes.

And worse, the sun was nearly set. Sureya could barely see.

But she saw Kalief make a surprising thrust with his dagger. It would've been a swift and deadly strike, had it landed. But the barbarian caught Kalief's wrist in his palm. Sureya could see the bearded man squeeze. His eyes squinted with effort, and she imagined his inhuman strength.

Kalief fought the hold, but his sword was pressed against the barbarian's shamshir—Kalief couldn't move. Kalief's dagger hand opened. Then his dagger fell uselessly to the ground.

The barbarian gave a terrible yell of success and punched Kalief right in his solar plexus with his left hand.

But Kalief must have been expecting it. He barely grunted as he pulled his elbow back, and thrust his sword toward the barbarian. The thrust was mighty. It didn't glance off the boiled leather armor—it penetrated. Deeply. The barbarian fell to the ground with a low and eerie moan.

Kalief withdrew his bloody sword and held it to the man's throat. Instead of delivering the killing stroke, Kalief bowed. "I'll let you make peace with your comrades and your god." Then in a voice loud enough for all to hear, Kalief said, "Well fought, barbarian."

"Finish it," the barbarian croaked in a thick accent. "Now."

Teron muttered, "When did they learn our language?"

"I'll not finish it now," Kalief announced to the man, to the crowd. "You should use these last moments to pray for the souls of all you have sent early to the afterlife."

"You'll regret this," the barbarian said. But Kalief turned his back on the man and began to walk away.

"Sire!" Teron shouted. He wasn't pretending to be tied any longer. "His shamshir!"

Sureya squinted in the tricky light, and saw that the barbarian had grabbed his weapon and was trying to roll atop the blade to kill himself.

Kalief bent to retrieve the weapon. He tossed it to Teron and said in a voice still heaving with exhaustion, "Make sure the Supplicant's family is returned to their home, and warn the priests that any similar actions on their behalf will lead directly to their ruin."

"Yes, sire."

"May I attend to your wound, my lord?" Sureya asked, eyes downcast. Other men would kill her for the mayhem she'd caused here.

But Kalief looked at her, and her heart nearly stopped. An intensity filled his gaze. As sweat poured from his brow, she knew she'd never seen anyone as gorgeous as he in her whole life. She'd never even imagined such rugged beauty in a man.

Kalief walked over to her and pulled her toward him. "I've come to collect my prize, Supplicant."

"Prize, sire?" she managed weakly.

He slowly leaned toward her, giving her every opportunity to move away, to turn her face, even.

But she didn't want to.

His salty lips claimed hers. Her shallow, quick breaths mingled with his. She swam in the luxury of his masculine scent, the scent of his hard-earned victory.

Ignoring the soldiers and the barbarians, he kissed her with deliberate slowness, holding her body crushed against his as if she could save him. His lips pressed harder against hers, and she tentatively returned the kiss. His lips were hot and skilled, tender and moist. Under his, hers grew warmer and bolder.

He withdrew for a moment, just long enough to look closely at her face. His eyes shone in the moonlight, sparkled, it seemed, just for her. Apparently he liked what he saw because he immediately kissed her again, harder and more possessively this time.

But he didn't need to take possession. She was his.

Sword still in hand, he touched her mouth with his tongue again, teasing and questing, until she shyly parted her lips, and she felt the intimacy of his tongue for the first time. Heat from his body enveloped her, and she wished he'd wrap her in his arms.

Her hunger grew, and she returned his kisses with growing

passion, tangling her tongue in his, yielding her body to his. Her breasts pressed against his leather armor, and she could feel him still heaving, still panting from exertion. Or was it from her?

Kalief worked his free hand into her hair. His warm fingers slid over her scalp. He tilted her head back, forcing her to yield completely. She opened her mouth to him as her pebbled nipples pressed hard against his armor.

Still ignoring the people surrounding them, Kalief slid a thumb over her nipple. The pad felt hard and calloused, even over the silk of her desert outfit.

"Do you desire me?" Kalief asked in a husky voice she'd not heard before now.

"I—" she began.

"Your words are irrelevant," he said, pressing hard against her hardened nipples. "Your body speaks for you."

"And it doesn't lie, my king."

After the little king and his soldiers rode off with the pathetic brown-skinned family, the watcher took charge of the small group of remaining warriors.

A number of men, including the healer, stood around the man who'd fallen in battle against the little king. As the watcher approached, he could see by the grim expression on the healer's face that the man wouldn't live.

"Leave us," he said to those gathered around the man. They scattered without question.

The watcher examined the wounds and concurred with the healer. The man would die—but he wasn't yet dead.

"Tal," the watcher said. "Can you hear me?"

"Yes, my lord," the man said, blood trickling from between his lips.

"Do you want some water?"

"Please, sire."

The watcher brought the flask to the man's lips and helped him drink. "You've done so very well today. I'm proud of you."

A faint light lit the dying man's eyes at the praise. "Thank you, my lord."

The watcher took the bloody man's hand in his own and said, "I know it's not easy to let another man win such a battle, but your sacrifice will go far toward victory for our people."

"Yes, my lord." His voice was fading. "It was an honor, my lord."

"She Who Loves Silence will save a special place in her bed for you, Tal," the watcher said. "And I know you'll give her good reason to love noise."

A slight smile crossed the man's lips, and he died.

The watcher stood, looking east, the direction the little king and his men had gone. He no doubt he could catch them by dawn. He hoped the false sense of complacency he'd planted in the mind of the king was worth the death of this remarkable swordsman.

Savoring the early morning cool, Sureya rode silently next to
Anhara and Turu, her horse. That victory kiss had disturbed
her almost as much as the new sun.

In the years since she'd come of age, she'd imagined herself
in love with Risham, only with Risham. And when he pro-
posed with Fajal's blessing, she'd thought all of her dreams had
come true.

But how did her love for Risham compare to—

"Tie the Supplicant's horse to Anhara's," Kalief said, turning
to Teron. "I don't want her bolting away again. And tie her
hands to her saddle, too."

"I won't run away," she said to him. But the words sounded
weak, even to her.

"Of that, I'm assured," Kalief said, smiling coldly. "Now,
Teron."

"But—" she started to say, but Firefly snorted and shook his
head. She couldn't complain, could she? Not after the trouble
she'd caused.

Sureya snuck a glance at Kalief's rugged profile. How would the weight of his hands feel pressed against her body? Brutal.

"We're coming to a village," Kalief said to her. "I'm going to ask my soldiers to surround you." His voice was rich, melodic even.

"If it's dangerous," she asked, "why are we going through it?"

"Water," he said simply. They'd ridden miles through this insidious sand. The horses would need something to drink, even if the men could manage with their canteens and flasks. Kalief motioned with his hand, and his men fell neatly into a box around them. A soldier toward the front bellowed, "Haloo!" as they approached the village.

No one answered, and she watched the muscles in Kalief's neck tighten, almost imperceptibly.

"Haloo!" a soldier cried again.

Silence. The blowing sand muffled even the jangling bridles.

Suddenly, a man from the front of the ranks broke off and galloped toward Kalief. "Captain," he said, "There're bodies shoveled into the irrigation canals, tens of them."

"Barbarians," Kalief muttered. "Tell Xat to take fifteen men and scout the buildings before we bring in the horses. Secure the place."

Anhara pulled her dagger from the loop in her pantaloons, and Sureya wished she could do the same. But she'd lost her dagger, having thrown it at the barbarian. Besides, her hands were tied. She couldn't defend herself even if she were armed.

She, Kalief, and Anhara stood in silence for a moment, waiting. Then the messenger soldier returned. "Barbarians raided the village, sire. Everyone's dead." In a quieter voice, he added, "I don't think the women want to see this, sire."

"We will see it," Anhara said. "The Supplicant needs to know more about the world, her world."

Her stomach churned. She'd seen exactly what barbarians could do. Every time she closed her eyes, she saw what they'd done to her family. And now, the haunted look of Risham's children appeared in her mind.

Kalief shot a glance at her and made a decision. "There's no need," he said. "Koit, take the women's horses to the well. You're correct—the women don't need to see this."

"No," Sureya said, in a voice so steady it surprised her. Her knees were shaking, but Firefly remained steady. "I want to see the village—it's not so different from the one in which I was raised."

Kalief looked at her a moment, then shrugged. "If it's clear of barbarians, suit yourself."

Anhara gave a matter-of-fact nod and legged Turu toward the plaza. Meekly, now that she'd won her way, Sureya urged Firefly to follow.

At first, Sureya didn't see much amiss. The desert wind had painted everything dust colored. Certainly, a coat of sand could obscure blood.

Then she noted the church. Glass lay smashed around the window openings, which had been boarded up—from the inside. The smell of roasting pork filled the air, and thick spirals of smoke wafted from the roof. Some of the wood panels covering the windows were charred black.

When she reined Firefly to an opening and peered inside, her mind couldn't grasp what it saw. Even before she could make sense of the horror, some logical part of her brain realized that it wasn't pork she smelled—it was the odor of cooked human flesh.

The people of this village had sought refuge from the barbarians in the church, and the marauders had set it on fire, roasting women and children as if they were chickens—or pigs.

Images from her childhood came crashing back. Her father, his bloody, gaping throat. Her mother. The metallic smell of blood, of foreign sweat. Burning flesh. The plump face of her little brother, still and lifeless.

Sureya kicked her horse, needing to leave, to erase this image from her mind. Firefly leapt blindly south, eating up a short distance in a heartbeat. Anhara and Turu were dragged behind.

But being a far superior horsewoman, Anhara caught Sureya's reins before she got too far. "Shh, my dove," she soothed, but Sureya could not be soothed. She leaned over her red horse's shoulder and vomited.

"Sureya," Anhara said. "Sureya. Look at me!"

Through her blurred vision, Sureya obeyed, seeking the reality of her friend's face. She wiped her mouth with the back of her hand.

Anhara untied Sureya's hands.

"Barbarians," Sureya panted, rubbing her wrists. "I hate them!"

Anhara's cool gaze assessed her for a moment. "That may be."

"They—" Sureya could barely speak. "They cooked the villagers."

"And yet look there." Anhara pointed to a grove of trees. A body hung from a rope. "That's a so-called barbarian."

Looking at the figure, Sureya cried out and wretched again over Firefly's withers. "I'd have hung him myself."

"Before you judge so quickly and so harshly, see what's actually in front of you." Anhara paused, giving Sureya a moment to digest her words. "The hanging happened first, little dove. And if you look closely, you'll see that the barbarian lost his eyes, and his fingers, and two of his toes before he was hung."

Sureya tore the veil from her face and ripped her hand through her hair. "I can't stand this!" she cried. "This is a horrible place."

"I would not belittle your anguish, little dove. Indeed, I hope you cherish it and hold on to it in these days to come."

"Why?"

"Because the world is not so clear as my cousin the king would try to make you believe—because there're always two sides to any story." Anhara pointed to the hanging man and asked, "Did the barbarians burn the villagers first, or did the villagers torture and hang the barbarian first?"

"Nothing could justify—" Sureya began.

"Look out!" a soldier behind her shouted. Other men shouted unintelligible words in answer. Plumes of dust erupted all around her. She heard the clatter of weapons, metal scraping metal as soldiers unsheathed swords, the cries of horses. But she could see nothing through the thick wall of sand that had arisen from nowhere.

"Sureya!" she heard Anhara call, but Sureya couldn't find her friend—couldn't see anything but the roiling waves of dust.

"Anhara!" she shouted, gripping Firefly's mane tightly in her hand, clutching his sides tightly with her calves. "Anhara!" she cried. Fine grains of sand filled her mouth each time she called to her friend.

Firefly whinnied nervously and danced beneath her, but he didn't bolt.

"Sureya!" she heard, but she couldn't tell who called her name—not even if the caller was male or female. Where was Anhara?

Then the whirlwind of sounds melted away, leaving an eerie silence. An impossibly tall wall of sand encircled her, blocking her senses of everything save Firefly beneath her.

The grove of trees, the church walls, everything was gone. And nothing moved. Every grain of sand remained perfectly still.

Sureya caught her breath, immobile with fright.

A figure appeared just before her, shimmering into existence. *He is going to hurt me!*

But Firefly gave a quiet nicker of greeting, nuzzling the man's upturned palm. His skin was a dark as the bark of the *baboab* tree. Ears pricked forward, Firefly nickered again. Sureya breathed a little easier, trusting her horse's judgment in a world without clues.

"You are the *nopuoc*," the figure said, breaking his eye contact with the horse to look up at Sureya. "And I have a gift for you, a gift of knowledge."

"Who are you?" But the figure—a man, she saw for certain now—didn't reply.

The man had broad features, hair as dark as Anhara's, and even darker skin. A fierce white tattoo of a jaguar pounced across his forehead, and he wore a thick jade hoop through the center of his nose. "You didn't ravage this village," she demanded. "You didn't hang that man, or cook the people in the church."

"I did not, my *nopuoc*."

"But who are you?" Sureya asked again.

"You have a good heart," the man said. His voice thrummed like a guitar playing quietly in the heart of the night. "My people have been praying for the appearance of a *nopuoc* for many seasons," he said. "A *nopuoc* with a good heart."

"I don't know what a *nopuoc* is," Sureya said, stumbling over the word.

"It is one mortal to whom the Corn God, the Rain Goddess, the War God, and the Fire Goddess listen."

The Supplicant. Sureya recognized both the description of her supposed powers and the list of foreign deities—they belonged to the Fierce People who dwelled south of the Mangoei Mountains.

"Are you here to steal me, then?" Sureya asked calmly. "Kidnap me back to your bloodthirsty land?"

He raised his eyebrows at her description of his home, making the ghostly jaguar on his forehead appear to leap.

It then occurred to Sureya—after seeing the hanged, tortured man and the charred church housing the dead, that perhaps her land was bloodthirsty as well. A longing for peace filled her, as palpable as the red horse beneath her.

But the man only said, "The gift I bring, offered from the very soul of my people, will bring you wisdom—wisdom to offset the folly of your youth."

This time Sureya blinked. She'd certainly demonstrated such folly yesterday.

"But it is not you I criticize," the tattooed man said. "All youth carries folly on its beautiful wings. It is its very nature."

Firefly bobbed his head, nudging the man with his muzzle. She stared silently at the man.

"And no one will kidnap you, not until you are . . ." The ebony man paused, as if looking for a word. ". . . dedicated to the god of your people in your basilica with your priests."

"We're on our way there now," she said as Firefly whickered softly.

"My time here is nearly at an end, *nopuoc*. Will you accept the gift of my people? You must accept it freely if I am to give it to you."

Sureya nodded. What else could she do?

"You will not be sorry," the man said. And as Sureya looked into the deep black of his eyes, she believed him.

"Please, give me your hand," he commanded.

Sureya held out her left hand. The man grasped her palm hard and laid his other palm on her forearm. A searing pain, an intense burning, ran right under her skin, and Sureya cried in agony, trying to jerk her arm away from the lunatic.

"I am so sorry, but just a moment more," he said in his thrumming voice. "I only need a heart—"

But Sureya couldn't comprehend his fading words. Amid the walls of sand, her world went black.

Sureya opened her eyes. A kaleidoscope of colors tumbled over each other. She closed her eyes again, inhaling deeply. The air smelled damp and cool, nothing like the desert.

"I think she's waking." The voice—a woman's—sounded far away. Sureya thought about answering, but the effort seemed too great. She sighed and let unconsciousness wash over her.

"Sureya," she heard. "Sureya!"

She groaned, wanting nothing more than to swim, to sleep. To swim through the wavelets of sleep. She'd swim back to her mother's arms, to a time when the world was safe and she was loved for herself.

"Wake up, Sureya!"

She'd swim back to a time when the One God was an abstract being, not some strange power that harkened to her orgasms, that ruined her life with his attentions.

"Sureya, wake up, little dove."

"Go away," she managed to croak. Her voice sounded like a frog's.

"Sit her up," a voice commanded. Anhara.

"Yes, Abbess," someone answered.

Anhara was an abbess? Of course she was, Sureya realized. With all of the clues—her religious knowledge, her authority— Sureya should have realized it earlier. The king's cousin would be someone important.

Deft hands pulled her up by the shoulders before she could swat them away. "Stop it," she said. "I'm fine." But the hands ignored her, worming their way under her arms. "I can do it myself," she insisted, opening her eyes and inching herself upright.

But when she managed to get herself into a sitting position, the room swam, spun. Blindly clawing the air for support, she found Anhara's arm. She'd recognize its strong grace even with her eyes closed.

"What happened to me? Where are we?"

"Oh, my little dove, we're back in San Mistofina—my abbey." Anhara brought a cool flask to Sureya's mouth. "Drink this."

"What happened to me? How long was I . . ." Cool and sweet, the water tasted as fresh as newly melted snow, and Sureya drank it all.

Setting the flask aside, Anhara told a woman—a nun, Sureya noted from the habit—to fetch the Abbot General. "A high priest from Tepetl brought a coatl for you," Anhara explained to Sureya. "He gave you one as a gift."

"A coatl?" Sureya searched her mind for a meaning but found none.

"We've tried to eradicate it, but we've been unable."

"Eradicate?" Sureya's heart began to pound. She so clearly remembered the man's face—not just his strange leaping tattoo, but his burning eyes. With a glance, he'd spoken volumes. His gift was important.

"We've tried to remove it," Anhara said, indicating Sureya's forearm, where an egg-sized lump had appeared. Burns and partially healed lacerations covered the lump, and Sureya knew the coatl had not caused them. "You tried to kill it!"

"It's growing in you."

Sureya caressed the thing protectively. "It won't hurt me. I need it."

"How do you know that?" Anhara asked with her quiet stillness. "Some coatl are evil."

"The man who gave it to me . . ." Sureya tried to explain. "He wouldn't hurt me. He said it was a gift from his people, from the soul of his people."

"His people sacrifice each other to a whole host of gods who insist on drinking blood. As the Supplicant of Marotiri, you don't speak to such wicked entities—you speak to the One God."

Perhaps I speak to whomever I please, Sureya thought. But she kept her words to herself. "Please, Anhara, don't try to . . . eradicate . . . my coatl. If it's dangerous, we'll deal with it later."

Anhara sighed and looked at her, making her feel like a stubborn child. "It'll hurt when it hatches," Anhara warned.

Sureya stifled a shudder, unwilling to let the other woman see any reluctance on her part. "You have medicine to allay the pain?"

"Yes," Anhara said, still holding her hand. "We can help the pain."

Sureya nodded, still too weak to speak overmuch. She felt like she wanted to cry, although she didn't know why, exactly.

Anhara dropped her voice to a softer tone. "I can see this coatl's important to you, little dove. If that's so, I'll help you keep it safe."

"Thank you," Sureya managed to say.

"And if you find speaking to the gods of the Fierce People helps you understand the world, then that's what you should do."

Sureya couldn't help herself. Tears ran down her cheeks.

"I'm so sorry for upsetting you," Anhara said, handing her the cool flask of water.

"It's just, my life..." Sureya floundered for words, but none were needed.

"Do you remember why you're here?"

"At the abbey?"

"Yes."

Sureya remembered. "The dedication." She scratched the coatl egg, which had begun to itch.

Anhara ran a fingertip across Sureya's brow. "My little dove, the dedication's in two days."

Sureya hoped she felt strong enough to walk down the aisle and murmur the appropriate prayers.

"And we need to prepare you." Anhara caressed Sureya's earlobe, sending a now familiar heat down her spine. "There's much I haven't told you."

"About?" Her heart started pounding again. Anhara didn't sound like she had welcoming news.

"About the next week." Anhara looked down at Sureya's hand. "About the dedication."

"Tell me."

"In the ceremony, you must play several roles. I'll describe the most challenging first."

The coatl egg began to itch beyond reason. "What is it?" Sureya asked, trying not to scratch.

"In the eyes of the entire congregation, you must be brought to orgasm."

Suddenly, the itching was gone. "Orgasm . . . ? Congrega—"

With a look of unhappiness, Anhara continued. "And then you'll be penetrated. Everyone must see that you're penetrated for the first time. Everyone must see the blood."

The room started spinning again.

"The Penetrator will pray to the One God, and all will see

that his prayer's answered," Anhara said in a tight voice that Sureya almost didn't recognize.

"But you—I mean, the butterflies in the caldera. Why do I have to—"

"These are the rules made by the priests, not me. The priests follow rules handed down over two millennia through Scripture." Anhara stroked her brow: small, soothing movements. "I'd never do this to you. My Order would never have imagined the trials the priests insist upon for dedicating a Supplicant."

"I don't feel so well," Sureya said. Why would the One God place her in such a terrible position?

"There're two other pieces of information."

"What? An orgy? Gang rape? What if I cannot—cannot—" Sureya couldn't even bring herself to say the word.

"Orgasm?"

"Yes! What if I can't in front of all those people? What if I can't for a—"

"Shh, my dove." Anhara stroked her forehead again. "Let me tell you the other two things."

"What?"

Anhara dropped her voice. "Keep this information to yourself—it's better for you if the priests believe you don't know this."

"What?" This time Sureya whispered.

"You can escape your fate. If you lose your virginity to anyone beside the Penetrator before the dedication ceremony, you'll lose all your powers. You'll live the rest of your life as a normal woman."

"And when I . . . orgasm?"

"You'll be like all other women. It'll be a pleasurable experience but not one the One God will heed."

"Oh." Sureya thought for a moment, and then said, "Did Risham know about . . ."

Sureya watched Anhara's expression soften. "I'm sorry, my dove. It's likely Risham knew. The priests probably told him."

"Oh," Sureya said again. That explained Risham's offer to save her by marrying her. Only he hadn't told her the whole story. He hadn't told her about her power—the Supplicant's power.

The cold fingers of reality twined around her heart. Risham never gave her the choice.

"Do you understand?" Anhara asked. "If the first person who penetrates you is anyone but the Abbott General, you escape your fate."

She had to lie with the Abbott General, probably some fat old military man with a curled mustache. "Yes," Sureya answered reluctantly. The coatl began to itch again. "I understand. What's the second thing?"

"The first wish after penetration is yours. It's for you."

"For me?"

"The Penetrator must ask the One God for whatever you wish."

"And I won't wish to back out because . . ."

"Because if that's what you want, you can run out this door and get one of the soldiers to take you," Anhara said in a quiet voice. "I have a very eager and willing man waiting, should you decide to forego this . . . honor."

"A . . . soldier?" Her whole adult life, she'd fantasized about Risham. But if she walked about back and let the soldier . . . fuck her . . . Well, then, her life would be her own. She looked at Anhara. "But why would you do that?"

"Don't ever doubt my faithfulness to my land, little dove. I love Marotiri with every pulse of my heart." Anhara's fingers were still now, quiet on Sureya's brow. "But if we violate the rights of our citizens, this'll be no place for anyone to live. If you've no desire to embrace the path fate has laid out for you, I've no desire to force you to take it."

"So if I don't accept—" Sureya paused, digesting the implication of Anhara's words. "Then I'm not patriotic?"

"Marotiri has survived without the aid of a Supplicant for generations. They can survive now without you, if they need to."

"But the barbarians . . ."

Speaking in a hushed voice, nearly a whisper, Anhara said, "If you remain a Supplicant, your life will never be easy. Men will continually try to use you as a pawn. People will always try to manipulate you to their cause. Common folk in the street will envy you and call you 'whore' with one breath and beg you to help them with the next. Marriage and family will not be yours."

"Not mine?"

"No Supplicant in history has every borne children."

In her mind, she saw the catbird tossing its eggs out of the nest. To her surprise, Sureya found tears rolling down her cheeks again.

"But—" Anhara stroked Sureya's hand. "You will have great power. The ability to heal will lie between your thighs—as will the ability to kill. You can change the shape of our entire land—not simply Marotiri, but the entire land—with your wisdom and your cunt. You can lay the foundation for generations of peace and prosperity. Or famine, strife, and hardship."

"If I walk out back and avail myself to that soldier, then I could get married and have children?"

"Yes," Anhara replied. "And you can ride the winds of fortune as the rest of us do. I'll never think less of you if that's your choice."

"And if I accept my fate?"

"If you stay and endure the next week, and if you're clever and generous"—Anhara placed a chaste kiss on Sureya's forehead—"then you can shape those same winds."

* * *

"Praise the One God she's alive," Kalief said to Teron as they marched down the polished cobbled floor toward Anhara's abbey.

"If we'd saved that accursed family just to lose the Supplicant to that freak sandstorm . . ." Teron didn't need to finish the sentence; Kalief understood exactly the frustration.

"But we lost not a man," Kalief said. In truth, his heart had lurched when that wall of sand appeared, and not only because he feared for the Supplicant. He'd miss his cousin if anything happened to her, despite their constant bickering. Anhara made him think.

"Teron, maybe we should talk to Anhara about the barbarians. Maybe she can help us devise some clever plan to eradicate them."

The clomping sound of their boots down the flagstone hallway echoed. Finally, Teron said, "How would the abbess interpret your vision, Kalief? The one where the Supplicant's fucking the white guy?"

He immediately understood his friend's implication. Maybe that terrible vision of the Supplicant servicing the common peasant would come about if he let Anhara get her hooks into the fire-haired Supplicant. Anhara had a way of worming women into positions of power and encouraging them to do outrageous things in the name of their country.

"You might be right," he said. As they strode purposefully down the hallway, he fought rising alarm within him. But taking a deep breath, Kalief shook his head. Anhara loved Marotiri as much as he did. As a leader, she'd made as many sacrifices as he had.

But that fact would not stop Anhara from pushing for reforms—not at all.

"Can I ask you something?" Teron said.

"What?"

"Why did you risk your life to save her family?"

"I didn't have a—"

"Don't start down that road, Kalief. You could have done any number of less risky things."

Kalief looked down at his friend as they walked. Teron was right. He'd like to say he saved the family because it was the right thing to do, but that wasn't the truth—not the whole truth.

"It was her eyes, wasn't it?" Teron asked. "The shade of gray. It's like, what? A dove's wing or something?"

"Teron," Kalief growled in warning.

But his friend wasn't holding back, not now. "There's something exciting about slumming down the classes, isn't there? That exotic skin, the color of milk? Makes you want to lap it up."

"Stop," Kalief tried to order.

"Am I right, though?" Teron smirked as they rounded a corner.

"Only a bit," Kalief admitted.

"The slumming it bit, or the trying to impress her bit?"

Kalief thought of the Supplicant's earnest eyes, gray like a spring sky just before a long, soft rain. He thought of how dedicated she was to saving that family. They weren't even her blood. "Maybe it's guilt."

"Guilt?" Teron asked.

"By the One, man," Kalief said, staring at the end of the hall. "Have you heard what the Scripture says we need to do to her?"

"No. How bad can it be?"

They turned left at a three-way juncture. "I'm sure every lord and lady in the realm knows that we have the Supplicant by now, and they're all reading up on it. A delegate from each borough gets to publicly fuck her, Teron. She's supposed to be on *dawa* for the rest of her life, to keep her amenable to fucking whenever we need her."

"By the One," Teron laughed. "A lifetime of orgasms. That doesn't sound too bad."

"For a man, maybe not. But have you ever met a woman like that?"

"Only whores."

"Whores stop whoring the minute they get rich," Kalief said.

"So, you're hoping to buy her off by saving her family?" Teron scoffed. "You're already treating her like a whore. Just get used to it, man." Teron clapped him on the arm.

"I don't have to like it," Kalief grunted, but his friend was right. The Supplicant would serve one function, and one function only. She would help him keep Marotiri's enemies at bay. If Kalief were wise—and he had every intention of behaving wisely—Marotiri's enemies would be forever smited with the help of the Supplicant.

Her life as she knew it was over for good. She'd never make another choice. She'd never select a lover of her own. She'd never bear children. How would the ex-nanny like that? Kalief almost felt pity for her.

"Think of it this way, Kalief."

"How?"

"You're sacrificing her freedom to save thousands of lives. Barbarians from just across the border killed her blood family. She might thank you."

"You haven't seen the platform for the dedication ceremony, Teron. She is not going to thank me. Trust me on that."

Light poured through the colored window above the entrance to Abbey de San Mistofina, bathing the main entry in a rainbow of colors. An intense scarlet hue bathed the door—where he knew he should knock.

But he didn't. "Stay here, Teron," Kalief ordered, and then the king simply pressed the latch and strode inside.

When he saw the girl—barely a woman—lying on the bed, his first emotion was fiercely protective. Someone should help her, keep her safe—get her away from the machinations of the priests and generals and nuns.

Someone should get her away from him.

But watching the girl struggle to keep her eyes open, he hardened his heart. The fate of his country lay between her thighs.

"Does anyone know when this thing on my arm—the coatl?—when will it hatch? I think it's exhausting me."

Is that what had happened in that wall of sand? By the One, every faraway culture, people from lands so far away they might be myths, were turning up to honor this woman.

"No, little dove," he heard his cousin answer. "We don't know when it'll hatch."

"The hatching time isn't the point, Supplicant," Kalief said before any of the fluttering nuns could answer. "It's not the coatl making you tired." With an anger that surprised him, he tore into his cousin. "Haven't you told this girl what's going on yet?" he demanded of Anhara.

"If you hadn't barged in without knocking, *sire*," she said, "you might have given me a chance to explain the details."

"I didn't know I had to ask permission to enter my own abbey."

"Are we behind in our payments? No? Until that point, I expect you to knock first."

"What's happening to me?" Sureya asked. She sounded groggy.

"My dove," said Anhara. "The priests require your purification and your education."

"High Abbess Anhara, you need to tell the girl how this works."

"I'm trying—"

"I'm not a girl," Sureya managed to say.

"It's a good thing," Kalief said. "You'll need the strength of a woman."

"Explain." Sureya's voice was weak. Kalief ignored what the sound did to his heart.

"You're going to fall asleep," he said tersely. "When you wake, you'll be in a grotto within the basilica—it's secret. Only the Abbot General knows its location. You'll be bathed and prepared, and the Penetrator will penetrate you." Kalief felt sweat springing from his brow, and he raked his fingers through his hair. "After he has completed his task, the Penetrator will ask the One God to grant your request. Since you've already proven your powers, you may request anything you wish."

"How gracious of him."

He ignored her comment. "After that, you'll be drugged and prepared for the public ceremony. I could give you the details of the ceremony, but you won't remember it. And for that, you should be grateful."

"And I'm tired because . . . ?"

"Because the High Abbess has drugged you."

"Like Risham?" Sureya shot a questioning look at Anhara, who only nodded.

"I'm sorry, little dove. It's part of the priest's requirements."

"Your offer's very tempting," Sureya said to him, as if he'd offered her something. Her eyelids were drooping. "Please leave me alone with Anhara a moment."

With relief he stepped away from the bed. He'd rather engage in an honest battle with an armed foe than sit at the bedside of a sick woman. Coping with this whore-to-be was beyond his abilities. His father would have delegated this job to someone else. For the briefest moment, he considered that option. But self-loathing washed that temptation quickly away.

As he stood watching, the women spoke in heated whispers.

Then tears began to stream down both faces. Black eyes and gray both grew rimmed with red.

Kalief had to look away, otherwise he'd find himself ordering their problems away. Women's tears unnerved him, made him behave senselessly. He carefully examined the mortar between the bricks in the red wall while the women sat in silence for a moment.

Then he clearly heard the Supplicant say, "I can accept my fate, Anhara."

Kalief thought of all that the following days were going to hold for this girl—this woman—and he thought of his role in it. Balls of sweat rolled down his brow, down his neck. How could this be happening? He saved women and children. He didn't torture them.

It's for the good of the country, he told himself. *Truly it is.*

Kalief looked at the young woman scratching madly at her arm. She seemed more like an urchin child than a nearly divine mortal. For a moment he was supremely tempted. *What would happen if he left the Supplicant with the Abbess?* he asked himself.

He'd never find out. Not in this lifetime. His land needed him. His people counted on him to make these hard choices.

Sureya awoke naked, drenched in early morning sunlight. Every part of her body ached—her forearm, her nipples, the pearl between her thighs.

She blinked, craving water, craving a blanket for cover. What had they done to her?

She looked down. Her nipples gleamed with gold. Sureya blinked, certain she'd seen incorrectly.

But no. A gold ring shone from each nipple.

With her pulse beating, she tentatively put her hand between her legs.

She found a metal ring there, too, right through her pearl. She'd been pierced.

Two novices entered the room, hair completely covered in rough brown cloth the same color and texture as their skin.

"What've you done to me?" she asked. "How could you?"

The girl with the plain face touched her own lips and then held her hands apart. *We can't speak*, her gestures said.

The other girl, with eyes of midnight blue and high-set cheekbones, efficiently brought water to Sureya's lips. She drank it all. "Could I have more, please?" Sureya asked.

While one girl poured more water, the other opened a small amphora. The aroma of camphor and something Sureya didn't recognize filled the air.

"What is that?" she asked, but the girls ignored her, busily examining her new rings, wiping up small drops of blood.

One girl dipped tiny fingers into the amphora and then gently wiped the amber-colored ointment around the nipple piercings. Sureya cried aloud at the excruciating, burning pain.

And when the novice reached the piercing between Sureya's thighs, the Supplicant did the only thing she could to bring relief—she began to faint.

But as unconsciousness wrapped a light finger over her eyes, through her brain, a strange image filled her mind. A thick verdant forest covering jagged mountains. The trees, the leaves, were emerald and jade and moss. Mountain crags jutted from the foliage, rough black cliffs against the seething green of life.

Her ears filled with thunder. Turning her head, Sureya found a magnificent waterfall. Its frothy cascade pounded down the mountain, sending diamond droplets whirling toward the hot sun.

Long feathers nearly touched her nose as a scarlet bird winged past, whispering in a language she didn't understand but felt like she should. A snake, thick as an ancient oak, twined through the tree, smiling as she met its gaze.

Pain. Pain so powerful she couldn't feel the gold rings, erupted from her forearm, and the jungle in her mind disappeared.

Sureya blinked, taking in the cool dampness of her room in the abbey, the staid brickwork, the high windows. She breathed the air deeply, grateful to find herself someplace that made sense.

Then something flew past. The red bird? A shadow crossed the corner of her eye. The shadow knew her heart, spoke words that her blood understood.

It wasn't the bird.

The creature landed at the foot of her bed. And, like the snake in her mind, it smiled.

Sureya realized, suddenly, the thing was a snake. With wings. And feathers. Sureya blinked, expecting the thing to disappear.

It didn't.

Still smiling, it coiled around her big toe. It fluffed its feathers—red as *boucei* petals, and began to preen the plumes under its wings, using its needle-thin fangs.

Unafraid, Sureya reached for the creature, wincing to discover how much her piercings hurt, how much her forearm hurt.

With a lightning grin, the creature dove beneath her legs, and Sureya gasped. But it curled around her calf and up her thigh, and the urge to scream dissipated. Its surprisingly warm body slithered over her mound in a flurry of feathers, as comforting as her own hand.

The creature crept over the shocking ring through her pearl, and the pain left. Sureya looked down. The ring remained. Only the pain was gone.

Thunder from the jungle's waterfall reverberated through her mind. She could smell the water, see it as it splashed over the hot rocks.

The creature roped around her belly, flicking its tongue over her navel with a mischievous smile. Sureya watched in horror as it opened its mouth and engulfed a nipple, gold ring and areola—but then the pain evaporated, like water under the sun.

Sureya closed her eyes, trying to remember the pain had actually existed. She breathed in relief.

In a caress of warm feathers, the creature slithered to Sureya's injured forearm, which bore a large gaping wound. Would the creature crawl back inside? Heal her and disappear?

"Wait," Sureya said, her voice thick with wonder.

The creature paused, met her gaze with its obsidian eyes.

"Who are you?"

An image danced across her mind. The same jungle, thick with steamy heat. Together, she and the coatl flew to the top of the highest crag and found the ancient gods. Squared noses bore fat gold pins, and *khal*-brown skin shone in the sunlight. Feathered serpents—like the one wrapped around her arm—adorned the gods' ankles, their wrists.

"You're from the gods of some strange land," Sureya guessed.

The coatl winked, nodded. It waited, like Sureya should ask it something more.

"I know!" Sureya exclaimed. "Anhara told me where your people are from." Sureya searched her mind for the name. "Tepetl?"

The winged serpent nodded, sending another picture to her mind. A village filled with *khal*-skinned people. Their irrigation ditches were dry. Their granaries were empty.

"They need help," she said. The coatl nodded.

"But how can I help them?"

Then another image. The coatl flying away from her, looking over its shoulder and waving. Sunlight caught the mango color of its inner wing and shifted it to silver, then scarlet, then saffron.

"You're leaving?"

Another image. Sureya standing in a dusty courtyard, surrounded by sand-colored walls engraved with odd images. She
held her wrists in the air and called. From nowhere the coatl
winged into existence.

The image evaporated. "But—"

Quick as spring lightning, the coatl kissed her eye, leaving
the smallest drop of venom.

Before she could wipe the droplet away, she slept.

When Sureya woke, moonlight poured through the ceiling window. Crawling from bed, she realized her rings didn't hurt, although her nipples felt sensitive.

Savoring the cold slate beneath her feet, she felt strangely strong, like power coursed through her from the light in the sky, through the stones beneath her. Was it the finger of the One God?

Looking around, she found a neatly folded pile of clothing on a chair. More green silk, she saw, holding it up. The gown was modest compared to the desert clothing—long sleeves, full skirt.

She slid into the flowing dress, relieved her nipples no longer ached, not even when she buttoned the form-fitting bodice.

Through the thin fabric, she could see the silhouette of her new nipple rings. Would Risham have liked them? Sureya found she didn't care—he had been planning to take her virginity without ever giving her the option to choose a life of the Supplicant's power.

Anhara gave her the choice, though.

She could accept or she could run. She looked up at the window, at the pinkish light filtering in with the moonbeams. Sureya sighed, picking up the hairbrush and running it through her hair. Tomorrow was never promised. A disease could eradicate Risham and his family. Barbarians could raid their village and kill the entire family.

The Supplicant's power gave her a tool—a tool she'd never imagined, but could imagine now. She'd do her best to—

The door swung open, and King Kalief entered the room carrying a spray of dragonflowers and a silver flask. He wore a humbled expression.

"Sureya," he said. "The novices told me—" He swallowed, obviously nervous. "You're awake. They said you'd feel— That you'd be awake."

"Sire," Sureya said, nodding her head in submission. "They brought me dinner not too long ago. I've been awake for a while."

Kalief put the flask on the table and stood there awkwardly with the flowers. "Do you like, um . . ." he looked down at the spray of white bell-shaped flowers set on long, graceful stems. ". . . whatever these flowers are?"

Sureya had to laugh. How could a girl as poorly born as she make the king of the land nervous. "They're dragonflowers, and yes, I like them."

He stuck them in a pitcher of water from which she'd been drinking, and then he sat on her bed. "I've come to apologize." He drank deeply from his flask and then offered it to her.

Sureya took a step closer to him then took a sip, unsurprised to find throat-burning *satra*. "Are you apologizing for . . . ?" Her head roiled with possible things. She guessed the most obvious, saying, "The rings?"

Kalief's face flushed with embarrassment. "For those, yes." Then he looked at the wall and ran his fingers through his hair. Sureya had noticed he did that when he was nervous. "I also want to apologize for the upcoming days."

"You know," Sureya said. "If you'd asked me first to submit to the piercings, I likely would have."

Emotions, clear as the new sun, crossed his face—first astonishment and then . . . was it arousal?

"I want peace and prosperity throughout the land, the end of the barbarian incursions." Sureya told him. "I'm told your heart craves the same."

He nodded slowly.

"The priests require these?" Sureya pointed toward her newly pierced breasts.

Kalief nodded again.

"Then I would have acquiesced," she said. And in a teasing voice, she added, "And maybe I've secretly always wanted nipple rings."

Desire darkened his eyes, even as he tried to appear nonchalant.

"Now it's my turn to apologize to you," she said, "for teasing you so mercilessly."

"No, it's—"

"But I still have my chance for revenge, don't I?"

"What do you mean?"

"I'm told," Sureya said softly, "that the first supplication after penetration is mine."

He swallowed hard. "That's true," he said tightly.

"I may just wish that you wake in the morning to find your nipples and foreskin pierced."

Kalief laughed and drank back more *satra*. "Some courts might find I deserve worse." He handed the flask to her again. "And we'll find out damned soon what your wish is."

"Why? Is the Penetrator waiting to drag me to the ceremony just on the other side of the door?"

"He's closer than that," he said, touching his chest.

"You?" she gasped. "It's not you." She'd been imagining

some old priest as the Penetrator, not this man with the burning kisses. Not the man who'd saved her loved ones, saved her.

Pained, he looked away from her. "I'm afraid it is. I'm both the High Abbot of Marotiri and the General al Marotiri."

"But that means . . ."

"That the king is the Penetrator and the Abbott General? Yes, it does. Our ancestors liked to make up titles, apparently. Or maybe during some period of reform, they collapsed a number of positions into one. Seems like something a power-hungry king would do, doesn't it?"

Sureya didn't answer that question. "You seem very . . . busy. I thought the king would sit on his thrown and order people around. But you don't."

"I take that as a compliment. My father was a wretched ruler, and I've tried to atone for that. I won't ask any of my men—any of my subjects—to take on a burden that I wouldn't myself accept."

Sureya paused for a moment, then said, "And that includes me."

"It does."

"I'm at a loss," Sureya said. "I thought that the Penetrator would be someone like the priests who tried to drag me from my home."

"And instead, you find it's someone who's had you pierced without consent, berated you for making me sleep, and who spied upon you when you thought you had privacy."

Sureya blushed, remembering her wild abandon with An-hara. "Well . . . yes. But you saved Risham and his family. You saved the children and me, even after I put the entire company in danger."

An expression of sudden seriousness closed Kalief's face. "My role in your life cannot be a good one, Sureya. I must do terrible things to you. The Order requires it. The One God requires it."

She tried to keep her tone light. "So, are you going to drug me? Take advantage of me? I believe that's been tried."

Kalief leaned so close that she could see the green flecks in his brown eyes. "I'd rather seduce you."

The *satra* was tingling in her veins. Or maybe it was just his presence. Her lips remembered the taste of his, and she craved another sample. "Is that because I'm the Supplicant?" That thought didn't make her sad, exactly, but it left her feeling . . . alone.

"Because you're the Supplicant, I must seduce you," he agreed. "But because you're who you are, I want to."

She looked up at the eerie light pouring in the window, and her heart beat madly in her chest. Now she understood something—the One God had made her the Supplicant. The desire that had haunted her when the new sun first appeared made sense. It was the hand of the One—*or maybe his hardened penis*, she thought sardonically. She'd been made to yield to Anhara. She felt the same pressure now with Kalief.

She wanted him to touch her, to show her. She knew it was right—the One God wanted it so. "You want me," she said to Kalief. It wasn't a question.

"Because you're beautiful." He ran a rough finger over her collarbone. "Your skin is beautiful—smooth. Like silk. Your face is beautiful." He touched her cheek. Running a finger over her brow, he said, "And your eyes take my breath away."

He had her. She knew he did.

"Your hair is as red as the setting sun, but it's kissed with gold."

His words drew her in closer, left her hanging in his thrall.

"But it's your heart that's captured me. Your loyalty to your family, your willingness to sacrifice your personal well-being for the sake of our land."

Sureya realized that this man, this king, saw her for who she truly was—and liked her. He melted her very soul. The One

God might demand that she lay with this man, but her heart demanded something too. She wanted to give herself to him.

But he couldn't take her tonight—he needed to save her for the ceremony. The crowd needed to see blood.

Tonight, she could tease. She could succumb to him, let herself be sucked into his seduction. It was safe, completely without fear or risk.

Sureya leaned toward his face, letting a wicked grin dance over her lips. "Then kiss me." She playfully threw down the gauntlet. "See if you can match Anhara's skill."

Kalief gently pulled her body to his. Her arms met his, embraced him in return, pulling him toward her, feeling him along the length of her body.

Where Anhara's body had been soft and giving, his was hard muscled and unyielding. His was strength itself. No soft breasts pressed against her now.

His eyes locked on hers, asking permission. *May I kiss you?* his eyes asked.

Yes.

He lightly touched his lips to hers, almost as softly as Anhara had done. With a brush of his tongue, he took her whole mouth in his. He tasted real—like strength and like truth. He rested his tongue at the entrance of her opened mouth, poised.

Tentatively, she touched him.

Then, he sucked her in, sliding his tongue over hers. He paused. Did she want more? Yes. Teasing, he forbade her tongue to meet his. Then he pushed against her, seeking, trying to suck her tongue into his mouth.

His kiss was truly as good, as enveloping, as she remembered.

Sureya realized, as her three rings throbbed in exquisite pleasure, in exquisite pain, that she loved to kiss him. That she preferred kissing him even to kissing Anhara.

She couldn't stop herself from moaning slightly.

But he caught her hands, held them away from him. "Hot," he said. "You make me burn as hot as a Kestralensday bonfire."

Her lips sought his, wanting to drink his strength.

"But not so fast, my love." Kalief retrieved a green silk scarf from the chair where her clothes had been placed, and he tied it around her eyes. She couldn't see a thing.

"You'll feel more when you can't see," he explained, biting her neck. "And I want you to feel every touch, every caress."

How could she feel more? she wondered, awash in these breathtaking sensations.

Then Kalief stopped.

Gently pushing the small of her back, he guided her to her bed. When the back of her knees touched the edge, he asked, "Do you trust me?"

Sureya considered. She trusted he wouldn't hurt her—that he couldn't hurt her. He couldn't even make love to her. Tonight, Kalief could only make her want him. And that was just fine with her.

"Yes," she said.

Leaving her blindfold over her eyes, his hands convinced her to sit—fingertips tracing her collarbones until they reached her shoulders, and then pushing gently until she slid down on the bed. It's safe here, his hands said, and Sureya believed him.

With her eyes covered, the sensation of his lips sliding over hers surprised her. Despite herself, she moved back and gasped.

"Trust me," he said.

Wanting to please him, to please herself, she let go of her fear, convinced herself to embrace the touch, as new as it might be.

He pulled away, removed his hands and lips from her skin. "Where are you?" she asked, but he didn't answer. Instead, he slid his hand under a clothed breast. Her nipples instantly hardened, and she felt a growing awareness of the weight of the rings against her areolas.

"You didn't jump," he said.

"No."

"Do you want more?"

"Mm-hmm." She did. She wanted a lot more.

With increasing firmness, he caressed the silk over her breasts, the gold tugging her nipples and pressing her areolas until she gasped.

Behind the blindfold, she gave her mouth to him. She caressed him with her tongue. Trusting him not to hurt her, she gave him her breasts, her rings, her nipples.

Use me as you will, her body said. And his agreed. He unbuttoned her bodice.

Slipping his hand inside the silk, he brushed an erect nipple with the side of his hand, running his fingers around the areola. Then, sliding the bodice off her shoulders, he nuzzled his head between her breasts before grabbing a ring between his teeth.

She lost her ability to breathe. Who was this woman she'd become? Who was she to toy with a man as powerful as King Kalief?

She was the Supplicant.

Sureya arched her back, offering him her breasts. Her heart. He accepted.

He tugged the rings, tracing her erect nipple, nibbling, sometimes nearly painfully hard, and she moaned. A direct connection existed between these rings and the one between her thighs. They pulsed in the same rhythm, to the tempo of his tongue.

Under his hands, her dress melted off her skin, leaving her naked in the moonlight still washing through the ceiling window—naked save the silk scarf over her eyes.

Their bodies pressed hard against each other, their hips moving together. Sureya sighed to feel his thickness through his clothes. She was delighted but alarmed by his hardness and her wetness and the power of their desire for each other.

"I can't stand it," he said, removing the blindfold. "I need to see your eyes."

Sureya blinked in the bright moonlight, in the pink glow of the new sun. His shirt glowed white. Her night with Anhara had given her confidence in her beauty, in her desirability. But when she saw the heat in his eyes, his consuming desire to have her, her confidence became unshakable.

And her alarm escalated. They couldn't walk away from a desire this strong, could they? And yet they had to, or forfeit the dedication.

Neither he nor she wanted that. She trusted that in him.

"Take off your clothes, Kalief. I want to see what I'm getting into."

"It's me who's getting into something."

"Perhaps," she laughed, understanding the implication. "But not tonight."

He stood and unbuttoned his shirt, removed his cavalry trousers. Sureya sat back down on the bed, savoring the sight of his naked body gleaming in the white moon.

Then she looked at his erection, the first she'd ever seen, and gasped.

Kalief laughed, but it wasn't patronizing or cruel. "It'll fit when the time comes. I promise."

"But it will reach to my throat."

He walked toward her and wrapped her in his arms. "I'll never hurt you."

"Except during the dedication ceremony." She felt his shoulders stiffen at her words.

"I wish there were some other way."

"But the priests," she said, resigned.

"Yes."

Sureya looked at up him, her king, and drank in his features. His hawk eyes were kind now, not fierce. The dark planes of his face begged to be traced by her lips and her fingers, but it was the depth in his eyes that called to her—that won her heart.

He brought his head down and kissed her. Not hungrily like his previous kisses. This kiss was loving, filled with promise.

Against her stomach Sureya became aware of his throbbing erection. The tip glistened.

"Every part of me wants you," he said, following her gaze.

"Come here," she said, savoring the pleasure of the weight of his body over hers.

Bold now, she began to kiss him, taking his lower lip between hers and sucking, running her tongue over it, moving until his tongue met hers. Their tongues found each other's, twined around and around until Sureya's head spun.

She moved to lie atop him. Their bodies touched only pubic mound to erection. He thrust his hips up, pushing his hardness against her belly. She leaned into him, savoring the pressure tugging the ring in her pearl.

He pulled back, as she knew he would—two hot, naked people, rubbing against each other could only mean trouble when her virginity needed to be saved. She sighed in frustration.

And also relief.

She didn't need to concern herself with a major life-changing event. At least not tonight. She still had time to back out—to live a normal life.

Sureya didn't think she'd choose that road, but the path was still open to her.

Kalief moved his hands over her body, slowly, like he was memorizing the texture of her skin, the curves of her ribs and hips and belly. Then he cupped her vulva, rocking into her.

Two of his skilled fingers parted her, and he slid a finger over the ring, flipping it first up and then down. The electric jolt of pleasure caused her to gasp his name.

"You're very ready," he said. "Very wet." He slid a finger inside of her, and she gasped again. Anhara hadn't done this, focusing her effort wholly on Sureya's pearl. "It's very erotic, Sureya."

"Mmmm." It was the only answer in her.

"We can do this now," he said. "We can dedicate you now."

"But how—" She fought the fear rising in her throat. "I thought that the ceremony was necessary."

"The only necessary component is that the first time you're penetrated, it's by the Abbot General, me, and that you achieve orgasm. The rest is for people—both secular and non."

"But the blood?" She swallowed. "And the priests?"

"The loss of virginity can be faked, the blood can be imitated—the actual dedication cannot. If you were to be penetrated by anyone else first, the One God wouldn't heed your climax."

"Oh," she said, feeling weak again.

"And I'm sure you'll come over and over again," he said, his eyes gleaming with delight in the moonlight. "If you want to."

Sureya felt something in her loosen. She could pretend all night long that she hadn't decided—but she had.

Not many people had the chance to make the world a better place.

"Then do it," she said, her voice thick. "Make me come all night long."

With one finger inside her, he ran a gentle fingertip over the ring between her thighs. He worked a finger over her pearl, electrifying her each time he slid over the ring. With his other hand, he slid inside of her, faster and faster, but he didn't penetrate her inner door.

Without stopping the finger dancing over her pearl, he arranged himself atop of her. With increasing pressure, he slid over the ring, around it. Her body trembled, anticipating the burst.

His shaft nestled between her thighs, and she felt it throb, against his fingers, against the ring.

She opened to him, pushing hard against his finger, raising her hips to meet his shaft, welcoming him. Inviting him despite her fear. She burned with such exquisite feeling that her head spun. "By the Above," she gasped. "That feels so good."

And just as she came, he thrust inside her, past her hymen. It stung, but not too much.

He stopped and looked at her, concern written on his expression.

"I'm not hurt," she said. To prove her point, she lifted her legs high, wrapping them tightly around his waist, guiding him tentatively into her.

He was tender at first, careful and slow. As he slid gently inside her, he ran his tongue over her collarbone, kissed behind her ear. Sureya relaxed into his touch, into his spell.

But then the pain was completely forgotten. She wanted him completely. She pressed her hips against him, shivering in delight as the full length of him slid deep inside her.

Again and again, he thrust into her, and with each motion, she moved to meet his tongue and lips, breathing herself into his mouth, making her part of him. She lost the ability to know where her skin ended and his began.

Under him, she could feel his sweat mix with hers and she wrapped her mouth around the side of his neck. He cried out and shuttered, and the force of his desire together with his pounding thrusts made her come with him.

After, she lay beneath him, panting, staring at the streams of moonlight pouring from the ceiling. The scent of him, the scent of sex, filled the room. A series of tiny ripples reverberated through her vagina. His shaft throbbed in response.

The quiet moment filled her with inner peace. The next few weeks, maybe even the next few decades, would be filled with turmoil and hardship—but right now, in this moment, she knew she'd chosen correctly.

"So, Supplicant," Kalief said, his voice still husky from their lovemaking. "What's your wish going to be?"

II

Kalief's fingers worked through her hair, wrapping chunky tendrils around his finger. "According to Scripture, the first supplication must be from you." The golden highlights in her hair shone in the moonlight. "And it's the only selfish wish you get."

"What do you mean, selfish wish?"

"The One God answers only supplications that are truly heartfelt. I can't just hold a sword to someone after he's made you come and order him to wish for a purple sky. Because I can't feel your prayer with my heart, I can't make your wish."

"Except for now?"

"Except for now. The first wish after penetration is yours. And it's your only one—it sets the whole tone for your reign—so choose it wisely."

He watched her expression focus, as if she had something very specific in mind. "World peace?" she asked, and he knew she was thinking of her blood family, her adoptive family, the marauded village. "The end of all war and violence?"

For a moment, his heart stopped. When he first saw the comet, as he was sitting on the parapet rooftop with Lady

Teanne, he'd hoped—fervently hoped—that the arrival of a Supplicant could help him end the barbarian terror. Toward that end, he would've drugged the girl and dragged her kicking and screaming into the bedchamber of every lord and lady in the land.

But maybe he wouldn't need to. He looked at her profile, lit by the moon and the comet's glow, and he realized this Supplicant might willingly help him make his land safe.

Kalief exhaled into the cool night air. "You amaze me," he said. "According to the records, the last Supplicant asked for immortality."

"By the Above," the Supplicant said. "Did it work?"

"Not exactly." Kalief began twirling her thick red locks around his index finger again. "She continued to live, although she aged normally. After more than one hundred and fifty years, she was desperate to die. Her longing for death led her to commit suicide in a variety of ways—poison, hanging, arrows—but nothing worked. Each attempt just made her uglier. She was green and filled with arrow holes."

Sureya sat up on her elbow, and peered into his face. "Are you teasing me?"

"Not at all," he said, shaking his head. She curled up with her head in his lap. The way she trusted him hurt something deep inside him. He should shove her away, let her know now exactly what he was going to do to her—what he was going to *have* to do to her.

But he couldn't keep his fingers out of her thick red locks.

"Is she still alive?" Sureya asked. She seemed unaware of the turmoil boiling inside of him, thank the One.

"No. No, she's long gone."

"What happened?"

Pale moonbeams played over her features, shrouding her in mystery. Even though he'd just had her, he wanted her all over again. All of her.

"Kalief?" she asked, interrupting his thoughts.

"She didn't come to a nice ending," he said. "Are you sure you want to hear it?"

"I'm sure." Her voice, melodic and even, sent shivers down his spine. Her country accent was adorable, made him think of a different kind of world, an easier one.

"Well," Kalief said. "She finally doused herself in oil and threw herself onto a blazing pyre on a windy day. The dust carried away her ashes."

"Not such a good wish, then."

He laughed at the understatement. "No. Not such a good wish."

"I suppose someone could ask for eternal youth," she said, stroking the ticklish spot behind his knee. Even that little movement was graceful and endearing. By the Above, what was happening to him? "That might get around the living-forever problem," she said.

"It might," he agreed, his voice huskier than usual. "I'd guess, though, that the One God would freeze you at one particular day, while time moved normally for everyone else."

"That might make the Supplicant insane, then."

"Yes, but anyone who made her come could still ask the One God for something," he said.

"So what about world peace?" she asked.

"I don't know that anyone has ever tried it, but I suspect such a plea, were it granted, might take away too much individual free will."

"And what would the One God do?"

"Likely grant it with an insidious side effect."

"How could world peace have a bad side effect?"

"Maybe everyone would forget how to fight as the wish requested, but they might also forget how to plant and till and shepherd."

"Then you could just unwish it with the next wish," she said.

"Maybe," he agreed. "If you remembered to."

"Your One God's insidious, then."

"He's your God, too," Kalief pointed out, as he needed to, given that he was the King of Marotiri. Abbess Anhara's liberal interpretation of Scripture appealed to him more than did the teachings of the priests, but admitting that in public would be political death. The one thing Marotiri didn't need now was religious controversy, not with the never-ending barbarian invasions.

The Supplicant said nothing, neither agreeing nor disagreeing. Finally she said, "What wishes have worked? Do you know?"

"Yes." He shifted so his hardened cock wasn't right beneath her cheek. "I know."

"Well?" she asked, moving slightly to keep his length beneath her head.

"Ahh," he tried to answer.

"Tell me," she insisted, pressing purposefully against him with a playful look he could just see in the moonlight.

"Well..." He thought for a moment. "The outcomes of particular battles have been decided."

"And Anhara filled the oasis with butterflies," she added. "That was ... fun."

His cock throbbed at her suggestion, and she laughed. To Kalief she sounded like tinkling bells. "What else?" she asked.

"People have been healed of disease or disfigurement. A man with a broken spine was made whole."

"So..." she teased, running her teeth gently over the silk sheet covering his cock. "I suppose a Supplicant and a Penetrator could heal ... fertility problems?"

"Mm-hmm." Kalief couldn't actually muster a real word.

"So, does Scripture list rules for wishing?" she asked, rolling off him. "Edicts or something?"

"There're some," he answered, wishing she'd curl up in his lap again.

"And what are they?"

Her hand, hot with life, snaked beneath the sheet. "You can't wish the dead back to life," he replied, knowing that wasn't his particular problem.

"What else?" she asked, capturing his cock.

"You can't make someone love or hate anyone else—you can't affect their free will."

"The One God seems to favor free will, doesn't he?"

"Free will . . ." he said as she rubbed the droplet of moisture that had formed on his head over his entire shaft, and he groaned.

"Any other rules?" she asked, running her palm up the entire length of him.

"You can't wish for more wishes," he gasped, wishing she wouldn't stop. "And wishes with 'and' or 'or' in them don't work at all, so they say."

"Small, specific wishes about yourself seem to work best?" she asked. He could see her impertinent smile, only half hidden in the shadows.

"Very small," he agreed, bending to place a tiny kiss on her pebbled nipple. The gold ring was warm from her body.

She arched up toward him, her hand still on his cock. "Not so small," she said.

"So what's your wish?" He watched indecision cross her face. He hated to distract her when they were both so close to finding oblivion in each other's arms again.

"Is there a time limit?" she asked, rolling to her stomach. "Do I have to tell you now?"

"You have to tell me before we make love again." He couldn't keep the promise out of his voice as he ran his hand over her silky ass. He wanted to run his tongue over the length of each of her new gold rings.

"So you'll be my lover from now on? I mean—after the ceremony. Anhara said the dedication itself would be brutal. But afterward, I'll be just yours? Is that how this works?"

Kalief held her hand and examined her fingernails. The little moon crescents shone where nail met flesh.

"What?" she asked.

"I'm not going to lie to you, Sureya," he said, locking eyes with her. "Your new life involves . . ."

"What?" Sureya demanded, but he still didn't answer. "Tell me!" She sat, clutching the sheet to her breasts.

"Everyone involved in the dedication orgy . . . Well, they'll have permanent access to you. For the good of the land. When they need something, they'll—pleasure you."

He watched emotions stampede across her face. First horror, then something calmer.

"It won't work," she said. "My heart wasn't made to work like this, Kalief."

"The priests require it, Supplicant. It's described in painful detail in Scripture." He hated himself in this moment.

"So maybe I should wish that I enjoy it, enjoy the hands and lips and—and cocks!" She choked out the word for what he suspected was the first time in her life.

"Shh," he said. "I'll be there. I won't let anyone hurt you. And there's *dawa*, an aphrodisiac. It'll ensure your bliss. The drug's so potent you're guaranteed to not mind the Ceremony of One Hundred Hands. In fact, I'm told that it dulls even the memory of anything that happens while you take it."

"Drugs . . ." she nearly whispered. "Maybe I'll wish there's no ceremony."

"The ceremony brings all factions of Marotiri together," Kalief said. "It unites them, ensures they remain allies against our enemies."

"Enemies," Sureya said, remembering. So many dead, hacked to death by invading barbarians. "So if I wish for an end to the whore's role, then the land's engulfed in war and chaos."

"Yes." He couldn't lie, not to her.

"The ceremony is tomorrow."

"Yes, it begins tomorrow."

"So tonight's my last chance to be normal, to make the choices other women take for granted—with whom I decide to lie, for instance." She looked at him. "After tonight, I'll be a toy for the great ladies, the great lords. Sometimes I'll be a public whore. Sometimes private. By the One, Kalief, no wonder you've come here to apologize."

Kalief thought of Anhara, who'd been making the same argument since she'd come of age. She'd made him wonder if all of the benefits of the Supplicant could be available even if he drastically changed the rules as laid down by Scripture.

Not that most priests—misogynists that they were—were interested in the dignity of women, especially women who had a more direct path to the One God than they did.

"No," he said slowly. "There's no time to redesign the ceremony without upsetting our allies. And after that, the lords and ladies no doubt expect access to you."

"I have my wish, then," she said.

And his heart sank. She was going to wish for time, time for the barbarians to organize, time that might affect the free will of Marotiri's allies.

"By the time the next Supplicant comes of age," she began, "I wish that the rules governing the Supplicant lie in the hands of the priestesses, conferring at least as many benefits to the land as it now confers."

"A legacy," he said, running his finger over her lips. "I suspect it's wise, but still it frightens me. The One God's trickier than we are."

"It's still my wish."

Kalief slid off the bed and fell to his knees. He said, "One God in the Above, please hear my prayer. I have granted You a

gift—the passion of Your Supplicant. Please grant my prayer."
He paused for a moment, adding Sureya's wish.

He stood and looked at the Supplicant. He saw heartbreaking
vulnerability. A moment of remorse sped through him, for the
lost opportunity to enjoy each other's bodies. But she needed
something more from him now.

He slid into bed and wrapped his arms around her. She didn't
object. When her muscles relaxed, when her breathing deepened, he knew he'd exhausted her. He'd tire her no further, not
tonight.

He stood and said to her, "In the morning your *khal* will be
drugged. Drink it all, and the day will pass easier."

Sureya stared at him wordlessly, fear clear in her expression.

"And Sureya?"

"Yes?"

"I really will do my best to protect you." He bowed for-
mally—as if she were the queen and he were the subject—and
he left her alone in the fading night.

Moments before her door opened, Sureya awoke, trepida-
tion constricting her throat. The ache between her legs reminded her: she couldn't go back to the girl she'd been three
days ago. She'd lost her maidenhead to the Penetrator.

There was no going back.

Early morning sunlight diffused pale beams throughout the
room. By the time that sun set, Sureya would be drugged past
caring, the focus of hundreds of strange hands and lips and
cocks.

She'd be the whole and complete conduit between her people and the One God.

Fear and hope grabbed her lungs, constricting her ability to
breathe. She didn't want to be part of an orgy. And after
tonight, how could she bear being the sex toy for Marotiri's in-
fluential folk?

But an image of her family raced through her mind, cold and blind in death, congealed blood thick around their necks. She saw the mutilated barbarian, the crisped people in the church. Then she saw Risham's youngest daughter, the child of her heart—held at knifepoint in a barbarian's grip.

Sureya felt her jaw clench in determination. If she could accept her fate, it'd be in her power to stop the barbarian atrocities.

Something hit the window above her with a soft *thud*. Sureya looked up and saw a shower of cherry blossoms. Even as her mind reminded her that spring was long past, that no cherry trees were in bloom during late summer, the flowers changed and morphed.

Three apricot-colored chicks peered in the window at her. The one in the middle cocked its tiny head at her and said, "Be smart."

"Meow," said the one on the left.

"Are you talking to me?"

But then the two mute novices entered the room.

"What are those?" Sureya asked the women, pointing to the ceiling window.

The women looked, but there was nothing. No blossoms, no birds.

Unbothered, the novices walked toward her, one after the other, bobbing their heads. Sureya slid from her bed, grabbing a sheet.

"There were birds," Sureya insisted. "At least, I think that's what I saw."

Without blinking, the prettier of the two girls retrieved the sheet and wrapped Sureya in a satin green robe.

As she allowed the girl to slip the robe over her shoulders, she spied bloodstains on the bed, evidence of her night's pleasure with Kalief—the Penetrator, the general and abbot and king.

The man.

Then the plain-faced novice spied the blood on the sheets. Wordlessly, she nudged the other girl, pointing with a nod.

Simultaneously, both novices bowed to Sureya, their foreheads nearly touching the floor.

With her heart in her throat, Sureya tried to stop them, pulling their shoulders. She was no one to whom bowing was required. She was a nanny who had the dubious luck of being born with red hair, the dubious luck of being unable to ignore the irresistible pull from the One God's fiery heart when its power throbbed between her thighs.

The novices bowed anyway, ignoring her attempts to stop them.

Now they would not meet her eyes, even as they fed her a sparse breakfast of dates, figs and unleavened bread. In a room with two women who would not speak or meet her gaze, Sureya had never felt so alone.

Then they handed her the *khal*.

She hesitated a moment before drinking. If she drank, she would completely surrender to the day and all it entailed. If she refused, she would need to face the travails with a clear mind. She might fight the ceremony, disgrace her new station.

As the novices watched, she drank the entire mug to the bottom and held the empty ceramic mug to them, asking for more. If Kalief hadn't told her it was drugged, she wouldn't have known. *Dawa* had no taste.

Having taken the aphrodisiac, Sureya sighed. Today, she belonged to the land. Now, she would not object.

Heart in her throat, Sureya finished her figs. Then she drank the second mug, trying without success to savor the steamy warmth. She carefully gauged herself. How long before the drug would take effect?

When she finished her meal, the novices indicated it was time to leave. Impassively Sureya walked with a straight back, unwilling to allow her fear and sorrow free rein.

Silently they led her through the still-quiet halls. Early morning sun made warm patches under her bare feet. The feel of her satin robe moving over her shoulders and thighs as she walked made her think of spring rain, of Kalief's caress. Of her lost childhood.

Sureya knew then the *dawa* was affecting her.

The young novices led Sureya through a maze of gray brick tunnels, each with windows set high in the wall. Finally they came to a door. Sureya tried to keep her fear under control as the novices swung open the doors.

Hot mist filled the room, and Sureya needed a moment to understand what she was seeing. Engineers had convinced a natural spring to dwell in the abbey, and the water chortled in several in-ground pools. Tiles in deeper blues and brighter pinks covered the walls, forming pictures of winged dragons soaring protectively over fields filled with laboring people.

Running supple hands over her back, the novices took her robe and indicated that she should enter the spring. Trying to cover herself with her hands, she turned away from the women and entered the tiled spring.

Warm water, hot almost, enveloped her to her calves. The novices gently pushed her, and she stepped deeper into the water. She plunged in and swam.

The soft, warm water slid over her body and lit up senses in her skin she hadn't known existed. The steamy heat washed away the ache of her first love making, and the *dawa* in the *khal* left her wanting more.

Sureya shook her head. After submitting to Kalief's hands and tongue last night, she knew she'd want more with or without the aphrodisiac. He'd touched her like he knew her heart, her every desire.

The mosaic caught her eye, then made her blink. The dragon in the mosaic took wing, began to fly across the wall, swooping over the farmers, grinning the whole time. Then he folded his wings tightly against his body and dove. By the time he hit the pool, he'd turned into a mermaid, complete with high, full breasts and a blue iridescent tail.

And she knew the *dawa* had done something strange to her mind.

The mermaid followed her to the shallow water. Its hair was as black as a night sky, and a constellation of stars speckled her locks. Sureya stopped and stared, knowing that a creature so lovely just couldn't be real.

Real or not, the mermaid swam to her. It wrapped a tail around her waist, and its black hair fanned around Sureya's face. So entwined, she found she could breathe underwater.

Then the creature kissed her, grabbing her soul and pulling it toward her heart. Above them, the moon pulled the ocean's waves.

You are the Supplicant! the creature rejoiced, pressing her slippery breasts over Sureya's.

Through the pleasurable thrill, she found an answer. *I believe I am.* Sureya replied in her mind as if she'd been speaking telepathically to mermaids her whole life.

You are! The mermaid blew bubbles around Sureya's face as it slid its breasts over hers.

Oh! Sureya said, as her new gold rings slid over the mermaid's pebbled nipples. Pleasure so intense it approached pain zinged to Sureya's brain. *Are you real?*

What is real? the creature asked, slithering its long tail between Sureya's thighs, over her gold-clad pearl. She could only moan, open her legs wider.

May I make you come? asked the mermaid—or was it a dragon? *May I have a wish?* Its tail skillfully dragged over her pearl, and it closed cherry-colored lips over Sureya's nipple while both swam underwater. *You won't regret it.*

Is your wish a good one? Is it kind? Will it hurt the people of my land or help them? she asked, even as she gasped in pleasure.

Surrounded by bubbles, the mermaid suckled one breast and tugged the gold ring on the other. Its tail slithered over the third ring between her thighs, pushing it back and forth, sending lightning-hot streaks of pleasure.

You have a good heart, the mermaid creature said. *I believe all beings in the land will benefit from your time as Supplicant.*

But you haven't answered my question, Sureya said, holding an orgasm at bay. *Is your wish a good one?*

You will not regret my wish, the creature said, pressing its tail hard against her pearl. It sucked her nipple deeply into her mouth, and its fingers worked their way between her thighs. Its tail wickedly twined around her torso, flicked over her nipples.

I hope not, she said, coming with body-wracking intensity in a sea of silvery bubbles.

The novices pulled her gently from the water and put a robe on her. Panting, she examined their faces for a clue. Was the mermaid real? Was the dragon? She shot a glance to the mosaic. The giant lizard was back protecting its people. It looked like it was smiling.

The plain-faced novice handed her another mug of *khal,* which she obediently drank. Then she lay back. Wondering. Her world didn't used to be such a strange place.

Her skin vibrated, singing a secret song of longing only a lover could hear. When she closed her eyes, the universe expanded before her. Stars popped into existence out of nothingness and grew so large they exploded. New universes were born.

Intent on watching the stars explode behind her eyes, she didn't object when the women slid her robe open, baring her breasts, exposing the nest between her thighs.

Opalescent slivers streamed past her vision in a glittering explosion, begging her to join the universe, which morphed into a growing river of cobalt and sapphire blues.

The women lathered her nest with something fragrant, something cedar-like, and the sparkling river in her mind crashed over rock-like thoughts. Dextrous fingers worked the suds, and Sureya felt each follicle luxuriate, relax into their touch. Shimmers of gold joined the silvery river collage.

The cold scrape of a blade added jagged streaks of electric blues to the river, the same color as lightning in a winter sky.

Sureya looked and saw her pubis was naked. Her familiar fiery hair was gone. The small, thick gold ring screamed its presence, unhidden now by the kinky red forest.

The novice with the high cheekbones retrieved a paintbrush and dipped it into a jar. Sureya closed her eyes. Each stroke of the brush felt like the lap of a tongue, and the river behind her eyes crashed though the rapids, sent cascades of stars plummeting across her internal sky.

Swim with me, the paintbrush cried in a voice as loud as thunder. Vertebrae along her back rippled, and her arms turned into fins, her skin into scales. Seaweed dazzled in brilliant green hues. Dodging rocks, swishing through turbulent pockets, slapping her tail to leap out of the water, Sureya swam the river.

Then the plain-faced novice held a mirror so she could see. Across her body, the novice had created a constellation. Her nipples glittered as silver stars. The new sun, with its pulsating red heart and lapis halo, throbbed between her thighs.

"You're an artist," Sureya breathed. The novice bowed low to the ground, but not before Sureya caught a glimpse of a pleased blush on the girl's cheeks.

Mist sprang from the river and Anhara appeared. Both novices bowed to her, foreheads well above the ground. With the galaxy splashed across her midriff, her breasts, her thighs, Sureya felt clothed. She stood, wanting Anhara to admire the mural.

When Anhara came close enough to view the work, she gasped. The sound echoed through Sureya's head, reverberating against the river's waves. "It's gorgeous," the abbess said, finally. "And it's on a beautiful canvas."

Anhara's feminine heat radiated across the small space that separated them, and silently she reached for Anhara, craving the warmth and safety of her embrace.

Anhara held up an elegant hand, fingers beautiful for their length. "I can't, my dove. I can't touch you. The *dawa's* thick in your blood, and if I touch you, you'll want nothing but sexual stimulation, and relief. I don't want to exhaust you."

A small bird-like noise came from her lips, a noise like a catbird. "Meow."

Anhara's eyes softened. "Be assured that in my heart, I'm cradling you, my dove."

Anhara took a step back. "I've brought these shoes for you." Anhara held up a pair of strappy things with extraordinarily high heels. Thin black leather ties slinked down from them. "I know they're not comfortable, but believe me, you're not going to be walking much."

Sureya took them, running her fingers through the supple straps. They felt like Maypole ribbons. The long heels themselves were spiked and made of etched gold. They caught the light no matter which direction she turned them, sending crazy sparkles dancing through the cedar-scented steam.

"I also brought this, which I'll let the novices hook for you." Anhara held up two long, thin chains. They were made of the same beaten gold as the spikes on her new shoes, the same color of the rings through her nipples and pearl.

The plain-faced novice took the gold lengths from Anhara, carefully collecting them in her palm.

"What are they for?" she asked, surprised that human words came from her mouth.

"I'll let the girls show you after they put up your hair."

Sureya tried to focus on her words, but they tripped away from her like chipmunks in the grass.

"Don't fret, little dove. You'll survive the day, and you'll survive it well."

"But the orgy," Sureya managed. "I don't want it."

"Shhh," Anhara said, looking like she wanted to embrace her friend. "I wish the priests wouldn't insist, but we must go through with it. Especially with that thing glowing in the sky throughout the day and night." Anhara waved at the ceiling. "The lords and ladies speak of only one thing—war. We need to rein them in, little dove. We can do it only with your help."

"I don't want to do it, Anhara." The *dawa* was too thick in her blood for her to wipe away her tears. A novice scurried up and dried the drops with a soft cloth.

"I know." Anhara held up her hands like she was going to embrace Sureya, but she stopped herself. "Just remember that you'll be safely back in my abbey by nightfall. It's just today."

But the drug's glittering river was flowing again through Sureya's mind. Without conscious thought, her fingers went to a nipple ring, gently tugging it.

The novice with the sharp cheekbones firmly pulled Sureya's hand back and nodded to the other girl. Together they worked the chain, clipping the ends to the nipple rings. They hooked the ends to the ring through Sureya's pearl, which traced up to her nipples. When they were finished, the glittering gold rang from nipple to nipple, and a length ran from her pearl.

A length remained in the novice's hand, like a leash.

They worked her hair into an intricate filigree, tight interwoven whorls. Several long tendrils were twisted into curls and left trailing down her back. Then the novices worked in handfuls of gem-encrusted pins.

When they held up a mirror, Sureya realized her hair looked like a fiery sky filled with summer stars.

The *dawa* receded long enough for Sureya to realize that Anhara was gone and she was bound in chains of gold.

12

Ignoring his man, Kalief strode quickly down the hall. "Sire." The castellan tried to interrupt the king's mad march. "You must take the *dawa* now. You should've taken it last hour." The man ran after him on his short legs, the leather soles of his boots thumping gracelessly on the cobbled floor.

"Go away, Echo," Kalief said. "I have too much to do and not enough time to do it." He was heading to the stables to inspect the Supplicant's platform.

"If I may disagree, sire," Echo said in a pleading voice. "All has been prepared according to Scripture."

Kalief thought about how Sureya chose to better the plight of the next Supplicant, without doing anything to help herself, without doing anything to harm his land. Her selflessness amazed him.

He'd decided that he could do no less than help her.

"Echo?"

"Yes, sire?"

"I want the warrior nuns to surround the Supplicant's moving platform."

"But, sire—" Kalief could hear the man choke.

"What is it?"

"Traditionally, that's been the duty of the brothers, the priests. They will be . . . unhappy . . . with this change."

Kalief thought the brothers would be a whole lot more than unhappy when the priests and bishops saw the half-naked warrior nuns surrounding the Supplicant with their short bows and orchid-colored quivers.

"Regardless," Kalief said. He was beyond caring. "Make it so."

"Yes, sire." Echo cleared his throat, indicating he had more to say on the subject.

"What is it, man?" Kalief said.

"Where shall we place the brothers in the procession? You're not thinking of excluding them altogether, are you?"

Kalief considered the muscle-bound priests and their quarterstaffs. Excluding them would send exactly the message Anhara would like—women could rule the entire ceremony.

But perhaps the time was too soon to cram that message down the Order's throat.

"Divide them in half," Kalief said. "Put half of them in front of the archers and half behind. Make them leave enough space so that if—may the One God forbid it—the archers need to shoot, they don't shoot the priests."

"Yes, sire," Echo said as he opened the thick oak door leading to the stable.

The sweet smell of oats, barley, and horse breath surrounded them as they entered the barn. The fine saddle horse Anhara had given Sureya stuck its head over the stall door and nickered to Kalief as he passed. He stroked its nose briefly, wishing he had time to ride it. The unfortunate creature wasn't used to being stuck in a stall.

"Show me the platform, Echo," Kalief growled, mentally preparing himself to control his temper. He knew he wouldn't like what they'd done.

"It's this way, sire. And if I may say so, I'm sure you'll be pleased. The brothers outdid themselves, while still following each of the edicts."

Kalief grunted his response as they passed rows and rows of spacious box stalls. Turning a corner, they entered a large open area used to store hay.

"Here it is, sire," Echo said, with a welcoming motion of his hand. "Isn't it perfect." It wasn't a question. "Father Antioch says it is perfection."

Kalief stopped in his tracks. The platform was as high as his shoulders, and it was covered in beaten silver and gold filigree. Bronze butterflies, symbols of the One God's love, decorated the entire thing. Perfection wasn't its problem.

A woman-sized butterfly had been welded into the center of the platform. Inside the wings were shackles, positioned so that a woman—Sureya—would be pinioned inside, arms and legs spread. The butterfly was opened so that hands from either side could reach her breasts, her ass, her cunt.

At the base of the contraption, smaller ledges had been built, and they were upholstered with thick sheepskins. Blankets of orange silk were heaped onto the ledges.

The molesters—him, chief among them—would ride in comfort. They'd rest in luxurious nests while the Supplicant was tied to the wall, her most private emotions and anatomy on display for the public to see, for the lords and ladies of the land to touch.

What in all the Above could he do about this?

But he was King. And he was a good king. Tradition would change today. "Echo, this thing won't work."

His castellan gasped, "Sire?"

"I can't let the representatives maul her," the King of Marotiri said. "Not in good conscience."

"But the land, sire."

"I know." Kalief stood looking at the thing. "Let me think for a moment."

To keep their land prosperous and free from invaders, each of Marotiri's boroughs sent one representative, sometimes a lord, sometimes a lady. And each representative rode on the platform as it was drawn through town for the common people to see. The lords and ladies would lick and suckle and caress and stroke the Supplicant as they were drawn through the town. They'd fuck her silly in the basilica, behind closed doors. And shackled by *dawa*, she'd be powerless to resist.

When the day was done, each lord and lady would scorn the unfortunate woman, distancing themselves as much as socially possible—as if they were embarrassed themselves by the public spectacle. They'd blame her white skin, though. It was unseemly to lay with anyone with skin as light as hers. May as well go out and fuck a peasant in the field.

"I wouldn't think of the ceremony as mauling her, sire." Echo interrupted Kalief's thoughts. "This is a blessed event, proof the One God loves us above all others. She's the embodiment of the One God's love."

Kalief sighed. "Why then should we subject the embodiment of the One God's love to such an exhibition? Would you want to be the person shackled to that butterfly?"

Echo stopped and looked at his king. "You sound like you agree with the priests of the Ezarc generation," he said slowly.

The last Supplicant had been found first by the priests—and they'd made her live her entire life chastely. But there'd been no kindness in their actions—they'd claimed to have prevented her from acting like the whore she was. All women were whores to them, and the Supplicant was the Queen of the Whores.

That his castellan likened him to those priests . . . "Echo, you're beginning to anger me."

Blood left the man's face as he replied, "Yes, sire. Sorry, sire."

"I'm not afraid of any woman's sexuality."

"I didn't mean to suggest you were, sire."

"Good," Kalief said. "Because what I'm suggesting isn't hiding this woman away from the eyes of the world. I'm not suggesting this woman be branded as a whore in any way."

"I don't understand, sire."

Of course he didn't. Kalief didn't understand himself. "This is what I mean," he finally said. "We should honor her as one should honor a gift from the One God."

"Sire?"

"Would you want your sister or your mother to be fondled by lords and ladies as they rode through town?"

"A particular kind of girl might enjoy it, sire. The *dawa* makes her into that kind of girl."

"But you didn't answer my question. Would you want your mother or sister to be that woman?"

"Of course not, sire. But it's for the safety of the land. And my family is quite dark in color."

As if he needed to be reminded of that.

When the procession reached the basilica, the orgy would begin in earnest behind closed doors. Traditionally, the lords and ladies would help the Penetrator get the girl near orgasm, and then the Penetrator would penetrate. After the Supplicant climaxed, he would make the official wish for the good of all the boroughs, for the good of the land.

After last night, he knew he didn't need any help getting Sureya to orgasm. He didn't need the lords and ladies to ready the lady. He didn't need them to make the wish for his land. "Where's the *dawa*, man?"

"Finally, sire," Echo said. Handing him a supple leather flask. "I'm glad you've come to your senses."

As he took the drink, he realized—he knew exactly what he was going to do.

* * *

Sureya stood still as a fawn startled in the woods while the two novices applied a shimmering cream to the few unpainted portions of her body. Their touch did nothing to her, made no rivers rise, made no constellations emerge.

Regardless, lacy fern fronds clouded her vision, and the scent of crushed moss filled her senses. When she first saw Kalief, she felt her doe's nose twitch, her deer tail rise straight into the sky. She recognized a hunter when she saw one.

Her gold chain rested lightly in his hand—her pearl, her nipples connected to his fingertips. Glittering gems studded the air around him. She could smell that he sought blood.

"Fireflies," Sureya said, reaching toward him.

"Your horse?" he asked, staying out of her reach. "He's in the stables."

Admiring the whirling cloak of sparkling lights surrounding him, Sureya could only repeat herself with more urgency. "Fireflies."

"He's safe, my love. Rest easy." His tone reached through the haze and reassured her. Kalief said something to the novices, who vanished into the steam.

"Thank you," Sureya said, watching an amber flicker above his head. Thanking him was easier than correcting the misunderstanding. Her doe's senses shifted, though. He was a stag, not a huntsman.

Then Kalief picked up the thin chain and said, "The public part of the ceremony's about to begin." Her flickering doe ears somehow understood the words.

Kalief carefully tugged the chain, and the intensity of the firefly glow around him grew, pulsated, as did the exquisite pleasure between her thighs. She could smell thick desire on him, his animal strength calling to hers.

But she battled through the pleasure—the aphrodisiac pleasure. Pushing away tendrils of delight, she croaked. "No orgy," she said. "Please." He was the only stag for her.

He tugged the chain again, and she took a step forward. She belonged in his arms. She belonged under him. She belonged next to him, leaping side by side through the ancient forests.

"No orgy," she said to her king. "And please—no *dawa*."

But he held up his hand.

"No, Sureya. Stop. Feel this." He tugged again.

A white-hot jolt of desire zipped from the ring in her pearl to the rings in her nipples. She saw the fireflies glow, only this time it wasn't around him—it was behind her eyes, in her mind. They coalesced into an amalgam and began to flow. Sureya wanted to do nothing more than lie down and surrender to the glittering pull of the molten river.

Instead Kalief closed the space between them with a hungry stride. He looked like he wanted to kiss her. She knew she wanted to taste him again. But he knelt at her feet, as if he were her supplicant.

"Please forgive me for what I'm about to do," he said. Then, running his lips from her ankle, over her knee to the top of her thigh, he spread the pulsating sun painted over her pubis, and licked her pearl. He sucked her into his mouth, and heat poured through her.

The beginnings of an orgasm quivered in the back of her mind, and she thrust toward him, wanting release after being sexually tormented since her first mug of *khal*.

He sucked hard, brutally, and she teetered closer on the brink. "Yes," she breathed. "Now."

And he stood back, leaving her starving for release. "No," she said. "Please, don't stop now."

But Kalief turned his back to her and used the chains to lead her from the steamy warmth to the cold, cool hall.

Her doe ears heard hounds baying far away in the forest. But they were coming closer, slobbery tongues lolling over unrelenting teeth.

"Kalief, please," she said. "Don't do this to me." But the fireflies surrounded him, and she knew he couldn't hear her.

Pink dragonflowers rained down upon them amid the cheers of the throngs. Kalief pushed a bunch of petals from his shoulder. Every man and woman in the street recognized the beauty of the Supplicant tied to the center of the butterfly. White-skinned peasants loved her as one of their own. Brown-skinned nobility appreciated her exotic beauty. The healing power she brought to the land made everyone adore her.

For now.

No one in the crowd seemed to notice the change to the butterfly contraption, which was no longer shaped according to Scripture. Although her arms were still tied above her, Sureya's legs were not shackled or spread. And no one was touching her.

Not even him, damn it.

Of course, Kalief realized, only the most scholarly people in the crowd would have read this part of Scripture. That ruled out most people in most crowds.

But it didn't rule out him.

As the procession poured down the main street, Kalief eyed Lord Auroch and Lady Wisteria, who shared the platform with him. As high-ranking nobility, they knew the benefits to which they were entitled as described by Scripture.

And they were supremely unhappy.

The hunch of their shoulders, their narrowed eyes, told him that his standing with them was precarious. Lady Wisteria kept straightening her perfectly pressed gown, coldly flicking pink flowers from her sleeves. Lord Auroch stood with a flat smile pasted on his face. His eyes reflected no joy.

Both carried ceremonial hammers, and the weapons looked menacing in their hands.

The other delegates—Lord Pentagrin, Lady Starliner, Lady Wolfitte, Lord Leeward, Lord Darrin, and Lord Hittine—

seemed content to have exchanged their traditional role for something different. They knew Scripture as well as Auroch and Wisteria, but these nobles bore their hammers with aplomb.

Kalief felt the thud of feet from the warrior nuns marching in perfect precision ahead of them. Their short bows were loaded with specially fletched arrows, a caterpillar painted onto each feathered tip. Kalief could see the orange fuzz of the feathers even from atop the platform.

The strap of each quiver snaked around a breast, pushing it up. To honor the Supplicant, the first in history they'd been asked to guard, each nun had painted a silver glittered star over each bared nipple.

Kalief didn't like it about himself—he couldn't help but admire the spectacular woman tied before him. Sureya writhed, probably seeing nothing besides a private manifestation of her own desire, a product of the *dawa* thick in her blood.

But when she writhed, her breasts shimmied and her ass called to him. Her skin begged to be memorized and caressed and savored. She'd never be more receptive than she was now. In the right hands, she could experience orgasm after orgasm after orgasm, granting wish after wish after wish.

The hands that would satisfy her ravenous desire, the hands that would bring salvation to the land would be his. And his alone.

With the help of this woman, King Kalief could bring the peace and prosperity—and dignity—to the land that his father and grandfather and great-grandfather had been unable to achieve.

The crowd began to chant. "Touch her. Touch her. Touch her." But he ignored it. When younger men rudely called out, "Fuck her! Fuck her! Fuck her!" Auroch and Wisteria shot him resentful glances. They agreed. They should fuck her.

But Kalief merely nodded at the hammer bearers. It was time.

As one, the lords and ladies turned toward Sureya and raised the hammers.

Kalief watched her eyes focus through the haze in her mind, and she opened her mouth to scream. She may have actually screamed, but the crowd shouted in frenzy, and he could hear only their voices.

Together with the lords and ladies, Kalief pounded on the wrought bronze until it collapsed in a heap. Kalief caught Sureya in his arms before she collapsed with the huge butterfly contraption at the feet of the nobility. Kalief caught her gold chains before she fell on them.

The *dawa* was still coursing through her veins, and as the Supplicant stood at his side, her stomach and thighs and breasts depicting the universe and their place in it, he lusted for her. The gold ring protruding from between her thighs glistened with the *dawa*-induced desire.

He shifted so that his erection was not on blatant display for the crowds.

"Whore! Whore! Whore!" The crowd's chant became louder as the platform approached the basilica's courtyard. "Fuck the whore! Fuck the whore! Fuck the whore!" shouted a group ahead of the warrior nuns. Behind them, Kalief heard, "Save the land! Save the land! Save the land!"

The King of Marotiri took Sureya's hand and stepped to the front of the platform. He held their hands high, careful of her chains, hoping she could stand on her own without writhing and pressing against him overly much.

He could protect her from others, but could he save her from himself?

"People of Marotiri!" he shouted, doing his best to override the crowd. "My people!" he tried again. The crowd uneasily hushed.

"People of Marotiri," King Kalief said. "I present to you not the whore tradition has led you to expect but a lady, well-bred and pure."

"She's white!" someone shouted.

"Fuck her! Fuck her! Fuck her!" the crowd replied.

Anhara's warrior nuns shifted uneasily, scanning the volatile crowd spread before them.

Keeping his voice loud, Kalief turned toward Sureya. "I present to you the Supplicant of Marotiri." Kalief tugged her chains, stimulating her nipples and pearl as surely as if he'd caressed them with his tongue, with his fingertips.

Sureya pressed against him, craving release. She grinded her hips over his thigh, completely oblivious to the shouting throng. "My love," Kalief heard her gasp. "Please."

"Fuck her! Fuck her! Fuck her!" The crowd did not relent. Her blatant desire fueled their hunger for a show, for an orgy.

Ignoring the lords and ladies, ignoring the crowds, Kalief stroked Sureya's cheek, trying to tell her with his eyes that he would protect her, even from himself.

Then, letting his throbbing cock free of his ceremonial garb, Kalief laid Sureya back on one of the benches and impaled her. High on *dawa*, she came immediately, and the tight, hot walls of her cunt pulsated around his cock.

But he needed to come too, for the One God to hear his most heartfelt prayer.

Kalief thrust again, this time penetrating her still deeper. She arched into him, so wet and so willing.

But it wasn't her, he thought to himself. Not truly. It was the drug.

And he felt dirty.

She said his name then, perhaps sensing his self-loathing through the *dawa*. "Kalief." A flower petal floating on a spring breeze might sound like her plea.

Something in his heart ached to live up to the way she called to him.

He knew then that he felt more than respect for this woman who'd sacrificed all she held dear for the sake of her land. His land.

He didn't want to kiss her lips, or run his fingers through her hair. Those gestures were too personal for this public display. He didn't want to ravish her breasts, tug those rings between his teeth until she begged him to satisfy her.

He wanted to give the crowd as little as possible—and still keep true to his cause.

He thrust.

And came with an intensity he'd never known. An autumn tornado whipped through him and spit him out in the palm of Sureya's hand. He came, and the orgasm kept tearing through him.

He came. Then he stopped.

On wobbly knees, he stood. In a voice thick with desire but still commanding, he, King of Marotiri, shouted for all to hear, "Thanks to the Supplicant." He gestured down toward Sureya, who looked far from queenly, "I can ask the One God, and he will hear my prayer!"

Kalief ignored the glowering faces of Lord Auroch and Lady Wisteria. They'd wanted to touch Sureya, to bring her to orgasm themselves. But he was the Penetrator and the king. His word was law. He hoped that they'd change their minds in the days to come.

"One God in the Above," he shouted so myriad people could hear. "Please hear my prayer. I have granted you a gift— the passion of Your Supplicant. Please grant my prayer."

"Save us! Save us! Save us!"

"I wish," he shouted over the crowd. "I wish to present to you, your future queen!"

The crowd shouted madly, instantly enamored with the surprise.

Ignoring the shocked expressions of the lords and ladies on

his platform, and ignoring the fact that they weren't yet married, King Kalief shouted again. "Queen Sureya!"

From the rear of the wild throng, the newly shaved man examined the onlookers with disgust. The naked faces of the men made him sneer, even as he ran his palm over his now-hairless jawline. The men in this country looked like boys. If he mourned the loss of his own facial hair, at least he'd lost it to a good cause.

When he'd seen the warrior women, each baring one black breast, he'd almost choked. He might have blown his cover with his shock, but most of the people around him were equally surprised, if for a different reason.

These people, weak as they were, objected to warrior women. But his objection was different—he couldn't believe this king was straying from Marotiri's precious Scripture. He'd heard that the little king was quite the religious scholar, could quote Scripture forward and back.

All of this gave the watcher pause. What was the little king doing?

Then the crowd grew silent, and the man cursed to himself. He should have procured a better position. He couldn't see the platform over the multitude. The watcher considered shouldering his way to the front, risking the possibility he might draw attention to himself.

But then he clearly heard the words voiced by the little king: "Your future queen!"

Then the watcher did curse aloud in the ancient language. "*Zewah!*" What was the little king doing?

He was completely fucking up the watcher's life. Stealing a Supplicant would have been difficult enough. But stealing a Supplicant Queen . . . ?

13

In a room full of people, Sureya sat alone. All around her, the well-dressed nobility sat in straight-backed chairs set in a series of ringed platforms. Women wore heavy brocades sewn with silver threads, giving them the plumage of iridescent birds. Men wore dress uniforms heavy with badges and medals.

Hushed voices rose and fell. As people's excitement grew, their hands fluttered over each other's, like butterflies over blossoms on a hot summer day. Well-clad knees and thighs pressed together, side by side.

Only virgins could touch Sureya, though, at least until the *dawa* was out of her blood, which would take many days. The touch of anyone else left her struggling against the rapids of desire—sometimes as a woman, sometimes as a fish or a bird or a frog. A woman in the hall had touched her arm, and Sureya loped over the plains as a wolf following the irresistable scent of her mate.

Regardless of her form, the scent always led her to her king. And Kalief gladly accommodated her, wrapping her in the safety of his arms, slaking the hunger of her madness.

Slaking his own hunger, too.

As the lunacy continued to exert itself on her, she tried not to panic. She found it easier to accept visions as they came rather than to fight them for grasp of reality.

So when she'd heard the words, "I will wed the Supplicant! She'll be my lady wife proper!" her first thought had been that another vision had her in its grasp.

Anhara had assured her marriage and family were not for her, and she had no reason to doubt her—not after the public orgy she knew must have happened. And girls of her class might sometimes be the mistresses or concubines of the nobility, but they weren't wives.

Still, wasn't that Kalief's voice she'd just heard, proclaiming her state of betrothal to him?

"Who?" she asked, perhaps not wisely. The people sitting in front of her turned to stare, and the virgins at her side hushed her, firmly grasping her arm to make their point.

She felt like an owl who'd been winging through the cool nocturnal woods where it belonged, then suddenly found itself swimming in the sun-studded sea.

Sureya took her slippery mind and held it loosely in control, wanting to understand exactly what was happening. Somewhere in her thoughts, she knew this meeting was important to her future, perhaps even critical.

She heard words and understood them. A volcanic voice said, "If you break your engagement with my daughter, Lady Teanne, I will have no choice, sire, than to break off our treaty."

The crowd collectively gasped, sounding like a thousand starlings taking wing at once.

"My Lord Auroch," she heard. That was Kalief's voice, she knew for certain. And it wasn't just Kalief—it was King Kalief. Despite the fact that he sat in the very bottom ring of the room, while she sat at the top, well protected by her mute virgins, she knew her king's voice when she heard it.

"My Lord Auroch," King Kalief repeated, "I implore you.

Please, do not withdraw from this treaty. Such an action will destabilize the entire region, and you and I—together—have worked hard to repair the damage wrought by my father and my grandfather."

"Your insult to the honor of my fief leaves me no choice, my liege. You promised the troth of Lady Teanne before all members of this parliament." Lord Auroch's face was red as lava.

Then the vision was upon her again. Auroch's red face took on the coloration of a monkey's behind. Then Auroch turned into a baboon and began screeching, running angry circles around the parliament, ripping clothing and hair of the people he passed. The women turned into baboons too—

"King Kalief, my liege," a voice said, cool and soothing. "Father," she said.

Silence fell over the members of parliament and the audience, both.

"Lady Teanne," Kalief said, bowing deeply to her. Examining Lady Teanne, her mind was once again her own. The lady was breathtakingly beautiful. Her auburn hair sparkled like sunshine. It offset the chocolate of her skin. Even at this distance, Sureya could see the elegant cheekbones, the long, straight nose.

"I beg your forgiveness, sire," Lady Teanne said to Kalief. "But I don't wish to marry you." She turned toward the man with the red face. "Father," she said, "I refuse his hand."

The crowd shouted this time. A jungle full of parrots screamed with the monkeys.

"But, daughter," Auroch said, befuddlement clear on his face. "Why ever not? We negotiated your terms for days—at your insistence."

Sureya detected determination in every line of Lady Teanne's posture. "I had a vision," she said clearly, so that everyone at the meeting could hear her. "And in this vision I saw our King Kalief needed to wed the Supplicant."

"Daughter!" Lord Auroch said. He was shocked, and she couldn't blame him. No king in the history of the land had every married a pale-skinned peasant.

"It's true, father. I saw her put the myrtle wreath on his head, and I saw him drink from her chalice—as in the ancient ceremony." Lady Teanne paused and looked at the crowd, at Sureya herself. "And then I saw butterflies float from the Supplicant's mouth."

"The Supplicant truly speaks for the One God!" someone from the gathering shouted.

"That settles it," Kalief said, rising to his feet. "Sureya, Supplicant of Marotiri . . ." He looked at her, on the platform high above him, and waited.

"Yes, my lord," she answered, prodded to stand by the mute novices.

Kalief sank to one knee in front of everyone at the parliament gathering. "Would you please be my wife? I swear to protect you and your name as I would my own."

She stood. "I—"

"She cannot!" a priest shouted across the room before she could answer. "The whore cannot marry the king! You may not wed her, sire!"

Kalief rose to his feet to answer the cleric, but the lords and ladies of his land interjected first.

"What about heirs?" Lady Wisteria asked, her blue brocade dress shimmering over her full breasts and hips. "Can this Supplicant bear heirs, or will you name someone else?"

The stark expression on Kalief's face told Sureya that the question hit home. Children were not possible for the Supplicant.

She herself had not thought about children, not about children fathered by Kalief. But now she imagined the tiny perfect features of their child. She could see the little fists waving helplessly in the air. And her arms ached to hold the babe.

She shook her head, hating what the *dawa* did to her mind.

"'Tis true no Supplicant has ever borne a child," Kalief said. "I will name an heir within the next two years."

Was that regret Sureya saw on his face? Surely not. Why would he want a cream-colored child?

"And what about the safety of our land?" Lord Pentagrin asked, flicking his long dark hair from his face. "If the lords and ladies can no longer petition the Supplicant with the needs of our land, are we to forgo the benefits she brings altogether?"

Sureya wondered the same thing—if they couldn't fuck her, how could they make their wishes?

"Lord Pentagrin," Kalief replied, "I will put a different tradition in place. The lords and ladies of Marotiri may come to me with any request. If I deem it beneficial for the land, then I'll bring the Supplicant to orgasm myself and make the wish."

"Well, that rather takes the fun out of it," Lady Wolfitte said, sotto voce. The women sitting around her laughed.

"That may be," Abbess Anhara said, addressing the crowd for the first time. "But it adds dignity to the station of Supplicant, a dignity that has been sorely lacking for millennia."

"The whore needs no dignity," the priest bellowed, his gray cassock flapping as he jumped to his feet. "No whore does!"

"Please," Kalief demanded. "I'll not have my betrothed discussed in such a manner. The next person to call Sureya or the Supplicant by that name will be imprisoned."

The crowd looked at him, perhaps too shocked to react. Her king took advantage of the moment. Kalief sunk to one knee again. He held one hand to his heart, the other toward her in entreaty. "My Lady Sureya," he said. His voice cracked. "Will you marry me?"

Sureya looked at the man below her, and in a moment of clarity so rare with *dawa*, she saw his beauty—the curve of his lips, the planes of his face, the breadth of his chest. But her heart saw deeper. Her heart saw the man who fought the barbarians for her family, who bucked a thousand years of tradition to ask for her hand in marriage.

Sureya knew that only one answer was possible.

"Yes, my liege, if it pleases you." The strength of her voice surprised her. She thought her words might come out as bubbles or feathers or frogs. "I accept your troth."

"It pleases me, very much," Kalief said. And the huge smile that took over Kalief's face opened up the shining galaxy of stars in Sureya's heart. She was truly loved!

Just then, the huge brass doors of the parliament room burst open. Several soldiers exploded into the room. "Sire!" one cried. "Lords and ladies!"

"What is it?" Kalief asked, his face as calm as his voice.

"It's the comet!" the shorter one said.

"What about it?"

"It's gone!" the soldiers cried in unison.

"Gone?" Kalief said, looking at the ceiling, although the room had no window. "Are you certain?"

"It's well and truly gone, sire," said the shorter soldier.

"As if it never existed," added the other.

"It's a sign," Lady Starliner cried, clutching her throat with a fluttering hand.

"I agree with Lady Starliner," Lord Leeward shouted. "It's a sign! The One God smiles upon this marriage!"

Kalief's eyes caught hers across the breadth of the room, and she read nothing but acceptance. She would be his. She shifted her weight and felt the gold ring between her thighs slip over her pearl, which was now wet with desire.

But far above her, above the closed-ceiling of the room, an eagle shrieked—high and piercing. Arrows fell from its mouth, and glinted in the sunlight.

Aware of the warmth of Kalief's skin so near to hers, Sureya looked at Anhara but couldn't comprehend the words. "You two cannot go through with this wedding ceremony," Anhara said.

"What? I—" Sureya began. She wanted to say *I love him,* but hadn't she thought exactly the same thing about Risham? Who'd believe her? She didn't know if she believed herself.

"Cousin, have you gone sun mad?" Kalief asked. "I'd have thought this was exactly the kind of reform you'd embrace."

"You misunderstand me, Kalief. It's the ceremony to which I object, not the marriage itself."

Sureya watched Kalief take a deep breath, as if marshalling his patience. "What are you talking about?" he demanded.

"All the signs point to following the ancient wedding ceremony—not the one sanctioned by Scripture."

Relief ran through her veins. Anhara wasn't trying to keep them apart. Sureya might not be able to insist on *love* when describing how she felt about Kalief, but being near him felt good, maybe even right.

"Exactly what signs are you talking about?" Kalief asked.

"Lady Teanne's vision, with the myrtle and chalice."

"Her vision! You've lost your mind. Lady Teanne didn't have a vision—she just couldn't stand the thought of being rejected, especially for—"

"Kalief, don't be daft," Anhara interrupted. But Sureya knew what her fiancé was about to say. Lady Teanne didn't want to be forsaken for a white-skinned peasant.

"What was the last ceremony you attended where the priests used myrtle and chalices?" Anhara demanded of Kalief.

Standing aside, Sureya watched Kalief shrug. "Those things are in every wedding ever painted."

"No." Another person might have flapped her hands in exasperation, but Anhara simply blinked at her cousin. "As a king, your exposure to new art is deplorable. Artists haven't used those symbols in hundreds of years. Neither have priests. Why would Teanne have mentioned them?"

Kalief pointed to a huge painting on the wall of his study. "Look," he commanded. The bride and groom danced together around a maypole while he placed a myrtle wreath on her head and she drank from his chalice. "Ha."

"That proves my point, Kalief. That artist died two hundred fifty years ago," Anhara said. Even to Sureya, the picture looked old.

"Look, cousin," Kalief said, pained patience dripping from his voice. "I don't know if she had a vision or if she saw this very painting." He ran his hand through his hair, making it stand on end. "All I'm saying is that putting too much weight in Teanne's words is dangerous. Her vision—real or not—gave her a way to assuage her pride."

"Why does it matter, Anhara?" Sureya felt like they'd forgotten she was there.

"Lady Teanne's vision tells me that you ought to honor the old ways with this ceremony."

"You'd have me aggravate the priests more than they already are? I know your agenda, Anhara." Kalief insisted.

"It's not an agenda. If Lady Teanne's vision is correct, honoring the old ways may give you both a stronger avenue to power.

"It's not an agenda—" Kalief began to scoff, shaking his head.

"Wait," Sureya cut in, wanting them to stop. A catbird meowed. "What if we do both?"

"Both?" Kalief and Anhara asked together.

"Both ceremonies. We can do the traditional ceremony in the morning, and the ancient one in the evening." She looked from Anhara to Kalief. "Would that work?"

Anhara nodded. "I think it would. What do you think, Kalief?"

Kalief laughed. Sureya thought it sounded rueful. "I think nothing in my life's as simple as it should be." He pulled Sureya toward him and kissed her. His touch. The *dawa* sent her mind skimming down the rapids, and desire splashed through her, hot and languid. "But that's a perfect compromise." His lips trailed down her neck, toward her shoulder, sending electric shivers through her.

"That's settled then," Anhara said.

Kalief looked up. "I'm not making any more compromises, though, cousin. The weddings," he emphasized the plural, "will take place tomorrow."

Anhara smiled and shook her head. "Have fun explaining that to your castellan. That'll make Echo very happy."

His voice sounded distant through the fog of *dawa*. "I think that's your wedding gift to me," Kalief said to his cousin, tantalizing Sureya with burning kisses along the edge of her ear.

"There's another sign, too, Kalief," Anhara said. "One that could fit in none of my so-called agendas."

His lips stopped in their tracks, and he said, "What?"

"Tomorrow's the autumnal equinox, the most powerful day of the year."

Sureya felt him sigh, then he said, "Be gone, cousin. I need time alone with my fiancée."

"The priests will be unhappy about the second ceremony, Kalief," Anhara said.

"Which should make you happy."

"I'm serious," Anhara said.

"Then don't tell them," Kalief said, pulling Sureya closer still. Into her ear, he whispered, "Shall we practice for our wedding night?"

There's no god here. That thought ran through Sureya's mind as she knelt with Kalief before the bishop. *The One isn't at this ceremony.* Maybe the unbearable weight of her gown, a full-length white thing encrusted with gems, muffled the One's voice. The crown dug into her temples, and maybe that was distracting her. Whatever the cause, the bishop's words slid over her mind without penetrating it.

His absence worried her. She'd have liked to know the One God blessed this union.

Finally, the bishop directed them to stand, turn toward the congregation. As she did, a figure dodged behind a gilt column, brown cassock swishing. Or maybe he just innocently shifted his weight, she didn't know. Her fingers itched to adjust the crown, relieve the pressure on her temples. But Anhara had told her not to touch it, and she wouldn't.

"In the eyes of the One God, the only God, King Kalief and the Supplicant are now wed!" the bishop declared in a booming voice.

Kalief took her hand in his, sending electric jolts jagging through her *dawa*-tainted blood, and held it high. The congregation politely clapped, but as her eyes scanned the crowd, she saw no joy, no happiness on the faces of the nobility. Where were Anhara and her nuns? They'd celebrate her moment, even if their noble peers didn't. Sureya saw her friends nowhere.

Then Kalief, in snug trousers of a rich cream cloth, released her hand and bowed to her. She curtsied in return, and he snuck her a private smile. And even though he wasn't touching her, even though he wasn't triggering the *dawa*, his smile lit her world.

"As his wife, the Supplicant is now Queen of Marotiri! Bow to your queen!" directed the bishop.

She watched all heads, brown skin and black hair, bow to her. If some of the nobility seemed reluctant, she couldn't blame them. She could scarcely believe it herself.

"My bride," Kalief said, for her ears only. Then he led her down the aisle toward the door. He stopped for a moment on the top step, pulling her to his side. Sureya watched the smile spread over his face at the sight of his subjects spread before him. Happiness twisted her heart, and she found herself near tears.

"My people!" Kalief called. "Thank you!" And he bowed to them. When the people applauded this time, she could hear their hearts in it.

Kalief led her down the stairs, and someone released thousands of butterflies. Their iridescent wings filled the air with fluttering yellow, and her husband laughed as he brushed one from her veil.

Then his lips claimed hers, masterfully. In front of anyone who mattered, Kalief declared her his. The shimmers from the *dawa* lit stars behind her eyes, but she knew she was his, regardless. Her blood ran hot for him, with or without the drug.

"Sire," a man called, sidling up to her husband, interrupting them. At the same time, their carriage approached, slated to take them to the feast in their honor. She recognized the short man as Echo, his castellan.

"What is it, man?" Kalief said, distaste clear in his expression.

"You're needed, sire," Echo said. He leaned toward Kalief's ear, and she couldn't hear what he said. With a final wave, her husband helped her into the gilt carriage and then climbed in himself—and climbed out the other side.

"What're you doing?" she asked him as the footman closed her door, separating her from the crowd.

"Echo thinks barbarians have been sighted just west of here. I need to check it out. I'll meet you at the feast." He winked at her and said, "Don't let anyone take my seat."

"Kalief, you can't just—"

But Echo handed Kalief the reins, and he climbed onto his warhorse. Kalief galloped away before the carriage could move, before the crowd could see the groom had disappeared into the thick forest.

Instinctively, she raised her hand to wave at the crowd, but she didn't recognize a single brown face. The carriage began to rumble down the narrow road before she could truly worry.

As the horses pulled the carriage up the steep hill, she watched the land fall away into a field of green. Jagged gray rocks dotted the hillside.

She tried to console herself. Anhara would be at the feast. Of course she would. She wouldn't leave her alone for long, hosting the nobility of this land.

Just then, the carriage rolled to a stop. She looked out the window, knowing they couldn't have returned to the castle, not that quickly. The door flew open, and a man in a long, flowing cassock jumped in.

"Supplicant," he leered with a toothy grin. His teeth were white against his dark face. His strong body odor filled the small area.

"Who are you?" she asked, shrinking back into the lush seat.

"That doesn't matter," the man sneered. "Not to the likes of you, whore."

She examined him. The cassock. The beads around his waist. But there was nothing pious about him. "You're not a priest, are you?"

He rolled his eyes. "Of course I am. Now shut your mouth." He rapped his fist on the roof, and the carriage began moving again, slowly at first, then with gathering speed. Sureya looked out the window and realized all six horses must have been running flat out up the hill.

"Kalief won't let you get away with this," she said with a calm she felt in her heart. "Neither will Anhara."

"By the time King Kalief discovers you missing, it'll be too late for him to do anything," he said. He spat a fat gob of mucus out the window and wiped his slug-like lips with his brown sleeve. "He'll thank me."

Sureya looked at him, letting scorn pour through her gaze as the carriage rumbled crazily beneath them.

"It might take awhile," the priest said, clutching the side of the carriage as it banked sharply around a corner. "But not even the king can disregard Scripture, not and get away with it." The man nodded, sending a greasy lock of hair into his eye. "He'll come to his senses."

"He'll kill you."

A beatific smile bloomed on his face. "Then I'll become a saint."

The man was mad. She looked out the window, wondering how badly she'd be hurt if she leapt from the carriage.

"Don't do it, whore."

"Don't do what?" she asked, flinging the door open and plunging herself to the rushing ground. She saw his hand grab for her, heard her gauzy veil shred. But then her voluminous skirt billowed around her legs, covering her face as she rolled down the hill.

Rocks and spits of green flashed by her face as she plummeted toward the bottom of the steep hill. She landed with a *thud* and then lay there for a moment, stunned.

"Meow," she heard. Sureya opened her eyes as a mass of black feathers shot past her. "Be smart," the catbird said. "Get up."

Good advice. She rose to her feet, tentatively at first. Her wedding gown was torn and stained, and her elbow was bruised. But she wasn't hurt badly. Her diamond tiara was gone, and that was a distinct relief.

"Uhnh." The sound came from her right, from a heap of brown cloth. The priest. She looked up toward the road, but saw no carriage. She saw no one. Perhaps the driver didn't yet know his passengers had bailed. Good.

"Priest!" She marched over and kicked him as hard as she could, aiming for his kidneys. The action bruised her foot through her wedding slipper, but she didn't care. "Priest!" His eyes were rolled back in his head, and his arm was twisted unnaturally, broken. She thought he might be close to fainting.

She squatted down and grabbed his greasy face. The contact between her palm and his face didn't awaken the *dawa* in her, thankfully. "Don't you dare pass out, virginal slime. I'll slap you."

"Uhnh."

"Where's Kalief? Where's Anhara? If you've hurt them, I'll kill you." Then she remembered his longing for sainthood. "I'll kill you and tell the world you raped me. No one'll believe you're a virgin or a saint. And if you're not canonized . . ."

"Uhnh," he groaned again.

"Where are they?"

"Bootless," he muttered.

"What?"

"Bootless errands."

"So they're not locked up? Injured?" She stopped herself from shaking him.

"Not hurt. Not prisoners. They were sent…"

"Sent where?"

"On fools' errands."

She breathed in relief.

"Never hurt king."

"I have news for you, priest," she spat. "Kidnapping me won't make him happy."

The black-skinned man focused his dark eyes on her. "Wouldn't hurt you either, whore."

She slapped him then. Hard. "I am not a whore."

"Stay," he tried to command. "Tonight." He clutched at her wrist, but she shoved him away and stood. He wasn't worth even another heartbeat of her attention.

Sureya began to walk away from him but he called to her. "Don't go. Honor the One and stay! Don't go to that pagan ritual!"

Ignoring his plea, she looked around her. The hill up to the road was too steep to climb, especially in her heavy gown and wedding slippers. She yanked off the silver cloak and tossed it to the ground.

Sureya walked east, toward the basilica, but after a distance, the vegetation became thick, impenetrable. She found no goat or deer paths. Raspberry and shrub-rose thorns grabbed her gown, snagging it to shreds as she marched past them. Pink stains bloomed on her white satin. Finally she came to a point where she could no longer go forward or back. The plants tangled around her angles and clothing. Red welts lacerated her wrists and ankles.

Too angry to cry, she sat on the plants, knowing they couldn't stab her. Her skirts saved her from that fate at least. She was hot and thirsty. She was frustrated, and her forearm itched. Had she gotten into one of the ivies? Had something bitten her? The crazed itching reminded her of . . . the coatl!

She jumped to her feet, ignoring the tearing sound of her dress caught on the raspberry branches. "Lord Coatl!" she cried to the turquoise sky. "I need your assistance!"

In a flurry of ruby feathers, he blinked into existence from the ether right in front of her face.

"It'sss about time, Sssupplicant."

"What?"

"I cannot appear if you do not asssk for me. It took you a long time to call."

She took a deep breath to curtail her exasperation. "Well, now that I've called, can you get me out of here?"

"You need to get to the ceremony Anhara sssset up for you and Kalief."

"I'd like that very much, Lord Coatl, but I'm caught in the brambles in the middle of nowhere." She thought she was stating the obvious, but the coatl seemed to miss the point.

"On equinox and sssolsssstice nightsss, doorsss open for all the godsss. Full moonsss open the doorsss, too. Tonight isss both the autumnal equinox and a full moon."

"I'd love to go." She held up her tattered skirt.

"A wedding between the King of Marotiri and the firssst Ss-supplicant in generationsss on ssuch a night will be very powerful indeed."

The feathered serpent winged toward her, flicked his tongue over her ankles and wrists. Her wounds disappeared. He flicked her elbow, and the dripping wound sealed itself closed, leaving no scar. Then he licked her face, and an ache of which she hadn't been aware disappeared.

"Thank you, Lord Coatl!" she said. "But can you get me there, to the wedding?"

But he disappeared into the ether.

"By the One," she spat to herself. "I'm surrounded by insanity."

"Did you say something, little dove?" Anhara asked, entering the glade. "Kalief would've come himself, but he's busy annihilating a particularly troublesome sect of priests." Anhara rode Turu toward her, and Firefly followed behind. "He assured me that he'd make it to tonight's ceremony, however," she added.

"I'm so glad to see you."

Sureya's blood bay nickered when he saw her and walked right into the brambles to lay his velvety muzzle on her cheek.

A full moon lit the glade, and the lilting call of flutes filled the air. From the moment Sureya set foot in the glade, the power of the One God hummed through the earth. Her ankles vibrated with His presence. Under the sea of stars, she felt Him flowing through her veins, appreciating the mortal feel of a heartbeat, of desire.

"Sureya." His voice rolled through her like a warm rain. Was this the first time he'd addressed her by name? "Wife," he said, holding the flat of his palm toward her in an invitation to dance.

The peasants, who'd been invited to this ceremony but not the other, brought their rough-made fiddles and flutes. They played folk music handed down from their grandparents' grandparents.

"Husband," she said, a smile playing on her lips as she placed her open palm to his. The intimate touch of his palm against hers in the starlight sent a delicious bolt through her three rings.

Of course, now she had four. Kalief had placed a gold ring on her right pinky in the moonlight ceremony. It, too, pulsed with the power of the One God.

Suddenly, the fiddles struck up an ancient tune from Sureya's hometown, and her feet flew through the pattern. Kalief managed to keep up, looking like he knew what he was doing.

"You know this dance?" Sureya asked.

"I didn't before tonight," he said as he danced the intricate footwork. "Do you feel the power churning from the ground?"

Sureya managed to nod as she twirled in unison with her new husband.

"It's teaching me the step," Kalief said, pressing his palm to hers again. "I'm sure I won't remember it in the morning."

"I hope you don't forget anything else," Sureya teased, as she leaned back in his arms.

"I'll never forget how beautiful you are tonight," he answered, his voice as thick as the morning fog on a cool morning. His eyes raked over her throat and breasts.

The song ended, leaving her wrapped protectively in Kalief's arms. Both were panting from exertion. "I mean it, wife. Your bravery won my heart." He caressed her cheek. "I love you. Completely. Wholly."

A halo of fireflies danced above Kalief's head. A crown. This was the One God's way of telling her that her new husband was the man with whom she could change the world, perhaps save her land.

Sureya leaned her face toward her husband's—*her husband's*. And he kissed her. The earth's pulsing welled up, through her toes and knees and thighs, through her pearl and navel and nipples, across the flat of her stomach, through her earlobes and fingertips. With a mighty crash, it reached a crescendo in her lips, her tongue.

As he kissed her, she guessed that Kalief experienced the same sensation. He opened his eyes at the same moment as she did. They were wide with wonder.

The crowd dancing around them fell back as electric-blue tendrils emanating from the ground coiled, surrounding the kissing pair. The air around them hissed, and fog formed around the coils. Melting into Kalief's touch, his mouth, she felt the tendrils of power caress her wrists, the soft spot behind her knees, the area behind her ears.

Now, she thought. *Now*. His tongue stroked and cajoled and caressed her, and she knew. Irrevocably, she belonged to Kalief, and he belonged to her. Nothing could undo the strength of this magic. Nothing could degrade them or change them.

"By the Above," she felt him mutter as their mouths finally parted. "By the Above, I find I have an overwhelming need that can be met only by my wife."

Then Kalief swept her up in his arms, gathering her like a bunch of flowers, and carried her away from the revelers. When he reached a silent glade, somehow shrouded in quiet fog, he spread his cloak on the ground and lay her gently upon it.

He leaned toward her, his mouth seeking hers. But she placed a pale finger against his lips.

"What is it, wife?"

"I've just realized something important."

"What is it?"

"Kalief, we are wed now, in the eyes of the One God and in the eyes of the earth. We're bound, beloved. We're truly bound."

Her words rocked Kalief to his core. Scripture mentioned the breath of the One God, describing it as lightning blue—like the tendrils that had curled around them. According to Scripture, the One God allowed his breath to be seen around something true, around something beautiful to the Above.

And that made Kalief's veins constrict in hope—every sign, every portent, indicated that his heretical marriage to the Supplicant, to Sureya, was right and just and true. Anhara had been right. Again. Dare he hope to see his land freed from the marauding barbarians?

But more than hope for his land filled his heart.

In the most sacred part of his soul, Kalief didn't know if he could live without Sureya. To keep her, to have her, Kalief might have abdicated his crown, even given up his god.

Instead, his cousin was right. Treating the Supplicant with honor and respect pleased the One God. Wedding her in the sacred glade under a full equinox moon made the One God sigh in pleasure, twine his sacred breath around them in delight.

And Kalief himself sighed in pleasure when her fingertips unbuttoned the bodice of her green gown. A delicate shrug of her creamy shoulder left her dress in a puddle beneath them.

The beauty of her white breasts, shining in the fog-filtered moonlight, made him tremble. Her high pink nipples begged to be tasted. How had he ever thought skin color mattered?

Kalief caressed one breast almost deferentially, and then he took the other in his watering mouth. With closed eyes, she arched her back toward him. Her silent appeal for his touch, his mouth, made his cock throb for her.

His hand moved down her ripe body, drinking in every

curve. She sighed his name, and he reveled in every whisper that fell from her mouth.

She shifted so that her hardened nipple slid under his thumb. Who was he to resist? Under his thumbs, both her nipples peaked and hardened as she pushed toward him, asking for more. He wrapped his tongue around a gold nipple ring and gently pulled. She gasped his name, and it sounded like a prayer.

He tugged the ring harder.

She shuddered then, and he gathered her in his arms, desire and devotion coursing through his veins. Kalief gently rolled her across his cloak, cushioning her in the fragrant moss. As she twined her arms around his neck, his love for her overwhelmed him, tightening his chest.

"Sureya, whatever trials we face with this unconventional marriage," he said, the tension in his voice surprising him. "I'll protect you with my life. I'll protect your name and give up everything I have to keep you safe if I have to."

"My husband," she said. "You have my heart."

And he believed her. The love shining from the deep pools of her eyes gave him all the assurances he needed. Like a bee, he drank in her honeyed kisses, reveling in the pollen of her touch.

Her breasts pressed against his chest, and he knew she was nearly ready for him. But he wanted her more than ready. He wanted her to want him like she'd never wanted anything in her life.

Wrapping one hand in the length of her hair, he crushed her lips against his. She opened her mouth to him, gave him her tongue, her lips, her breath.

His tongue found her lips swollen with desire, and a moan escaped him. Perhaps desire gave her confidence. His bride rolled from beneath him and straddled him, sliding the tip of his cock over her throbbing pearl.

When her knees clenched his hips, when her nails sank into

his chest, he though she might be there, ready for him. As she leaned toward him, he memorized one lush breast with his fingertips and palms, even with the back of his hand. He stroked one nipple between his fingers while he sucked and licked the other. His teeth and tongue toyed with the irresistible gleam of the rings.

Now that they'd forsaken all of the Scripture's instructions, she could take them out, but Kalief hoped she'd keep them. He tugged one gently with his teeth, licking the tip of her pebbled nipple as he pulled. She arched toward him, sliding her wet pearl over his cock. He didn't think she'd need much convincing to leave the rings in place.

She wanted him. Now. His hand descended down her stomach, past her navel. Kalief lightly traced his fingers over the line of her soft hair, and then lower, until he found the molten heat of her. She arched toward him, wet and hot. Ready for him.

And finally, finally, Kalief could take her in good conscience. No guilt now. He was her husband, and she was his wife. She belonged to him. Only to him.

Taking his cock in hand, he slid the wet tip over her pearl, gently at first, then more insistently.

"By the Above, Kalief," Sureya said, pressing into him. "That feels good."

He slowly pushed his cock into her, teasing her with the promise of fulfillment. She sat down hard, trying to fill herself with him, but he chuckled and held her back. A small animal noise escaped her throat.

Kalief purposefully pushed a finger deep inside her, then sank another. She groaned with pleasure and pushed against him. "You're ready for me, my queen." He hoped—no, knew—he was right, but he teased her and withdrew.

Sureya cried out and lifted her hips toward him.

"Don't stop, Kalief!"

He wanted her, no doubt, but this wasn't about him. Not on

their wedding night. Kalief slid his fingers inside of her again, savoring the look of satisfaction that crossed her face. By the Above, he wanted her. Kalief pulled out his fingers and—

And then she captured his throbbing cock in her grasp. He lay helpless as a newborn foal as she rolled off his body and dipped her head toward his cock. Kalief knew then what she wanted, what she was going to do. The beads of sweat on his brow spread, covering his whole body in a fine sheen.

Sureya's fiery locks spilled across his stomach, over his thighs, obscuring his cock. She ran her tongue over the thick length of him, sucking him deeply inside her beautiful mouth.

Then she sucked hard, and Kalief nearly came.

Perhaps sensing his imminent orgasm, she slowed. Languid and sensual, she moved her mouth over his pulsing erection. He filled her completely. The eroticism of having his cock buried in her mouth, her gold-studded breasts pressed against his thighs, nearly undid him.

"Stop," he said. "Please." Desire had thickened his voice, and he knew she heard it. Kalief rolled her over and gazed down at her. "Now?" The word emerged hoarse and eager. Kalief needed this woman more than life itself.

She nodded and spread her legs, wrapping her thighs around his waist. Her movement fit his thick length against her pearl, almost where it belonged.

"Don't stop," she murmured, grabbing his hips. She raised her own and buried him deeply inside of her.

Kalief needed no further encouragement. He grabbed her ass and pumped into her. He thrust over and over and over.

"Kalief, my love." She clung to him like her life depended on it.

"Sureya," he nearly whispered. "I love you." Then Kalief cried out in raw pleasure, in exhilarated ecstasy. He bellowed in triumph and release.

She came with him.

The same ozone-blue tendrils that wrapped around them during their wedding kiss now swirled up from the damp earth beneath them. As the orgasms wracked through them, the tendrils spun in a dreamy vortex.

Her new husband cloaked her in his arms. "My queen," he said in butterfly words and then promptly fell asleep.

Sureya's heart took wing at Kalief's tender touch. "I love you, too, my king," she whispered after he was asleep. Her words came out as a barn owl's hoot.

He'd astounded her. Though their shared orgasm had funneled the world's power into a cobalt whirlwind, Kalief didn't fall to his knees and make a wish—although surely the One God couldn't have ignored it.

Tears of happiness slid down Sureya's cheeks. She'd finally found it—the place where she would be loved and cherished for herself.

She'd found a home.

"Caw," a crow called into the star-spangled night.

Sureya looked up and saw that the crow, too, was weeping. "Why do you cry, crow?" she asked, whistling like a whippoor-will.

But the crow flew away, its tears cascading down toward her. Its tears joined Sureya's, and together they puddled into a lake of crystalline blue and sapphire white.

14

Amid people bedecked in finery and jewels, Kalief had eyes for only one person at the feast. His wife.

Sureya's yellow silk gown made her hair shine like the flames on the giant hearth, and the smoky gem at her throat glowed like her eyes.

"So, my queen," he asked her over the lute music. "How're you adjusting to your new life?"

When Sureya turned her sparkling eyes toward him with that little smile on her lips, something strange happened to his heart. She had that effect on him.

"Anhara's been very gracious in showing me around," Sureya said. "And she's been introducing me to the appropriate people." Her voice reminded him of moonbeams, cool and soothing.

"Exhausting you, you mean?"

"Not as much as you have, my lord."

Kalief laughed at her demure expression, at her oblique reference to their passionate nights granting the wishes of Marotiri's lords and ladies. "My lord, is it now?"

"Anhara tells me that it's appropriate to address you so," Sureya said from behind dropped lashes. "At least in public."

He watched the smile playing on her lips, and if the pheasant weren't plattered on the table between them, he'd devour that smile in one hot kiss. "That sounds like my cousin."

"Are you talking about me?" Anhara asked. Her hair had been twisted into black ringlets atop her head.

Lady Wolfitte, sitting between Kalief and his cousin, said, "I do think they're talking about you, Anhara." She held up a fine crystal glass, as if in a toast. "You'd better get to the bottom of this." The violet hue of her dress matched her unusual lavender eyes.

Anhara returned the toast and said, "Seeing the gleam in Sureya's expression, I believe Kalief generally gets to the bottom of things. Isn't that so, sister?"

Sureya took a sip of mulled wine. Kalief could see her mind racing for a clever comeback. "Well," his wife said, "when something needs to be explored in depth, my husband can generally rise to the occasion."

Anhara and Lady Wolfitte laughed in delight. "You'll make good company here in court, sister," Anhara said. "I'm so glad that you're here."

"I agree," Lady Wolfitte said, then she playfully swatted her king's arm and said, "but I'm still angry with you for depriving us of Sureya's company in bed. Look how beautiful she is, and now I can't even touch her. Just think of all I could have taught her, all the trouble I could have saved you."

Minions would have to walk the earth before he'd share his wife with Lady Wolfitte. "You know, Lady, if you have a supplication, we're more than happy to implore our One God on your behalf."

"I'm sure you are, you hedonist," teased Anhara, her tapered crimson nails elegantly contrasting the silver stem of her goblet. "Oh, Kalief," Anhara said in a playful falsetto, "Do you think you can ask the One God to repair my broken fingernail?" Then in a deeper voice, she said, "I'll get right to that, lady. Sureya! Come here!" Anhara shimmied her shoulders suggestively.

"Or what if I implore you to ask the One to share your lovely bride," Wolfitte asked with a grin that matched her namesake. "My dear lord," she mimed, holding her hands together as if in prayer. "Kalief's new bride is so lovely that I can't sleep at night. Could you please let me have her for just one tumble?"

Kalief rested a possessive hand on Sureya's milky-white shoulder, bared by the cut of her gown. The feel of her smooth skin under his fingertips drove him to distraction. "The sheets are still warm from our wedding night, Wolfy, and you're already offering to join us in a threesome."

"I was actually hoping to get Sureya to myself," Wolfitte said. "But a threesome might have its rewards." She reached across the table and stroked his chest.

"Greedy thing," Anhara said, swatting Lady Wolfitte's hand away from Kalief. "I thought I was enough for you."

With a mock evil look in her eye, Lady Wolfitte said, "I'd suggest a foursome, but—"

The cousins howled in disgust.

"Prudes," Wolfitte said, shrugging her *khal*-colored shoulder. "I guess I could settle for a night with Sureya alone."

"I highly recommend it," said Anhara.

Kalief cleared his throat, hoping his discomfort wasn't apparent. Sureya belonged to him and him alone. He wished his cousin had never lain with her. Sureya was his.

He held out his hand for Sureya in an invitation to dance. The soft pressure of her fingertips in his palm, the knowing look in her eye, made his cock instantly hard. Kalief held back a growl as he led her to the dance floor.

Seeing the king and queen step onto the floor, the band

struck up something exquisite. Kalief noted that his wife—the movements of her feet, the waves of her red hair—matched the intricacy of the melody perfectly. As graceful as if she'd learned the dance in childhood, Sureya synchronized her steps to his. *One-two-three. One-two-three. One-two-three,* the lute and flute nearly hummed together.

Given the privacy of the dance, Sureya apparently felt bold enough for direct eye contact. "So, my lord," she said, "surely there is a supplication for tonight?"

"Does my lady hope?"

She softly laughed, reminding him of quiet brooks. "I hope that if there weren't," she said, "I'd still have your very thorough attention."

Kalief pulled her tightly against him so that she could feel his hard desire for her. She was so close his fingertips caressed the clean line of her collarbone.

"I've only thoughts for you, Sureya."

Sureya sighed in pleasure as Kalief pulled the long pins from her hair and let it tumble down her bare back. "That feels better," she said.

Then she turned to him and loosened the band tying his dark hair back from his face. She pulled him toward her as she lay back in their decadent bed. His kisses held magic for her—a strong magic. When his tongue twined around hers as it did now, every bit of her yielded to him, wanted to be his and only his.

As her lips drank in the feel of his mouth, she rolled him beneath her, letting his hard thickness press against the apex of her thighs. She knew she was wet enough to take him deep inside her. She knew she was excited enough to come in a heartbeat.

But Sureya wanted to prolong the pleasure, to revel in his

strength and his scent, the play of his muscles under her hands. She pulled his hand to her breast and arched into him, moaning softly at the lightning zing of pleasure it sent coursing through her.

She opened her eyes just a bit to see the heavy desire in her husband's expression, and—

Screamed.

Kalief's castellan, Echo, appeared at the side of the bed, just outside the gauze netting. The man cleared his throat.

"This better be important, man," Kalief growled.

"Sire," Echo began, speaking quietly, "the barbarians have attacked the Ascelpian Monastery."

"The healers?"

"Yes, sire," Echo said, his lean face grim.

Sureya sensed Kalief's growing rage. She knew helplessness must be at the root of his anger.

"The buildings?" Kalief asked.

"They've figured out some way to set fire to the bricks, sire." Echo swallowed; Sureya could see his throat bob. "The monastery burns," he added. "The night watch on the western parapets can see the glow."

Kalief turned toward his wife and said, "I must ride, beloved." He stood naked and said to his man, "Echo, prepare my horse and alert my best fifty soldiers."

"Yes, sire."

Sureya watched Echo disappear as quickly as he'd appeared.

"I'm sorry, my lady," Kalief said. His eyes weren't seeing her, she noted.

"Perhaps we should supplicate the One God before you go," she suggested.

He stopped and looked at her a moment, and she felt certain he'd come up with a clever wish to ameliorate the problem. But Kalief, tight lipped, shook his head and said, "I'm too angry."

"Perhaps we should wish for the recovery of all who survived," she suggested. "Or maybe we could wish that the flames were extinguished."

"Sureya," he said, pulling on his fawn-skinned cavalry trousers, "I need to go there first. Then I'll see what we need."

She sat up and pulled the satin sheet to her chin. "The fire needs to be put out right away," she said. "And we can't hurt anything by wishing for the health of the survivors."

"Unless they're all barbarians, Sureya." He was buttoning his shirt with tense fingers.

"But—"

"I'm leaving. That's it. No argument." Kalief pulled on his coat, which was split up the middle to accommodate a horse. "I want you waiting for me when I return," he said. "We can make the appropriate supplication then."

Anger laced through her with his words, but he was gone before she could argue.

"Damn him," she muttered, lying back on the pillows.

But sleep was impossible. No matter how she twisted the words around in her head, she knew she was right. Together, they should have put out the flames. And maybe, if he were worried about healing the barbarians, they could've wished to heal the people of Marotiri, or anyone who'd been in the monastery for more than a day.

Something, she thought, slamming her fist into the pillow, hating her own helplessness. *Anything*.

Now she had to worry about him racing toward a burning castle filled with insane barbarians. Surely she could wish the flames out—then it wouldn't be so dangerous when her beloved arrived.

The thought froze Sureya in the warmth of her bed. Could she—by herself—wish the flames of the burning monastery out? Did she need a partner?

Making herself come might not be as difficult as all that. She was still wet from their foreplay, which had begun over dinner.

During the first days of their marriage, she thought her overwhelming desire for him was due to the *dawa*, which was slow to work out of her system. Then later she thought it might be the hand of the One God upon her—after all, she'd imagined Anhara in great detail before she'd met her.

But Sureya was just coming to realize her desire for her husband was due to something else altogether. She loved him.

She loved his bravery and honor and the way he tried so hard to be a good king, to rule fairly. He'd defended her honor, too, bucking centuries of tradition and the Scripture.

When it came down to it, though, Sureya had to admit it was the way he looked at her that grabbed her heart. Like tonight. When his gaze fell her way, something inside him lit up. He glowed. He made her feel loved.

Sureya tentatively slid her fingers between her thighs, wondering what full penetration by herself would feel like.

She'd kept her pubis shorn. She and Kalief both liked the way the thick gold ring invited his fingers and tongue. Like the ring, the novelty of her shorn pubis still enticed her hands, beckoned her fingers. Desire rippled through her. She felt as famished for this as she'd ever felt for a meal.

With the touch of one uncertain finger, the first orgasm of the evening threatened to crash through her before she could truly begin.

With hunger burning deep inside her, Sureya had no choice but to use multiple fingers, imagining Kalief's hands and tongue. She slid over the entire surface of the nerve-filled pearl, gasping at the thrill of it.

Using two fingers, then three, then more, she caressed herself. Then she slid one finger slightly inside, surprising herself with her own tight heat. Her mind played her the sound of

Kalief's moan, and she came with an amazing intensity that left her breathless.

Keeping one finger sheathed while another pressed against her pearl, she came again, bucking in pleasure.

Ignoring her sticky fingers, the scent of desire pervading her bed, Sureya fell to her knees, and began the ritual words.

"It won't work like that, little dove."

Sureya jumped in surprise, then stood, wrapping herself in the sheet.

"Anhara!"

"The One God can't hear prayers evoked from a partner-less orgasm," the abbess said, surrounded by a stillness Sureya wished she could emulate.

"That's what Scripture says?"

Anhara nodded her chin slightly. "Yes."

"I could still try, though." Sureya asked. "It wouldn't hurt anything, would it?"

"It wouldn't hurt anything." The abbess gave a slight shrug. "Perhaps you should try petitioning the One God. We've been surprised before."

"Okay." She pulled the satin more tightly around her breasts. "I've already . . ." Even now, she felt embarrassed discussing her sexuality so blatantly.

"Come?"

"Yes." She couldn't meet Anhara's gaze.

"Send your prayer then, little dove," Anhara said. "Were you going to pray to extinguish the flames?"

"In the monastery," Sureya nodded. "Yes."

"I'll send a servant to the parapet to see if the flames go out," Anhara said, "while you send your supplication."

Anhara left, leaving behind a swirling scent of something exotic and rich.

Sureya sunk back to her knees and prayed.

After several long moments, Anhara returned.

"The fire?" Sureya asked.

"It still burns."

Sureya heard herself moan as she collapsed onto the bed, sick with worry over Kalief's safety.

"Together we can help him," Anhara suggested gently, sitting on the bed.

"You mean . . . ?" Again, Sureya couldn't bring herself to say the words.

"Yes, if you want to." Anhara looked more worried than she'd ever seen her. "I want Kalief to come home safely."

"But we can't wish for that!" Sureya said. "It might stop him from completing his job. He'd never forgive me."

"No, no," Anhara said. "I didn't mean that as a supplication." Anhara leaned over near her and said, "We should concentrate on the flames."

Sureya's sheet of midnight blue satin fell away from her breasts, but Anhara's hands and fingers and tongue kept her warm.

Trying to keep the tread of his boots light on the floor so as not to wake his wife, Kalief walked into his bedchamber, brushed the netting back, and sat.

Sureya sat up. "Thank the Above," she said. "You're safe."

"Were you worried about me?"

"You know I was." She wrapped her arms around him. "It was all I could do not to ask the One God for your safety."

But that would mean—he found himself thinking. No. Then a small sleepy sound emanated from the lump under the blanket next to his wife. She wouldn't! Kalief ripped the sheet off the lump.

"How could you?" he demanded of his wife, who blinked, her confusion obvious.

"What do you mean?" Sureya asked.

"How could you cheat on me? How dare you sleep with

someone else?" He fought to keep from shouting, fought to keep his rage under control while Anhara calmly stood and dressed.

Sureya rubbed her eyes, maybe hoping this was a bad dream. "Cheat on you?" she asked. Sureya grabbed the blankets and wrapped them around her protectively. "I didn't cheat on you."

Anhara finally spoke, "Cousin, you need to get a hold of yourself. We put out the fire in the monastery. To keep you safe. *You*." She pulled the belt of her robe tight around her waist.

"You have no right to touch my wife!"

"I couldn't do it alone," Sureya said. "I tried."

"I didn't need your help!" Kalief felt his eyes bulge with the rage pouring through him, even as he watched something cold settle over the face of his usually amenable wife.

"This is our land, too, husband. And the fire needed to be extinguished."

"It would have gone out on its own."

Sureya stood and, like Anhara, very deliberately pulled on her robe and pulled the belt tight around her waist. She put her hands on her hips and glared at him. "This speaks to a bigger problem," Sureya said.

"And what's that?" he asked.

"I'm a Supplicant."

"I've noticed," he said. "And you're my wife. Not hers!" He gestured at Anhara who, uncharacteristically, looked like she didn't know if she should stay or go.

"I'm a Supplicant," Sureya said coolly. "And that means I'll send prayers to the One God as required."

"When I ask them!" he roared.

"When you ask them, true," Sureya conceded. "But also when I see fit."

The coatl's vision came crashing back to Kalief. "So if some *servant*," he spat the word, "wants to save his son, you're going to fuck the servant?"

"If I have to," Sureya answered, her voice still maddeningly calm. "But I'd rather make love to you to see the servant's prayer answered."

"I'm not going to fuck you for a servant!" he bellowed, knowing even as he said the words that he was being irrational. He turned on his heels and headed for the door before he said anything else that he'd regret—anything he'd regret more.

But his mouth wasn't finished with him. When he got to the door, he found himself saying, "Pack a light bag, wife. I have to slaughter those barbarians before they get back to their own land, and you're coming with me."

"Kalief—" Anhara said.

"I've heard enough from you, cousin. Don't even think about coming with us. I'll be bringing the monks to keep our precious commodity safe."

15

The man watched the royal party ride out from the safety of the castle. The king's cape billowed in the wind, making his shoulders and horse seem monstrously large.

But the party wasn't big, and that's what caught his interest. Maybe ten hulking horses that wouldn't last a day in his land. Some soldiers, bulky armor impeding their agility.

And something more interesting . . . The Supplicant rode with the royal party. Her red hair, uncovered, shone like a beacon. She beckoned him like a coatlfly to a flame. Even better, only two warrior monks guarded her.

At first he thought arrogance made them careless. Where were the warrior nuns? He knew an entire battalion was at the king's disposal. Their deadly arrows made him very cautious, even as their bared breasts distracted his junior officers.

But no nuns guarded the brazenly uncovered Supplicant. Only monks, with their paltry staffs, stood stiffly at her side.

What could require the king to bring his precious queen out into this unprotected desert? Did he need her for something?

Then he noticed something else. The warrior monks weren't

guarding the Supplicant as much as frog marching her. He rethought his idea about royal arrogance and royal need.

The monks were telling the Supplicant Queen where she could and could not go, and the king wasn't riding by her side. In fact, as he spied through the glass he saw the king's back was unusually stiff, his ass jamming against his horse's back as he trotted. Unusual. The little king rode well enough under most conditions.

He observed other telltale clues. The Supplicant Queen wasn't speaking to anyone, wasn't turning her head to look at the burning monastery.

Only one conclusion was possible. The couple looked angry—at each other.

He smiled to himself. Had the little king and his peasant queen fought so early in their marriage? It'd been less than a month. His people seldom permitted love matches, as this one was rumored to be. When love matches blew up, they blew up spectacularly, and that was bad for politics . . . as was the case here.

Peering through the spyglass, he studied the king's face. The little king was glowering. Ha. Perhaps anger led the little king to escort the Suplicant right into his hands.

His mouth practically watered. The king and queen might be so busy feuding with each other they'd become careless with her safety.

He put down his spyglass and rubbed his naked chin. He looked forward to the day when he'd once again sport his golden, bead-filled beard.

Capturing and returning the Supplicant would allow him to wear a very special bead—red in color. Like her hair. He wondered briefly what color the hair above her cunt was. Probably as red as blood.

* * *

Regret washed over Kalief as he headed the party over the deep sand toward the monastery, tendrils of smoke still curling from its slate roof. The flames were out, and he should be grateful. Instead, jealousy burned in his heart.

She was his wife. His. Bucking Scripture and centuries of tradition, he'd rescued her from a hellish life, from whoredom.

Was fidelity too much to ask of her?

Still, the soldier in him scanned the countryside. He shouldn't have brought her here. He'd been so focused on keeping her from fucking anyone else, he hadn't thought beyond his own pride.

She slept with another woman to keep you safe, fool, a small voice in his head said.

Fuck you, he said right back to it. *She's my wife.*

She *was* his wife, and he needed to keep her safe. Kalief held his hand for his second-in-command to see, and then circled his fingers around in a spiral. *We're turning around,* he told his second, in their silent language of war.

Sureya seethed as Firefly danced beneath her. Her anger obscured the surrounding scenery, painted it red. "How dare he?" she asked her horse, who snorted in reply. The warrior monks at her side gave no indication they heard her talking to herself.

She observed the object of her wrath. Even angry as a Minion, Kalief sat his horse with skill. His broad shoulders looked powerful, and he rode his huge chestnut stallion with ease.

But he was stiff in his saddle, and not stiff in a good way, either. From under her eyelashes she saw the furrow on his brow, and thought a childish, *ha.* He wasn't any happier than she was, the lake scum.

Then she saw Kalief give that strange hand signal, looping his fingers through the air. What was he doing? Telling his soldiers he was crazy? When the entire group turned around, heading back toward the castle, Sureya asked the monk next to her, "What're we doing? Why're we going back?"

But he didn't answer. Of course he didn't. The monks, the warrior monks, anyway, obeyed their king blindly. Sureya wished the warrior nuns were here—at least they were Anhara's creatures and perhaps more reasonable then these silent, judgmental men.

Tired of being treated like a prisoner, Sureya tried to ride toward Kalief, but the monks blocked her way. Kalief was acting like a child. She'd slept with Anhara for his own good, and if she had the chance to do it over, she would. And just because he was angrier than a snorting bull, Kalief had no reason to keep her in the dark. She was his wife. She loved this land, and she loved her husband.

Filled with self-righteous determination, Sureya kicked Firefly hard in the ribs, and the blood bay lunged forward, quicker than the monks or their mounts. With a snort, her horse flew out of their reach.

Giving a shout of victory, Sureya kicked Firefly again, reining him toward Kalief—who was finally looking at her, at least.

"Kalief," she said, ignoring the soldiers and monks. "Talk to me. Please. I hate arguing with you."

But she watched in horror as an arrow hissed through the air and sliced into Kalief's thigh. Before she could scream, his stallion collapsed to the ground with a horrible, bubbling shriek, an arrow protruding from its throat, another protruding from its chest, a third from its eye.

"Kalief!" she shouted, looking wildly around for support from the soldiers or the monks.

One of the monks grabbed her bridle. He turned toward her as if to say something, but then he, too, crumpled to the ground. The fletching of the arrow sticking from his throat was black and yellow. Sureya's stunned brain noted the individual vanes of the fletching, could almost feel the feathers between her fingers, before she ripped her gaze away.

Wildly, she pointed Firefly's nose toward the castle walls. She kicked him, but he needed no urging. He flew like the arrows searing the air around her. She leaned forward, pressing herself against his neck, grabbing his sides with her legs. The wind whipped his mane into her face, lashing her cheeks with his coarse hair.

And then they descended upon her.

"No!" Sureya shouted, but there was no one to hear. She kicked Firefly, assaulting him with her heels. But his brave heart and swift legs couldn't save them, not this time.

A rough rope whizzed through the air, and the loop snagged Firefly's head. Courageous as he was, he ran headlong into the noose, which choked his breath from his lungs. The lasso jerked his legs from underneath him, and he blasted toward the ground with her on his back.

The sand and rocks beneath Firefly's feet rushed toward Sureya's face, and she prepared herself to hit the ground hard. But a strong arm jerked her to his horse, to safety. The arms could belong only to one person.

"Kalief," she breathed in relief, leaning against his broad back and inhaling his scent. "Thank the Above."

But as hooves pounded beneath her, Sureya realized the scent wasn't his, and neither were the muscles beneath the man's shirt. Her stomach sank. Surrounded by dozens of men with horrible blond beards and amber skin, her captor reined his tiny mount at full tilt toward the deep wood south of the monastery.

"No!" Sureya shouted, realizing barbarians had captured her.

As easily as he might lift an infant, her captor reached behind him and dragged Sureya to the saddle in front of him while the horse under them madly galloped. He wrapped his brawny arms tightly around her.

Sureya couldn't even jump to her death.

Where was her beloved? Sureya tried to look behind them, but her captor's shirt flapped in her way. Then she remembered the way Kalief's horse had collapsed, the arrow in her husband's thigh.

She would not be saved any time soon, not by the people of Marotiri. Not by her Kalief.

Knowing that she'd rather be dead than used against her land, against her husband, Sureya nuzzled her face into the thick arm, hoping to distract him for even a moment. He didn't move away, and she was pretty sure she felt his cock stir behind her ass.

Then Sureya bit into the muscle with all of her might. She felt sinew and flesh crunch, and even though her teeth ached with the effort, she bit harder. Her captor yelled, but she kept her hold, digging in until her eyes began to hurt.

Her captor's mount began to veer as he tried to shake Sureya's teeth away from his arm. Unrelenting, Sureya squashed his testicles and cock between her palm and the hard seat of the saddle, even as she dug her teeth in further.

The barbarian howled in pain, and she threw herself from the saddle. She hit the sand hard, elbows first, then face. Her first thought was to run. She felt no pain but saw blood on her hands as she scrambled to her feet.

Her plan to escape the barbarians had reached no further than getting out of her captor's arms. Now barbarians on scrubby horses swarmed past her, ignoring her. Perhaps they hadn't realized their captain had lost his captor.

Like a cornered rabbit, she stood absolutely still for a moment. Breathing heavily, she scanned the horizon, still hoping to see Marotiri's soldiers, to see figures on horseback in the distance. Even if she could find Firefly . . .

But Sureya saw nothing.

A short distance to the west of the smoking monastery stood a towering rocky outcrop like the one she and Anhara had used for refuge. An inselberg, Anhara had called it. Sureya remembered the oasis, where no violence could take place. Perhaps this was similar.

With her heartbeat loud in her ears, Sureya ran toward it. The barbarian who'd captured her would waste little time in retrieving her, Sureya knew. And that thought lent strength to her legs.

The towering refuge wasn't far away—Firefly would need only a handful of strides to get there. But she wasn't her horse, and she heard unintelligible barbarian shouts behind her. With a mighty effort, she sprinted toward the outcrop.

And she was there! Rough volcanic rocks appeared beneath her bloodied palms. Sureya darted blindly toward the first opening she found, hoping it was a tunnel leading to a caldera protected by the One God.

She was in. Darkness shrouded most of the cave in which she found herself. Believing herself momentarily safe, she stopped for a minute, panting, heart pounding. She needed to catch her breath.

But just outside the opening she heard male voices speaking the old language. She didn't understand them, but she knew without a doubt they were Marotiri's ancient enemies—the barbarians. The people who'd killed her family. The people who'd nearly killed her adopted family and who'd roasted an entire village in a church.

Sureya had only her dagger with her, on her hip. She doubted she could hold her own against even one of these men, but she might be able to surprise them. Failing that she might be able to take her own life. Even killing herself would be better then helping the barbarians.

She heard a new voice speaking unintelligible words, and it

spurred her into action. Better to escape than to kill herself. Keeping her hands against the rough rocks, Sureya followed the wall into the darkness.

As she tracked what turned out to be a tunnel, Sureya banged her shin once or twice, wishing she'd worn something more substantial than the flimsy green silk. As if Kalief had given her a choice. The air grew cooler but not brighter. And after some immeasurable amount of time, Sureya realized that she hadn't heard even the muffled voices of the barbarians in awhile.

A different kind of fear filled Sureya now. What if she never found her way out of this tunnel? Could she find the center of the world this way?

But still she kept going. Backtracking would lead her back to the barbarians, who, for all she knew, were tracking her down this very same tunnel. Keeping her hands on the volcanic rock, Sureya kept walking.

Minutes passed this way. After her harrowing escape and desperate sprint through the desert sands, Sureya's mouth was as a dry as the sand beneath her feet. The darkness had grown so cold, colder than she'd been in her life, but her thirst was making her crazy.

She couldn't see a thing. Hand after hand, she worked her way down the tunnel, cautiously placing each foot forward so that she didn't hurt herself. She tried to stay quiet, certain the barbarians were following her. In places, the tunnel grew so narrow that she needed to crouch to get through, but so far she hadn't come to a dead end.

Suddenly she found herself in a small grotto. The volcanic tunnel led her to a huge rock, long and narrow, hanging from the ceiling. She knew this because she could see it.

Not that sunlight had somehow entered the cave. Instead, the narrow rock glowed an eerie green. Tentatively, she touched it and found it damp to the touch, slippery.

Immediately, her mouth craved relief. Using the tip of her tongue, she licked the glowing rock. It tasted like water. True, it had a funny aftertaste, but she was in no position to complain. She found a puddle at the rock's base and drank it too.

Kalief's face flickered through Sureya's mind. His expression glowed with respect and kindness. And desire. Then twisted in fury at her perceived infidelity.

Right now Sureya missed Kalief with a pain so intense she could almost touch it. She smelled the masculine scent of his sweat. She saw his teeth flash as he smiled, saw the dimple on the right side of his cheek. Remembering the fire in his eyes as he confronted the entire religious community on her behalf made her long to have his arms around her right now. And that made her think of his gentle touch in bed.

His teeth grazed the length of her neck and followed the line of her collarbone. She arched her breast to him. "Suck me," she said in her imagination, much bolder than she was in real life.

He sucked one breast greedily, making small moans escape her throat, as he tugged the nipple ring until pain met pleasure with equal measure.

"My heart is yours, Kalief," she'd tell him. "And my cunt loves you the best."

He'd plunge into her, writhing in ecstasy. The orgasm would wrack his body, leaving him spent and fulfilled. She'd come with him, her body vibrating with his like a violin's bow against the strings.

"Be mine," he'd say.

"I'm yours."

"But Anhara . . ."

"I'm yours," she'd repeat.

In the darkness, Sureya sighed at the fantasy, wishing it were true.

But none of her dreams changed the fact that she knew she

was right. Being with Anhara to put out the fire he'd been marching into was the honorable thing to do.

Even if it broke his heart.

Sitting in the cold, dark tunnel, new images trickled through her mind. A lame man approached her and asked her to heal him. She took him to bed and he walked away—soundly. A woman came to her and asked for healthy crops. Sureya took her to bed, and the woman left with a bushel of vegetables.

Listening to the water drip off the narrow rock into the puddle beneath it, Sureya knew she would help anyone who needed her. She knew it was the right thing to do—even if it hurt Kalief. Which it would.

A sudden flapping surprised Sureya. She heard a bird fly down the tunnel toward her. It landed right beneath the glowing rock and looked right at her. "Meow," the catbird cried.

The catbird extended its wing like it was introducing someone, and a nest appeared in a tiny cherry tree, which had suddenly grown from the green puddle. The bird purred its laughter and hopped onto a branch as the trunk thickened and the branches extended in growth.

As the bird hopped up to the highest branch, the cherry tree burst into flowers, frothy and pink. The catbird threw back its head and sang like a mockingbird.

As if answering his song, the eggs hatched, and three tiny chicks appeared in the nest.

"They're adorable," Sureya said, taking in their large, dark eyes, their almost smiling beaks.

"Take them," the bird said, then disappeared. The cherry tree, the blossoms—everything vanished. The babies were gone, too.

Blinking in consternation, Sureya stuck her hand into one of her voluminous pockets and found three unhatched eggs. She shook her head, certain they'd be gone the next time she reached into her pocket.

Sureya stood, put her sore hands on the wall again, and began to walk. The barbarians could stumble into her at any moment. "Meow," she said to herself, careful not to bump her pocket against the wall.

As she walked away from the glowing rock, the tunnel grew dark again, and it stayed that way for hundreds of steps, maybe thousands.

Then something strange began to happen. The tunnel began to grow warmer. Sweat soaked her filmy shirt, and it stuck to her torso. Beads formed on her brow and dripped uncomfortably down her face.

Anhara had said volcanoes had formed these strange outcrops, so when her eyes detected a faint light, Sureya wondered if it was lava. But as she neared it, she saw sunlight. She began running toward it, stumbling over the rocks.

It *was* sunlight, Sureya realized as she rushed into the cave's grotto. Only it wasn't a grotto. It was some sort of dusty courtyard. She froze and looked up. If a barbarian lurked here, she had no protection, no darkness in which to hide.

But something about this place seemed familiar. Of course she'd never been here before. Had she dreamed it? Awed and confused, she looked up again.

Running along the top of the walls, nearly at the ceiling, ran intricate carvings in the stone. They depicted a life cycle of some sort. Eggs. She saw eggs. Then further along, bordered in intricate runes she didn't recognize, the eggs were shown hatching. Tiny lizards poured out.

There was something familiar about them . . .

One wall gave way to the next, and Sureya gasped. She recognized the creatures. They had feathers. They had wings. Coatls. Like the one that had hatched from her forearm.

A memory came crashing back. Shock made her sit hard. She remembered where she'd seen this room before. She remembered exactly. The coatl who'd hatched from her arm had shown her the problems of his world. He'd shown her this dusty room.

Hope danced a crazy waltz in her heart.

Following her memory of the vision, Sureya stood. She faced north, as she had in the dream, and held up her wrist. In her mind, she asked the coatl to appear.

Nothing happened.

Sureya tried again, holding both wrists aloft, offering her hands and arms as a perch for the creature. This time she spoke the words aloud, quietly, still afraid of the barbarians. "Lovely coatl, I need your help. I need it now."

The coatl didn't magically appear from the ether this time. And for a long moment, it seemed that nothing had happened.

But then Sureya heard a snuffling sound from the tunnel ahead. A snorting sound. Something hard clomping over the rock.

Her heart stopped, and she leapt toward the shadows of the tunnel.

But it was too late. The newcomer spied her.

With a whinny and a toss of his elegant head, Firefly trotted to Sureya and nuzzled her face.

"Where'd you come from?" she whispered, relieved he'd survived and found his freedom. She knew talking to a horse was insane, but her world had shimmered into something unbelievable.

She needed to escape the barbarians, get back to the castle. But when she snagged the reins of Firefly's bridle and led him toward the tunnel, he dug his hooves into the sand and refused to budge. Sureya looked at him and said, "What? Don't stop now. Let's get out of here."

But the horse shook his black mane. "Your work in this courtyard isn't finished," he said.

"I'm losing my mind," she said.

The horse snorted at her, shaking his head.

A sudden cool breeze filled the grotto, instantly drying her sweat-soaked silk. A flurry of scarlet feathers filled the dusty courtyard. Then a familiar face appeared, complete with red forked tongue.

"Lord Coatl."

"At your sssservice, my Ssssupplicant Queen," he said.

Sureya felt no fear, only relief. "I need to save Kalief, Lord Coatl. I need to get home. Can you help me?"

"Your king livesssss, my Ssssupplicant Queen," the coatl said, flicking his forked tongue between words. "He'll fully recover from hisss woundsss."

Sureya collapsed to the warm sand in relief. "Thank the One God."

"Your Abbessss Anhara rode out with her warrior nunsss and vanquished all of the barbarianssss, sssave one—the captain."

"So I can go home now? Am I safe?"

The coatl wrapped himself around Sureya's waist, tickling her sides with his feathers. Sureya saw its cherry color shift to peach as the feathered serpent slithered. Wings tucked, the coatl twined his feathered neck up her torso, snaked around her breast.

Then her coatl grabbed the gold nipple ring through the flimsy silk covering her breast. He tugged it gently, then more urgently, and she couldn't help herself. It was nearly impossible to fight the delicious sensations assaulting her body. She gasped and pushed her coatl away, knowing her actions wouldn't please him.

"My Ssssupplicant," the serpent hissed. "There isss worssse in ssstore for you, I fear." He flicked his tail to her pearl and vibrated it quickly, pulling away just as she grabbed for him.

"What're you doing?"

"The barbarian captain will do worssse than I'm doing, my

Sssupplicant." The coatl made a quick lunge for her nipple. His hot mouth lashed her with exquisite pleasure before he slithered away. "He will touch you assss I'm touching you, and more."

"Then help me get home!"

The creature hissed, twitching his tail between her legs. She no longer fought him. "The world requiresss sssomething more of you."

"What more can Marotiri ask?"

"No, my Sssupplicant, it iss not Marotiri that assks—the world assks." His snakey face dove between her legs, and his hot mouth inhaled her pearl. She felt the pressure and pleasure immediately. Sureya squirmed at the sensations that thrilled her.

"You need to ssssurrender your very will to the barbarian, my brave Sssupplicant," the coatl said, releasing her pearl for a moment. "And he will not make it eassssy for you, for he'sss a rough man."

Sighing, Sureya lay back, yielding to the serpent.

"Thisss iss better, my Sssupplicant." The coatl slithered so that his tongue flicked rapidly over her nipple and his tail vibrated against her pearl. "Don't you agree?"

Sureya's heart began to race, and the serpent wrapped his tail through her pearl's ring and tugged. His fangs hooked her nipple ring and tugged at the same time.

Sureya bowed her back as surges of rapture crashed through her. Her moans of ecstasy reverberated against the granite walls of the courtyard.

Even as the orgasm wracked her body, the coatl began his prayer. "One God in the Above, pleasssssssse hear my prayer," the coatl hissed. "I have granted you a gift—the passssion of Your Sssssupplicant. Pleasssse grant my prayer."

"What are you doing?" Sureya demanded.

"Pleassse permit your Sssssupplicant Sssureya to take the

path toward world tranquility with calm and happinessss in her heart. Allow her to take the indignitiessss she will ssssuffer in the handsss of people from foreign landsss with beauty and nobility."

"But what about Kalief?" Sureya asked. How would he ever accept her sleeping with their sworn enemies? "He won't take me back after I do what you ask. I know he won't."

"Let me show you sssomething," the coatl said, slithering around Sureya's arms, from wrist to wrist. "Clossse your eyesss."

Sureya closed her eyes, and she felt the coatl place a kiss first on one eyelid, then the other.

Behind her closed eyes, Sureya felt the world shimmer and shift. Time bent. She was back in the village where she'd lived as a child, where she'd known her mother's love, her father's devotion, and the adoration of her little brother. She could see for an amazing distance through the clean, crisp air.

"Watch," the coatl said in a catbird's voice.

Sureya shrunk to her child-sized self. "What—" she began to ask, but she looked up with joy as she saw her mother.

A large clay water urn was balanced on her mother's blond head, so the grown woman looked at her daughter through her lashes, without turning her head, without bending toward her. "What is it, Sureya?"

"Momma!" Sureya said. Cool water droplets were condensed on the urn's side under the hot noonday sun. Sureya watched as a fat droplet slowly worked its way down her mother's neck. "I'm just so happy to see you!"

A smile played in her mother's eyes. "I know," she said, obviously playing along with her young daughter's game. "It's been such a long time! Since breakfast at least!"

Then Sureya recognized where they were. And when.

"Momma!" she said. "We must flee! We've got to run and hide!"

"Why, Sureya?"

"The barbarians are coming! They'll be here any minute!"
And they'll rape you and kill you while I hide in the urn, listening, biting my lip to a bloody mess so that I don't call out. Afterward, I'll stumble home and find Papa's throat slit, and my baby brother will be nearly unrecognizable as human, eviscerated and scalped.

"Sureya," her mother said in a voice thick with chagrin. "That's a rude word to use for our lovely neighbors."

Sureya stopped in her tracks. "The men with the yellow beards are our neighbors? Our *lovely* neighbors?"

"Of course they are. They're our friends." Her mother picked up her pace, obviously annoyed with her daughter. "What's gotten into you?"

"How're they friends?" Sureya asked, taking advantage of the fact that all seven-year-olds ask too many questions.

"They helped your father raise our barn, for one thing, miss." Sureya watched a fat water droplet disappear down the back of her mother's orange *kameez*, which waved a bit in the slight breeze.

"They did?"

"Yes, miss," her mother continued. "Friends help each other. We helped them develop a vaccine for their plague and they helped us with building things. They're very clever."

Before Sureya could marshal a reply to that, she heard the telltale sign of thundering hooves. Faint vibrations shook the earth underfoot. "They're coming!"

"I don't know what's gotten into you, Sureya, but if you're fresh to them, I'll tell your father, and he'll *not* be pleased."

"Father's alive?"

"Sureya!"

But her mother couldn't chastise her any longer because the barbarians, astride short, narrow-necked horses, were upon them.

"Honifa!" the leader shouted toward her mother. "How fare you on this fine morning?" He spoke their language with a thick accent, but Sureya could understand him. "Young miss," the leader said to Sureya, bowing low across his horse's neck. "Good morning to you as well."

"Otte," her mother said in her dulcet voice that still haunted Sureya's dreams. "It's nice to see you." She turned toward her daughter with the grace required by a woman carrying an urn on her head. "Would you like to say 'good morning,' Sureya?"

But Sureya only stared at the colorful beads in the man's beard: tiny blue and green figurines. His horse had similar beads worked into its mane: small clay animals and globes painted with unusual patterns.

Sureya read irritation on her mother's expression, but she said coolly to the barbarian, "She needs a nap, Otte. Please forgive her bad manners."

"Of course—there's nothing to forgive," Otte replied in his heavy accent. "A lady always retains the right to say nothing, especially a lady as charming as Miss Sureya."

Otte waved his hand at another rider and said, "Take her urn, Selat."

"Thank you." She nodded to the man after he lugged the thing to the saddle in front of him. Then her beautiful momma turned back toward Otte. "You are looking for Leinad?" she asked.

"No!" Sureya blurted. Leinad was her father. These barbarians must be kept away from the rest of her family.

"I am," Otte replied to her mother. "Why, little miss, don't be upset. I'm sure we'll still have time to play 'find the vole' together."

Sureya only blinked her reply.

"Leinad'll be very happy to see you. He hasn't been able to get that mill to work, and he thinks you can help."

"Well, I'm off, then," Otte said.

And the vision faded away.

Sureya was sitting in the hot sand surrounded by a talking horse and a mythical coatl. She wiped away her tears.

"That's just cruel, Lord Coatl."

"It'ssss what the world could be if Marotiri and the people you call barbarians could learn to coexist."

"My family will never live again," she said.

"That'sss true," said the coatl. "But not all other familiesss must sssuffer as yoursss hasss. You've ssstumbled acrossss a path that will yield a long-lasssting peace between the Marotiri and her ssso-called barbarian enemiessssss."

Sureya had no reply. Again, she faced the choice—should she choose greater good for the world over personal happiness? Could she live with herself if she didn't?

But could she live with herself if she did?

"Your horsssse knowsss where to go," the coatl said, fluffing his scarlet feathers. "Keep him near you. He'll help you get home, when the time isss right."

"After this, I'll have no home," Sureya replied, knowing she was not exaggerating. Kalief would never forgive her if she accepted this path, if she subjugated herself to the hands of the barbarians.

"Hooome," the coatl said. A cobalt blue mist began to coalesce again in the courtyard. Amorphous ruby feathers filled the air.

"You're leaving me," Sureya said, her voice lacking any trace of emotion.

"But not without giftsss," the coatl said, its voice ephemeral, coming from everywhere and nowhere. "You'll be able to ss-peak and understand the tonguesss of Marotiri's enemiesss, now," the coatl said. "You'll be able to ssspeak and undersss-stand all languagesss."

"Thank you," Sureya said, but she couldn't stop her voice from sounding forlorn.

"By the way," the coatl said in a voice as thin as the wavering mist.

"What?" Sureya called into the silence. But he didn't answer. "Are you still there?"

"Yesss. Remember thisss. The barbarians call themselvesss the Jatiss. It will help you befriend them."

"I don't want to befriend them, Lord Coatl."

But the creature had disappeared.

16

As sunlight filtered through the dust, one ruby feather floated slowly to the ground. It landed right next to a small vial halfway buried in the sand. Sureya looked at the bottle for a moment before she reached over and picked it up. Had the coatl left it for her?

"What is it?" she asked aloud.

Firefly snorted.

The vial was almost hot in her hand. She held it up to the light, admiring its color. It was the same color as a papaya, a deep and decadent orange.

"What is it?" she asked again.

Firefly snorted again and then said, "I suspect it's *dawa*, and taking it now might not be a bad idea since I heard the barbarian creeping down the southern tunnel at this moment."

Sureya blinked. "What do you suppose he'll think when he meets a talking horse?"

Firefly shook his head, blowing breath from his nose. The action sent his black forelock floating through the air.

"Fine," Sureya said, ignoring her wobbly knees, her pounding heart. "Be that way." She ran her hand through her hair, wondering whether she should drink the *dawa*, slit her throat, or try to surprise the man sneaking down the tunnel and slit his throat.

"Which is the southern tunnel?" she asked the horse, questioning her sanity.

Firefly tossed his nose in the direction of the tunnel to her left.

Sureya looked above the opening. Wouldn't it be nice if there were a ledge above it? Then she could perch on it and jump onto the barbarian when he passed below. She could slit his throat. Or perhaps, better yet, she could shove the *dawa* down his throat.

But no ledge existed.

Besides, Sureya wasn't trained in fighting. She might be able to punch a priest to unconsciousness by surprise, but she doubted she could take on a trained warrior—even if he suspected nothing.

Firefly looked at her with a pointed expression. He tossed his nose at her. She didn't doubt for a heartbeat the barbarian was only footsteps away.

Sureya picked up the scarlet feather, and turned her back to the approaching barbarian. She shrugged off her diaphanous shirt so it fell off her shoulders and then she sat in the hot sand in front of the south tunnel.

With the vial in her lap, she began to braid the red feather into her red hair, thinking of the last time Kalief ran his fingers through her locks.

He crept with near silence through the tunnel. All tunnels led to the courtyard with the mythical coatl friezes, and he figured his quarry would eventually end up here.

When he finally spied sunlight, he stood still and opened his mouth to better hear. Sound bounced better over the bones in his head through an opened mouth.

Still, he couldn't hear anything—angry blood pounded too viscously in his ears. The bitch he hunted had caused every single one of his top warriors to be massacred by women, by women in a land that didn't even honor female warriors. He himself had only just escaped with his life.

Padding silently forward, he planned to take out every droplet of his anger—and humiliation—on the Supplicant.

He could see her now; the graceful length of her neck seemed particularly long as she coiled her long red braid loosely atop her head. She'd woven a strange red feather into the fiery mass.

Capturing her would be as easy as capturing a baby rabbit. She'd be as tasty, too.

From inside the courtyard, he heard a horse snort. That gave him pause. He knew for a fact she'd lost her mount before she'd sought shelter in the inselberg. Did that mean she wasn't alone?

"Barbarian—" He heard, then, "Excuse me, I mean *Jatis*."

He froze. Where had this Supplicant learned his tongue?

He watched her creamy shoulders lift as she sighed. Her back was still to him. "Please, Mr. Jatis. Do come out of the tunnel."

He rushed out of the dark tunnel into the blinding light, tackling the woman, who was even slighter than he'd thought when she'd been on his horse in front of him.

He wrapped one arm cruelly around her neck. Holding the razor-sharp obsidian blade to her slender throat with his other hand, he shouted, "I take the woman or kill her—either way she's mine."

He saw no one. Her blood bay gelding stood in the center of the courtyard, looking at him like he was crazy.

Wondering how a horse could give him such a look, he kept the Supplicant snug in his grip and spun her around, scanning the small empty room for any other occupants, examining even the ceiling.

No one.

"What's your game, *zewah*?" he asked, expecting no answer, but the horse shook his head and rolled his eyes, giving every appearance of exasperation. He wondered whether he'd been too long in the tunnel without water.

"Please unhand me, Mr. Jatis," she said in a voice as cool as one of those rare winter snows.

"My name's Forkbeard, not Mr. Jatis." He pressed the blade against her milky throat, but aside from a slight tensing of her muscles, the Supplicant did not react. He became increasingly aware of the pressure of her ass against his cock. As he'd seen after months of spying, the Supplicant had a splendid ass, and he didn't try to stop himself from reacting to it. He'd be taking plenty of advantage of it soon. "Are you here alone, *zewah*?"

"Except for my horse, yes," she said, her hands cool against his forearm. "Please release me," she repeated. "My name is Sureya."

Only then did he detect the small vial in her grasp.

"What's in the bottle?" he demanded. "No tricks." Forkbeard shook her to make his point understood, but she seemed undaunted. The swell of her breasts under his arm distracted him more than anything he did to her.

"*Dawa*," she said.

"I do not know the word. Explain its properties, *zewah*." Forkbeard jabbed her with the knife until a small drop of blood welled to the surface. "Do not lie."

"If I take it, I will enjoy anything you do to me." Her voice seemed breathy, almost husky.

Forkbeard grabbed the vial from her. "Anything you enjoy from my hand will be from my hand." Even to him, he sounded like he was growling. He jammed the vial into his pocket, but this, too, failed to bring a reaction from the Supplicant.

"You cannot rape me, Mr. Forkbeard."

"I can do whatever I please, whore."

"If I do not achieve an orgasm, you will be unable to petition the One God."

"You are working under the misunderstanding that I cannot fuck you as many times as I please—I can rape you then make you scream to the stars in pleasure."

Sureya wondered if the small dose she'd drunk from the papaya-colored vial would be enough to help her through this.

It has to be, she told herself. *Especially with the coatl's wish, she could surrender to this man's touch. She could.*

The aphrodisiac was already working; Forkbeard didn't strike her as repulsive as most barbarians. Perhaps because he wore no beard.

Then again, maybe it was his eyes. Piercing blue, they filled with desire as they examined her. Maybe the people of Marotiri were right—maybe she was a whore. Because when she looked at this murdering, underhanded, cunning man, felt his overwhelming strength—she wanted him.

The drug definitely brought out the whore in her.

He was pressing his cock against her ass, but she didn't feel threatened. She moved her fingers over the length of his arm. His muscles were like hewn oak.

"Say my name," he said.

"Forkbeard," she said, aware that the 'r' sound came out softer when she said it than when he did.

Forkbeard let one hand trail over her body while the other kept its grip around her neck. Rough fingers caressed the curve of her waist, the flat of her stomach. When his huge palm cupped her breast, she felt tiny, like a wren caught in someone's hand.

His fingers found her nipple through the green silk, found the ring. He lightly traced her areola with a grace Sureya found surprising in so large a man. Her nipples stood erect and hard.

Deep inside her sex, desire caused a pain so exquisite that

she moaned. Unable to keep her legs together, she shifted her feet apart to ease that inner ache.

The *dawa* was definitely working.

Forkbeard pressed her up against one of the four pillars in the courtyard. Sureya didn't fight him. She didn't want to.

But that didn't stop him from assaulting her.

He unbuckled the supple brown belt from his waist, and he used it to lash her hands above her head and around the column.

"I'll leave your feet free," he growled. "But not out of kindness—I have only one belt. If you try to kick me, you'll regret it."

Anger crackled from the man's skin, from each shift of the planes of his muscles. But he needed to make her come. Sureya knew then that she was done for.

He would hurt her.

He would pleasure her.

And no longer did she have a choice in the matter. The ache between her legs spread like cream in morning—fresh *khal*, reaching its delicate tendrils to her breasts and fingertips and toes. The sensitive flesh behind her ears and knees tingled with the desire to be noticed by the hulking barbarian—the Jatis.

But Forkbeard wasn't noticing her knees. His hands were rough, ungentle, as he yanked the gauzy green halter from her shoulders, from her breasts. He ripped the silk away from her hips. Shredded tatters floated to the ground.

"No," Sureya moaned, but her traitorous breasts gave her away. Her nipples couldn't have been stiffer or pinker. They begged for the the touch of the barbarian's mouth, and as his head descended upon them, she knew he would satisfy his hunger.

He inhaled one lush breast entirely into his mouth.

Wild sensations whirled unchained throughout her body.

There was nothing courtly about the barbarian's approach to lovemaking—to fucking. Groaning, Sureya closed her eyes in ecstasy.

Forkbeard brought his fingers to her mouth. "Suck them," he commanded.

Sureya obeyed.

She rolled his calloused fingers over her tongue, tasting the masculine salt and sweat. She pushed a finger between her teeth and bit, hard—not hard enough to hurt, but hard.

He was the one to groan this time. Then he took his slick fingers and caught a pert nipple, rolling it between them. He pinched, not immediately hard, but with a slowly growing pressure.

Just as pain was equally balanced with pleasure, the barbarian reached down and flicked the nipple with his hot, wet tongue.

Even as she struggled against her bonds, Sureya felt something deep inside of her soften, yield. Her pearl was presented like a gift on her shaved pubis. Bared from her clothes, it throbbed. The scent of her desire perfumed the air.

He smelled it too, she knew.

He moved his hands from her breasts, appearing to savor the deep curves of her waist. Then he cupped her ass in his insistent hands, kneading his fingers into her muscle, again perfecting the balance between pleasure and pain.

The stone column dug into Sureya's naked back, but she didn't care. The cold pain added to the hot delight.

Naked, arms tied to the column above her head, she hung her head in near-shame. Sureya saw the slickness of her desire making the gold ring in her pearl shine. The sultry heat between her thighs pervaded all of her senses.

"Spread your legs, *zewah*," Forkbeard commanded.

And Sureya wanted to comply.

He shrugged from his trousers, releasing his hard, throbbing cock. He pressed himself, almost gently, against the naked folds of her sex. She was wet and open, and she knew that no protest on her part would convince him that she didn't want him.

Then Forkbeard plowed into her, filling her completely. His actions bore no resemblance to anything genteel. But Sureya didn't mind. As her muscles stretched wide to accommodate him, she longed to dig her nails into his back, to leave long bloody tracks down his muscular back, across his honed ass.

He slid his cock, nearly pulling out, then burying himself fully inside of her. Sureya felt herself crashing onto the shores of the *dawa* river. The small dose—the merest swallow—yielded an almost tame ride through the rapids, but as Forkbeard slid so deeply inside her body, she knew she was moments away from riding the orgasm's crest.

Forkbeard buried his face in the side of her neck, moving his mouth hard over her flesh. He bit and sucked hard—pleasure outweighing pain, then pain outweighing pleasure.

Just as the orgasm tightened the muscles deep inside her, Forkbeard grabbed her breast and squeezed it slowly, inexorably. Even as his cock slid in and out, the pressure of his hand on her breast brought increasing delight.

But he didn't stop there. He squeezed harder. "You will not come yet," he said. The pain was exquisite. So was the thrill of pleasure.

Forkbeard molded both hands to her breasts, trapping her nipples between massively strong fingers. He closed his fingers, squeezing her nipples.

The black river called to her, beckoned her. She could barely contain herself. Each muscle and nerve in her body hummed and vibrated. His slow, exquisite torture sent the dark *dawa* river spiraling around her.

Crying out, Sureya came with a shocking intensity. She didn't crash on the soft sand shore as she had with Kalief. With this man, she nearly drowned in the whirlpool.

But he had no mercy. He continued to brutally slam into her. His thumb pulled the ring between her thighs, and as he plowed into her again and again, he pinched her pearl between his fingers. He pushed against her flesh, then he pulled back and stroked the base of the ring as gently as if he were petting a kitten.

He bent his head to once again capture a nipple and he gave a wicked suck and an evil nip. His teeth were so insistent she wondered if she bled. Then he sucked most of her breast into his hot mouth and bit—and she decided she didn't care.

She came again, internal muscles spasming around his cock. He pumped once more, running his fingers cruelly over her. Her overly sensitive flesh shivered beneath his touch and, for the first time since he'd touched her, she tried to sidle away from him.

Forkbeard grabbed her hip with one hand and continued to work her pearl with his finger, stroking and petting, ripping one more orgasm from Sureya's body.

Finally, finally, he came.

It seemed to her that his orgasm nearly incapacitated him.

Then Forkbeard fell to his knees, submission evident in the slope of his shoulders, the tilt of his head. In his own language, Sureya heard him say, "Beloved Lreya, please hear my prayer. I have granted You a gift—the passion of Your Supplicant. Please grant my prayer."

As his seed dripped from her, she examined Forkbeard with dread. What horrible thing would the barbarian request?

Lord Coatl, she reminded herself. *He said this would bring peace between our lands.* She took a deep breath and forced herself to relax in her bonds.

"Dearest Lreya, Goddess of All . . ." Forkbeard began, then he hesitated, perhaps searching for the right words.

Who was Lreya? Sureya wondered. If this man dedicated his

actions to the wrong god—or goddess—would his prayer still be answered?

"Please," the man continued, giving every appearance of humility. "Please allow Your Supplicant to see the world from the eyes of the Jatis, to understand us as You do."

An image of her parents, hacked to death in a barbarian massacre, flitted through Sureya's mind. Only the strongest god could grant her empathy for these people.

Forkbeard yanked up his trousers, retrieved his belt, and hefted the Supplicant over his shoulder, not giving her even a moment to rub her wrists, which must be sore. She was as light as a kitten. He strode over to her horse and dumped her onto it, her head hanging from one side, her feet hanging from the other.

He used his belt to tie her hands to her feet around the horse's belly, unable to shake the feeling that the horse was giving him a nasty look.

"I can ride," the Supplicant said when she understood his plan. "I'm not going to run."

Forkbeard rubbed his arm where she'd bit him that morning in the melee. He didn't believe a word she said, regardless of how compliant—and pleasurable—she had been just moments before.

"Please," she said, her voice muffled against the horse's flank. "Let me ride properly."

Forkbeard looked over at her, eyeing her heart-shaped ass so perfectly presented. Through her whorish silk pants, tattered now, he could just see the outline of her cunt. His cock hardened yet again—and he shook his head at the power this woman had over him.

Too bad he didn't have time to put her in her place.

Instead, Forkbeard opened his palm and spanked the Supplicant hard on her ass.

She was right—he didn't want her to hate him. But throughout his life, Forkbeard had found that a little pain went a long way toward making a woman amenable to nearly anything.

And she needed to understand his people, anyway.

He spanked her again, hard, finding himself hardening again at the tiny mewling sound she made. Forkbeard wished he had time to fuck her, but his pleasure could wait.

For now.

17

Ignoring the stabbing pain in his thigh, Kalief whirled his replacement stallion, a hulking dark bay, toward Anhara's warrior nuns and shouted, "Fall back! We're not going to find them on horseback."

The nuns, each with one breast bared, fell back obediently. The warrior women had expertly slain all of the barbarians, picking off each one with their pink and purple arrows. Apparently Anhara had been scrying at exactly the right moment, because her warriors had arrived none too soon. One even led a new warhorse for him, saddled in the king's silks. It'd been a sight to behold, those arrows hissing through the air, each landing in the chest or eye of a leather-clad barbarian.

But where was his wife? And where was the beardless barbarian leader?

The barbarian must have been camouflaging himself as a man of Marotiri. That would explain his shaved face. The realization made Kalief's blood run cold—the barbarian must have been watching him for a long while. Had he learned the Marotirian tongue? None of his soldiers had been able to infiltrate the barbarian hordes—their skin was too dark. None had learned the barbarian language.

Anhara galloped up to him on her tiny desert horse, its dark head flashing in the sun. It wasn't even lathered, unlike his hulking mount. "What are you going to do, cousin?" she asked in a tone that suggested she knew the answer and didn't like it.

Holding his overeager stallion steady with his legs, Kalief nodded toward a tunnel into the inselberg. "There," he said, marshalling his strength. His left leg ached and wasn't as strong as his right, so the wretched horse kept sidling to the left. "I'm going in there."

"Kalief," she said. "You can't." Chagrin dripped from her words. "How far do you think you'll get on that leg?"

"I must, cousin, and you know it." He knew she could hear the pain in his voice, the fatigue. "That puss-ridden barbarian cannot take the Supplicant. We'll never hold the bearded hordes at bay if they have her."

Anhara looked at him steadily. Her dark eyes named him as a fool although she said nothing.

"What is it?" he demanded, trying to compensate with his rein for his injured leg. It wasn't working. The horse kept dancing sideways.

"You assume Sureya has no ability to think on her own," she said. Even with dead barbarians scattered over the sands, Anhara's demeanor was quiet and controlled, unlike this cursed horse he rode. "Your Supplicant has great power," Anhara added simply.

"She gives the people who fuck her great power," he corrected.

"Is that why you want her, Kalief? For the power she brings you?"

"No!" The animal beneath him quit prancing, perhaps sensing the shock Anhara had just give him. "I—"

"You what?"

Searching for words, Kalief looked away from his cousin, toward the still-smoldering castle across the leagues of sand. His eyes didn't see the dead bodies. Instead, he saw Sureya's warm smile, directed toward him. Her gray eyes shone with love. "I just don't want to see her get hurt," he finally answered.

"Why not? I'm here on the battlefield with you. You ask your people to take risks for Marotiri all of the time."

He knew what she was after, and it made him angry. Fed up, Kalief snapped, "Why should I spell it out for you, Anhara? What difference could it possibly make if I actually say the words?"

"What words?" she asked calmly, raising one inky black eyebrow.

"I love her," he growled. "It's not seemly for so many reasons, but that woman . . ." An image of Sureya asleep on his lap flashed through his mind. The way she implicitly trusted him left him helpless in her hands. It didn't matter that she was the Supplicant or that she was from the lowest class. It didn't matter that her skin was as pale as the moon. Sureya had captured his heart as surely as the One God answered her prayers.

"Then I'll help you find her," Anhara said.

"What?"

"For power, I wouldn't drag your bloody lame ass through these tunnels," she said in that controlled voice. "But for love, I would."

Sureya didn't make even the smallest sound of complaint as Forkbeard led Firefly through the maze of tunnels, although her stomach muscles ached and she saw stars behind her eyes from the blood rushing to her head. Riding a horse like a sack of grain for hour upon hour hurt, but she'd gathered the Jatis valued endurance. To honor Lord Coatl's supplication, she wanted Forkbeard's admiration.

Walking beside Firefly, Forkbeard led the horse through tunnel after tunnel, in never-ending darkness. And never-ending silence. He said not a word. It wasn't until she sniffed cool night air, so clean after the closed-in tunnels, that she realized they'd left the inselberg.

Using the last vestiges of her strength, she lifted her head and looked around. She thought she saw small bonfires in the distance. But she dropped her head in exhaustion before she gained her bearings. Her neck ached.

Finally the barbarian—no, the Jatis—brought Firefly to a stop and pulled her off his back. He dumped her in a heap onto the ground, which was covered with thick, soft grass.

Struggling to sit, she thought she might faint as her fingers and toes regained circulation. Sitting quietly, she willed the nausea to recede.

But his actions did nothing to calm her. Flashing her a wicked smile, Forkbeard poured the slightest drop of *dawa* into a leather flask.

"I thought you said you didn't need help winning women to your bed," she said.

But he only grinned again, something steely in his eyes. "Drink," he commanded, handing the flask her.

He could force it down her throat, if he wanted so she didn't fight. She drank deeply, expecting *satra*, but it was water. "May I empty it?" she asked, amazed how words in the foreign tongue fell easily from her mouth.

Forkbeard grunted in response. "Finish it. We're nearly home."

"Home?"

"Remember your place," he snarled. Forkbeard strode over to her. He crushed a kiss on her lips, brutal and hard. At the same time he cupped her vulva, caressing his finger against her pearl. Pain and pleasure. "Your place isn't to ask questions, Supplicant. It's to crave my touch and heal this land."

She didn't like it, the way her body responded to his rough touch, but she couldn't help it, either. She arched her breasts into his massive chest, and she pushed her hips toward his hand. Within a heartbeat or two, her thighs ached with desire.

She saw his nostrils flare and knew he smelled her need. "Does the aphrodisiac make you respond like this to just me, since I gave it to you, or to anyone?" He squeezed a nipple between his fingertips before she could answer and said, "Don't lie."

"You're not that special, Forkbeard. *Dawa* lets the hand of the One God weigh hard upon my heart—"

"Your cunt, you mean."

She shrugged, unwilling to be baited. "The One God wants to feel the thrill of mortal lust again, and the drug lets him," she continued. "It makes me crave the touch of anyone who will pleasure me."

He laughed at her impertinence, standing before her, legs apart, arms akimbo. "You have it wrong, little queen," he said. "But it's not your fault. Your people are a presumptuous lot. It's not any one god that answers the Supplicant's prayer, it's Lreya, Goddess of All."

She was too exhausted to argue theology. "Whether it's Lreya or the Worm Queen who answers the supplications, they *are* answered."

"I saw the butterflies," Forkbeard said, in a voice that rumbled like distant thunder.

"If you know about the butterflies, then you know that my husband won't let you keep me. He'll chase you to the ends of the earth to return me to his land."

"Ah, you have a lot of confidence, little queen," he said, caressing her breast, her nipple, as gently as a bee climbs over a flower. "The last time I saw your beloved husband, he appeared to be overtaken by anger." He ran the pad of his thumb over her nipple ring and said, "A great degree of anger."

Her nipples were hardening under his fingertips. She could feel her pearl, the very core of her, calling to him. "He was upset with me, it's true," she said. "But he loves me. He'll hunt you down like a rabid wolf."

Forkbeard cupped both breasts now and pinched both nipples hard. He smiled when she groaned and pushed toward him. He could certainly get to love how she responded to him. "He may chase me down, Supplicant, but it won't be because he loves you—not after he sees what I do to you." The shadow of fear that crossed her face even as she squirmed with pleasure at his rough treatment made him rock hard.

"What are you going to do?"

He was trying to humiliate her, but that seemed impossible. Whether it was the drug or her own inner strength, he didn't know. "Your little king won't hunt me down because he loves you—he'll hunt you down for the power you bring to him."

"But what are you going to do to me?" She asked this with as much grace as if she were sitting on her throne instead of squirming with desire, his cock a mere hand's breadth from her face.

"I'm going to take you to my sister's village while the heat of the aphrodisiac is burning you alive. We'll see how many of their problems you can alleviate." He helped her to her feet and said, "Let's go."

He let her ride Firefly properly this time, although her hands were bound tightly behind her back. He rode behind her, so her hands couldn't help but brush against his cock.

"If you smash my cock again, Supplicant, you'll live to regret it."

She believed him but wasn't tempted. The *dawa* whispered in her ear, tempting her to caresses him, stroke him.

She, Forkbeard, and Firefly entered the small encampment under the light of the moon. Silence lay all around them, like a snowfall in winter.

"Hallooo, Clan Beloved by my Sister!" Forkbeard yelled into the night, breaking the quiet. Folk streamed out of animal-skin tents. Happy noises assaulted them.

"Brother Forkbeard!" she heard a woman cry.

"It is I, my sister." As he answered, Sureya felt his chest heaving behind her. The muscles of his broad chest pressed against her back as he shouted his greeting. "And I've brought our salvation! I've brought the Supplicant!"

At this, the villagers began ululating, high and loud. Coyotes from the plains answered the cry, and nightjars took wing with a feathery *whoosh*.

Like wildfire, fear raced through Sureya's veins. From what did these people need salvation?

Forkbeard pulled her head back, and poured more *dawa*-laced water down her throat. Not wanting to surf the river of insane desire, she tried to spit it out. She wouldn't harm her own people to save these. But Forkbeard wouldn't permit her to do anything but swallow. "Drink," he growled, rubbing her throat until she complied.

In three heartbeats, the shimmering river of desire was back, beckoning her, inviting her. But Forkbeard must not have given her as much *dawa* as the novices had, because she resisted the pull, resisted the craving.

"Build a fire!" Forkbeard commanded of the amber-skinned crowd gathering around them. "Make a bed of skins large enough for many."

The scent of the river tantalized her nose. It smelled green and welcoming. She longed to jump into it, to feel the cool water caress her, sluice over her neck and breasts and throat, soothe the ache between her thighs left by Forkbeard's huge cock. She'd turn into a fish again and—

Sureya knew that resisting the river would only hurt herself, but she did it. She resisted.

Every wish Kalief made between her thighs was aimed at securing Marotiri's position against the barbarians. Why would the barbarians be different than the Marotiri? They'd want to protect their borders against her people.

She wouldn't aid the people who had slaughtered her baby brother, her parents. She wouldn't aid the people that roasted villagers—women and children—in a church.

She wouldn't.

"Pour the *masato*," Forkbeard cried from behind her, still astride Firefly. "Begin to drink, but don't get drunk! Each of you has a job to do! A wish to make! Be prepared."

Keeping one hand on Firefly's reins, he pulled her toward him. Her hands cupped his hardened cock. His muscular chest pressed against her back. With his free hand, he found a nipple ring. Under the dark sky, he slowly flipped it up while grazing his teeth over her neck. He slowly turned the ring down.

Sureya squirmed, pressed her pearl against the unyielding saddle. She moaned, unable to resist the promise of his rough fingers.

He ran his teeth up her neck, stopping just below her ear. Tugging gently now on her left ring, he bit the fleshy part of her earlobe. He slowly bit harder, tugged the ring. As she yielded to him, he whispered, "Remember, Supplicant, all pleasure among my people comes with pain."

Then Forkbeard lifted her off the saddle and plunked her into the pile of skins near the fire.

As her cheek registered the soft wolf-fur skin, too many hands to count were upon her.

"Volepox," she heard someone sob. "My daughter. Reffye."

"My son," another voice. "Yreve's dying."

Voiced melted into each other as fingers melted over her back and arms.

"What do you mean?" Sureya said over the roar of the *dawa* river. Although no one had touched her intimately—not her breasts or hips or lips—she could feel the stream's cool wavelets tickling her toes. "Are your children dying?"

"Yes," someone whispered. "Of volepox."

"Boils and pustules," she heard. "Trumin, my son." Cold mossy stones under her feet invited her to swim in the river. She could let go and allow the current to carry her.

"Rewolf, my daughter," she heard. "Fever and death."

"Everyone dies."

"Every child," another corrected. In the distance, Sureya heard a catbird. "Meow," it said. "Swim!"

And then she heard a choice. "Will you help us?" someone asked. A woman.

"Help us save our children?" a man asked. His voice cracked.

"Your children are dying of *volepox?*" the Supplicant asked. Mist rose in curling tendrils above the river, and she heard water trickling calmly past her.

"Yes," someone breathed in horror. "Volepox."

"Yes," a man agreed.

"Yes," said a mother.

"But there's a vaccine," Sureya said over the sound of rushing water. "For many years there's been a vaccine."

"Your fine little king will not share it," Forkbeard said. He sounded far away, and she heard fire in his voice.

Sureya was astounded. While in Marotiri, she'd never once heard anyone mention the vaccine. Surely Kalief would have traded—

"Will you help us, Supplicant?"

"She'll help you," Forkbeard growled. "Or I'll—"

"No," Sureya interrupted her captor. "Don't threaten me." Then she looked at the people on the pelts. "Of course I'll help you save your children."

Forkbeard tossed her the flask of *dawa*-laced water, and she drank deeply.

A catbird purred in the distance.

Shrugging out of her rags, Sureya succumbed to the touch of a mother. She yielded to the mouth of a father. She ignored bead-filled beards. She ignored amber flesh. She floated on the river of desire, slowly at first. Then hands and mouths and cocks and cunts became more insistent, and the river rippled over the rapids.

"She's almost there," a woman said.

"Touch her," a man commanded. "Everyone."

Someone wrapped their arms around her hips and pulled her pearl to their face. Someone—beardless, a woman, then—nuzzled her face into Sureya's sex. She slid her tongue into her, sliding over the ring, her pearl, with exquisite care. Sureya felt the wild rapids calling to her. Finding the nerve to leave the shallows wouldn't take much. Already tiny jolts of pleasure zigzagged throughout her body.

As a tongue slid in and out of her, someone else's fingers began to explore. A foamy wave hit a rock, hard, as a finger swirled past her pearl, past her opening, toward her anus.

With the river flowing in her mind, between her thighs, the exploring finger was wet, slippery. It easily slid into her. And out. And in again.

Her stomach tightened instantly, her thighs too, as a sizzling crack of pleasure slammed through her, sending foamy waves crashing over the rocks and into the air. Sureya could hardly catch her breath as the finger slid in and out of her ass, as a tongue rolled over her pearl. Another mouth had latched onto a nipple, and a tongue rolled over hers.

Every nerve was inundated with pleasure.

The wave Sureya rode exploded on the shore. Wild light

flashed behind her eyes and she screamed in pleasure with the impact of the orgasm.

But even as her flesh quivered with the orgasm's strength, the village folk were leaving her. As one, they fell to their knees, and together they said, "Beloved Lreya, please hear my prayer. I have granted you a gift—the passion of Your Supplicant. Please grant my prayer."

Firefly ambled toward her, head low to the ground. He stepped carefully around the kneeling people.

"Please," the voices continued. "Please, save . . ." And here the voices blurred together as each parent named a child or children. ". . . from Volepox."

"Don't let my beloved die!" one woman cried.

Firefly nuzzled Sureya's ear, and she reached up from the skins to stroke his velvety nose. As he snuffled over her, he said in a near whisper, "Kalief, Anhara, and the warrior nuns are about to reach the top of that knoll."

Sureya sat up, peering into the darkness and seeing nothing. "Are you sure?" she asked in a hushed voice, but she didn't need to take such precautions. The folk were rushing back to their tents to see how their children fared.

"The children?" she asked.

"Can't you smell anything? The sickness no longer hangs in the air. They live." Then Firefly nudged her, and she stood. She quickly dressed in what was left of her clothing, and her horse tossed his head back. *Get on*, his action said.

Sureya obeyed and hugged low to the horse's neck, not wanting to draw any attention to herself. She needn't have worried. Cries of joy came from each tent. The children, of this camp at least, were spared.

Firefly slowly walked away from the campfire light. When he got far enough away, he began to trot, then canter, toward the knoll. Light from the campfires faded as Firefly brought her to her beloved. Then she heard a distant clink from a bridle.

"Kalief!" Sureya couldn't help but shout. "My love!"

She heard hoofbeats galloping toward her. "Sureya!" she heard. "My wife!"

When he saw her horse approach, Kalief leapt from his stallion and pulled her from her mount. Leaving Anhara and her warriors behind, he crushed Sureya to his chest, wrapping his arms around her, burying his face in her hair.

"You're safe," he said. "Praise the One."

She tilted her face toward him and he saw tears streaking down her face. "I thought you were dead," she said, running her hand through his hair as if to convince herself that he actually breathed. "When I saw your horse fall on you, and that arrow in your thigh . . ." She kissed him: his chin, his cheeks, his lips. "And then Lord Coatl said you were safe, and I—"

She broke off, and Kalief could see she was at a loss for words.

But Kalief didn't need words. He captured her lips in his and drank deeply. How could he have been such a fool? Did he care if she'd lain with someone else? No, it'd been his cousin, and it'd saved his life. How could he care? He should never have risked her life in his fit of rage.

"I was so afraid you wouldn't love me anymore," she said, her voice cracking with emotion. "After—everything."

"And I thought you'd come to your senses and forgotten me." He kissed her hard, savoring the glide of her lips under his. "I'll always love you," he answered. "Always."

"No," he heard a voice grumble with a guttural accent. "You will not love her. Not when you know the truth about your whore wife."

At his side, Sureya gasped and drew in close to him. "Forkbeard," she hissed. "He followed me from camp." Protectively, Kalief wrapped his arms around her. "You have what you need," she said to the Jatis. "Now leave me in peace."

"But I could have so much more, Supplicant. With you by my side, I could rule the world."

"I've helped your people. Be satisfied and go," she said.

"Barbarian," Kalief said, anger menacing his voice. "I have fifty warriors on the hill. At my word, they'll attack you—and your encampment."

"Kalief, no," she said, clutching his arm. "There're children down there."

"See?" Forkbeard gloated. "She's a whore. She slept with all the parents—an orgy of parents with sick children—to save tens of lives. Barbarian lives."

Cold dread filled him. He looked down at his wife. "It's not true." But something in her face stopped him. "An orgy?" he asked her. "Willingly?"

"To save the children, Kalief! They're dying of volepox."

"You wouldn't sleep with the lords and ladies of Marotiri to stop the barbarian incursion, but you'd save a bunch of barbarian brats?"

"It's not like that!" she insisted, but he couldn't hear her words. The beardless barbarian's icy leer drowned out any reason.

"She's a great fuck," the barbarian said. "Very willing."

He needed to wipe the evil, knowing look from the barbarian's face. With cold precision, he reached for his sword.

"No!" Sureya shouted. "Let's leave this be. Kalief, let's go home."

"Shut up, whore," he growled to his wife. His sword glittered in the starlight. His dagger, in his off hand, glittered as well.

"This is more to my liking," the barbarian said, pulling his curved shamshir from behind his back. "The winner takes the whore."

"No!" Sureya shouted loud enough to be heard by Anhara and anyone still awake in the camp at the hill's base. Eyes locked on the barbarian who padded like a deadly lion, his shamshir shining with deadly promise.

As the barbarian lunged toward him, Sureya's horse bolted toward her. She jumped on and kicked the beast wildly. They dashed off madly into the darkness.

Again.

As his sword clashed against the shamshir with bone-jarring power, Kalief mentally shrugged. After he killed this beardless barbarian, he'd hunt down the Supplicant and bring her home to his castle.

He parried the barbarian's vicious thrust with his dagger. *Dawa* would control her hot temper.

Your horse knows where to go. Lord Coatl's words echoed through her mind as, blinded by tears, she let Firefly gallop with seeming randomness over the grassy plains. She rode without a saddle, and Firefly's hot body heaved beneath her. His broad muscles flexed under her thighs, under her hands on his neck.

That Forkbeard had been right made her want to vomit. The evil man had said he'd make Kalief hate her, and bending her husband to his wicked will had been simplicity itself.

She'd saved children, and he loathed her, thought she was a whore. Would he have done differently in the face of a population ridden with volepox? Could he have? She doubted it.

Beneath her, Firefly's gallop had slowed to an easy canter. She sat up a bit. "I've had enough, Firefly," she said, wiping tears from her eyes. "I've had enough of being told what to do, of being told how to use this power."

Her horse snorted.

"That's right," she agreed. "I didn't ask for it, but now that I have this power I'm going to use it how *I* see fit."

Firefly slowed to a trot, then he stopped completely, sides heaving as he stood.

Sureya slid off his bare back, hands clutching his wiry mane. She knew, the moment her feet touched the earth, that she was someplace special. Power poured through her toes, filled her blood. This place was magic, like the glade in which she and Kalief had been wed.

And the thought broke her heart.

And then it made her angry. Who was the One God to use her like this? Who was Kalief to give with one hand and take away with the next?

Sureya stepped away from Firefly and held her hands over her head, palms upturned toward the sky. Bathed in starlight, she stood silently for a long moment, letting the energy pour from her feet into the sky.

Real fireflies lit up the plains with crazy intensity. Heartbeats of gold and emerald and sapphire pulsed over the grassland. A flock of quails, asleep for the night, took wing with alarmed chitterings.

But still Sureya stood with her palms turned up to the sky. She tilted her face toward the moon and closed her eyes, savoring the thrumming magic, channeling it into the sky with a vengeful heart.

Even behind closed eyelids, Sureya saw the sky darken, and her skin grew gooseflesh as a cold breeze blew. She opened her eyes and gasped.

A huge dragon soared toward her, blocking the moonlight. Gliding on outstretched wings, it winged toward her. It looped over a hill and blew a huge plume of flame. Silhouetted against the flame, she saw Kalief and Forkbeard crossing swords.

But before she could worry about Kalief's safety, the dragon turned its eye toward her. Sureya felt the great beast assessing her soul. It judged her, and yet, approached.

Still, electrifying power poured from the earth beneath her feet, through her body, and into the sky. Conducting the energy, Sureya knew a truth. She wasn't the dragon's inferior. She wasn't Kalief's or Anhara's or Forkbeard's.

Locking gazes with the dragon several leagues away, she found the crackling energy gave her something new. She could see right to the dragon's very core. His heart pulsed with justice and certainty. With every beat she welcomed his arrival.

Greetings, Supplicant, he said to her in mindspeak. *I'm Ekal, friend of all people of this world.*

Greetings, Ekal. I'm very pleased to meet you.

With a mighty flap of his wings, he curved toward her with a powerful swoosh. She felt no fear, not even when she saw his glittering talons grab the earth as he landed a hand's breadth away from her, leaving long, deep furrows in the billowing grass.

When the great beast lowered his head in submission to her, she wasn't surprised, not with the One God's—or whoever's—power thrumming through her.

I've frightened away your horse, my lady.

And Sureya realized that Firefly was nowhere to be seen. Poor baby. He'd been so brave since she'd first met him. But dragons ate horses, she gathered.

Then I suppose I might ride you, mighty Ekal. Sureya sensed his grin at her answer.

Climb up my wing, Supplicant. Ekal lowered a massive arm. Under the moon, Sureya saw its muted blue color. *My watery cousin Eria perused your heart at your dedication ceremony. Do you recall meeting her?*

Sureya remembered the mosaic dragon who'd flown from the tiled wall into her pool. The beast had become a mermaid and stolen an orgasmic wish from her.

I remember. Sureya climbed up the leathery wing, surprised at its warmth under her feet. *She did more than peruse my heart.*

Ekal chuckled at her wry words. *It's true that Eria fancies human cunts and breasts. She often sticks her tail where it doesn't belong.*

And you? Sureya asked, finding a place to sit on his broad warm back.

My heart has been stolen by a thief. She gets offended when I fuck someone without inviting her to join us.

Why have you come to me? she asked.

Eria extracted a wish from you—when you were ready to see the world with opened eyes and an opened heart, I would serve as your guide.

And this does not go against your personal will?

She was correct in her assessment of your heart, Supplicant. Thank you for worrying about my will. But Eria selected me because she knows that justice rules my actions.

Justice?

Yes, justice. And injustice. Ekal turned away from the moon and extended his wings. *Clasp those small horns by your hands, Supplicant, and prepare to fly.*

With excitement and fear filling her heart, Sureya obeyed.

I have much to show you of your world.

18

"He still loves you, Sureya," Anhara whispered.

Sitting in the auditorium at the seminary, Sureya and Anhara were supposed to be contributing to the conversation—why supplications were answered even when the prayers were directed at gods and goddesses other than the One. Officially, the priests declared that as the One God's conduit, Sureya should have some insight into the issue, but in reality, the all-male order didn't pay her opinions any heed.

"What did you say?" she whispered back to her friend, even though she'd heard her—very clearly.

"You heard me."

"Can we leave this thing without causing a scandal?" she asked.

"As if you care," Anhara said with a smile, graceful despite its irony.

"Let's go," she whispered. "Back to the temple?"

Anhara nodded and stood with her quiet elegance. She gathered the skirt of her crimson gown. Sureya followed her out of the auditorium, ignoring the nasty looks from the brothers.

Anhara pushed huge brass doors open, and the two women

walked onto the cobbled street. Throngs hurried over the red bricks, apparently intent on their business. "The City of Mistofina has certainly become more interesting since your temple was established," Anhara said.

Eying a tall woman with moon-white skin striding toward a weapons shop with authority, Sureya could only agree. "You're right."

Two amber-skinned Jatis bought persimmon from a brown man with a cart. And a short man bearing the broad features of the Tepetl hurried north, wrapping his burgundy cloak tightly around him despite the day's warmth. His inward expression made Sureya guess he was heading to her temple. She'd likely meet him tomorrow.

Through the plate window of the weapons shop, Sureya watched the tall, white-skinned woman heft a huge longbow, testing its balance. "I can't imagine a servant being permitted to purchase a weapon a year ago," Sureya said. "Not in Mistofina."

"No," agreed Anhara, "and yesterday a pale-skinned king from someplace in the frigid south came to court. He made quite a sight paying homage to Kalief. Next to him, Kalief looked like he was made of obsidian."

Him again, Sureya thought, but aloud she said, "And how did our king take meeting a royal with skin like mine?"

Anhara gave her that no-nonsense look of hers before she answered. She wasn't fooling her, she knew. She was dying to hear any news about her husband, and Anhara knew it.

"Oh, Kalief was fine with him," Anhara said. "In fact, I'm not sure he noticed the man's complexion, since the foreigner rode the most astounding horse. The man—the king of Nifland, I mean—sat back on the animal and moved the reins a hair's breadth onto the beast's neck and the horse spun in circles, like a dancer or circus performer."

"Anhara—"

"And when he asked the horse to gallop, it took off like Minions were chasing it, but when the Nifland king sat back, the horse stopped so fast, it nearly sat. It left a furrow at least—"

"Anhara!" Sureya interrupted. "You know I don't care about the cursed horse."

"I'm sure Firefly would be happy to hear that." Anhara stopped at a stall selling long silk scarves cleverly painted in watery shades. She ran one through her fingers. Aquas and emeralds shimmered in the midmorning sun. "This would suit you," she said, holding it next to Sureya's cheek.

Sureya brushed it away with a huff of impatience.

Finally Anhara met her gaze. "You should talk to him, Sureya. He misses you."

"Firefly?" Sureya purposefully misinterpreted.

"I'm serious, my dove."

She looked away from the intense look in her friend's eyes. "*He* should talk to *me*," she insisted.

Anhara captured her hand and began walking north, toward Sureya's new home, her temple. "Kalief gave you permission to build your temple here," Anhara said. "That should tell you something. He wants your presence. He wants to accidentally encounter you here on the street."

She gave an angry huff. "As the Council of Dragons pointed out four seasons ago, my temple brings great honor to Mistofina," she retorted. "And much commerce." She shook her head. "Kalief's approval of my temple had nothing to do with me."

"You're wrong. You should talk to him, little dove." Anhara took her hand more firmly in her own, brought it to her lips, and kissed it. "I know his heart, and he longs for you. Who could blame him?"

They walked without speaking for a moment. A *somosa* vender hawking his little meat-filled pastries brushed past them. The spicy scent wafted around the women.

"I've tried to talk to him," Sureya finally admitted, the anger gone from her voice. Humiliation replaced it. "He won't see me. His wretched castellan returns my notes. They're all un-opened. Kalief wants nothing to do with me."

"Really?" Anhara stopped midstride, arching one of her black eyebrows. "You've sent notes and they come back to you unread?"

"Yes—"

"Excuse me," a woman said. It was the tall warrior woman they'd seen testing the long bow in the weapons shop.

"Yes?" asked Sureya, thinking the foreigner sought directions.

The tall woman, with her kinky black hair falling down to her shoulders, kept perfect eye contact with Sureya as she held out her hand. "My name's Larkspur." The woman oozed self confidence.

Sureya tentatively took the proffered hand. "Oh?" She shot a questioning look at Anhara, who gave a tiny shake of her head.

"You're the Supplicant, yes?" Larkspur asked, enveloping Sureya's hand in a strong grip.

She nodded. "I am."

"Good," the woman said, nodding. "Ekal sent me to you."

"Oh!" she said. "Ekal!" She turned toward Anhara and ex-plained, "Ekal's the dragon who gave me the tour of the lands." She turned back to Larkspur and asked with a smile, "Are you the 'Thief of His Heart'?"

Larkspur blushed and opened her mouth to answer, but An-hara beat her to it. "Pay no attention to Sureya, Larkspur. If you want to make *her* blush, ask her with whom she slept to quiet the volcano threatening the Tepetl. And then ask her which position they use to—"

"Anhara," she admonished. "Please—"

"What?" Anhara teased. Looking at Sureya, Anhara pointed to Larkspur and said, "Her lover's a dragon. You think there's anything she hasn't tried yet?"

The comment did little to reduce the pinkness on the woman's cheek, but Sureya watched Larkspur take a deep breath and say, "Enough!"

She said it with authority, and Anhara and Sureya looked at her in stunned silence.

"Our apologies, Larkspur," Anhara said. "I'm afraid we've endured too much priestly seriousness for our own good."

"Still, tell us of our favorite dragon," Sureya said. "What news does Ekal bring?"

"He brings an invitation, Lady Supplicant," Larkspur answered. "From the Council of Dragons."

Welcome to my home, Supplicant.

Thank you, Ekal, she said, comfortable with mindspeak after months of working with the dragon. *Your home is lovely.*

Rubies and agate made his nest. Ekal lay amidst tiny beasties carved of gold and crystal candelabras as tall as a huge man.

And that comparison snagged her mind. *A huge man . . . Kalief,* her mind whispered.

But she shoved the image to the back of her thoughts. He couldn't stand what she'd become, especially after he'd done all he could to protect her from this fate, the perceived whoredom.

But that was his problem. Not hers. She was no whore. Now mistress of her own fate, she slept with whomever she saw fit.

She'd sleep with him, if he'd let her.

You mourn, her dragon friend noted.

Sureya shrugged. *Not unlike others.* She let out a deep breath, letting her sorrow go.

I'm glad you're here. Ekal brought his massive head toward her and flicked out his long, dry tongue. It caressed Sureya's cheek as gently as a mother's palm over a fevered brow. *I enjoy my time with you.*

Thank you, she said.

You've grown your hair longer. Ekal sent her a playful mental image of Larkspur grabbing a handful of Sureya's thick red hair, tilting her head back far enough so that the thief could run her luscious tongue along the length of Sureya's exposed neck. Sureya's breasts were crushed against Larkspur's. Erect nipple slid over erect nipple.

Sureya laughed. *You like it, then, my long hair?* She shook it flirtatiously. A tiny portion of her mind wished she were having this conversation with her husband.

I like many things about you, he replied. This time he sent an image of himself in manform, shockingly tall and broad with raven-black hair and eyes as blue as a springtime sky. He ran a careful fingertip over one of her nipple rings.

Not like that, dragon, she teased. Sureya sent back an image of a strong brown hand palming her breast. A tongue circled her nipple, flipped the ring up and then down. Then teeth grabbed the ring and tugged until Sureya arched her back, desire etched on her face.

Mmmhh, Supplicant, Ekal grumbled. *I'd get Larkspur in here right now, before the meeting, except . . .*

Except what, beast? Are you all talk?

Ekal laughed at her teasing. *Not all talk, Supplicant. I'd stroke you and pet you and lick you and suck you with the help of my wondrous thief until you cried for mercy—except you've made it clear it's not* me *you desire.*

Not you?

Ekal flashed her image back to her. Then Sureya realized— the hands on her breasts belonged to Kalief. The lips and tongue sampling her nipples were her king's. The teeth tugging her gold ring belonged to her husband.

* * *

In dragonform, Ekal led her through a wide, snaking tunnel from his nest to the council chamber.

Two massive doors stood at the end of the tunnel, reflecting Ekal's soft green dragonglow. As they exited, the sight that met them took her breath away.

The gold-gilt ribs of the vaulted ceiling rose so high that Sureya couldn't see the apex. The chamber exceeded in size any chamber Sureya had ever seen throughout her travels.

A butterfly banner hung on the wall. Dragonglow—Ekal's green, Eqil's orange, Etol's aqua, Emex's vermillion, and colors from dragons she didn't know—filled the room, bathing it in watery rainbow light. The prism colors danced over the walls, over the banner.

Twelve massive dragons had arranged themselves in a semi-circle. Walking next to a dragon as massive as Ekal was breathtaking, but greeting twelve mighty beasts at once made her mouth run dry. *Hello,* she managed to say.

They nodded silently at her greeting.

You know Eqil, Etol, and Emex. Ekal nodded his huge head at the first three dragons as he said their names.

Yes, Sureya said. *Of course.* Eqil had brought her to his land to help eradicate the weevil threatening the crops. Etol and she had calmed volcanoes so they didn't solidify the ancient forests. Emex, like Lord Coatl, had scarlet and crimson scales. Sureya had helped him save the local sheep from a wasting disease. *How are you, my friends?* she directed at them with her mind-voice.

Hello, Supplicant Queen. The voices jumbled together as they rolled over her brain.

These other eight, Ekal nodded at the remaining dragons, *will not be familiar to you.*

Hello, Sureya thought at them.

As a barrage of greetings fell over her, Ekal's voice rose

above them. *These are Ewof, Eluy, Edas, Enip, Ecaz, Eroi, Ejal, and Egri.*

Sureya scanned the new faces, a riot of purples and greens and blues. Tiny curls of smoke wafted from the dragons' nostrils, ebbing and flowing with each breath. The curls sunk to the ground, making the great beasts seem as if they lay on one huge cloud.

May I know the purpose of this meeting, my lord dragons?

Very well, Ekal said. *The people of your land don't know this—it wasn't permitted to be recorded in your Scripture. But Egri, with the help of the Council of Dragons, has advised the last twelve Supplicants.*

But doesn't that span— She was at a loss. *Thousands of years?*

Eight hundred and ninety seven, to be precise, Egri agreed in a rumbling voice. His scales had a more metallic sheen than did the other dragons—flashing silvers and golds.

Have you told this to King Kalief? Sureya asked. It hurt her heart to say his name.

It is you with whom we wish to speak first, Ekal said, a gray plume of smoke curling from one nostril. *Although we understand he's the best scholar among you humans on this topic. It's convenient he's also the Penetrator.*

Her knees trembled at that thought.

Let me come right to the point, Egri said. *We wish to know if you'd like to retract your first wish, the wish you made for yourself.*

Retract? asked Sureya. *I thought the wish was binding, I'd get no other.*

Ah! said Egri. *That's true, but only for the most part. We find very few Supplicants make wise choices with their first wishes, and we can help them reformulate that wish.*

It's time to bring in the Penetrator, Ecaz said, citrine dragonglow smoldering off his amethyst scales.

Kalief's here? Her voice sounded like a child's. The keeper of her heart was here!

Just then Larkspur entered the room. In a commanding voice that filled the cavernous space, Larkspur said, "May I present Lord Kalief, King of Marotiri?"

The huge doorway dwarfed them, but Sureya saw him. Her fingers longed to caress the dark planes of his face, drink in the hard muscles of his chest and arms. She wanted to bury her face in the curve of his neck and inhale his masculine scent.

But he didn't even look her way.

If you'd be seated, please, and listen, the purpose of this meeting will be clear, Ekal said to Kalief.

Thank you, Ekal, Kalief said with a small bow. His mind-voice was shaky, as if he were uncomfortable with it.

Egri turned toward her and said, *You've been unusually wise, Sureya. No other Supplicant's been brave enough to visit volcanoes, or lay with a dragon to keep her territory safe.*

No other Supplicant would have saved the sheep in my land, added Emex.

Or stopped our weevils, said Eqil.

Furthermore, her friend Ekal spoke now, *throughout the last nine hundred years, few other Supplicants have aided as many peoples as have you. The Jatis and the Marotirians are no longer at war. You've cured the Jatis of volepox. You've stopped droughts and floods throughout the land by putting your personal desires behind the needs of others.*

Sureya squirmed where she stood, uncomfortable with the praise. She'd only done what was right. Then she looked at Kalief, seeing what she'd given up to make her land a better place. He couldn't love her. She couldn't have a family.

But these were small sacrifices in the face of the gains.

I've found, said Egri, *that most Supplicants grow with wisdom as their reign progresses.*

I hope that's true for me as well, Sureya said. But she

watched Kalief shift so that he no longer faced her. He, apparently, did not agree.

Most Supplicants come to regret their first wish, the only true wish they receive, according to human Scripture, Egri said.

Sureya considered that for moment. *The Penetrator himself approved my wish,* she said. Sureya nodded at her king, remembering the moment, remembering the tender way he'd wrapped her hair around his finger, the hunger of his kisses. *He said my wish was a legacy. Is there a reason I should retract it?*

We don't know what your wish was, Supplicant Queen, Egri clarified, his metallic sheen shining in the dragonglow. *We've simply decided that you, more than any other Supplicant in our history, deserved a second chance.*

Unlike the others, Kalief spoke aloud now. "Her wish took the fate of the next Supplicant's dedication and rule out of the hands of the priests and put it into the hands of the nuns, the abbess."

What's your new wish, Supplicant?

She considered. For what would she wish were she a regular girl? Health? She had that. Wealth? She'd never desired riches, and now she had more than she'd ever need. She couldn't wish for Kalief's love—free will could not be manipulated. Would she make a wish on behalf of a loved one? If she had a family . . .

I can think of no personal wish, Lord Egri. I've been blessed in abundance in this life.

A tension that she hadn't noticed previously suddenly lifted from the room. It was as if the shoulder muscles of all twelve dragons relaxed simultaneously. Curls of smoke filled the cavern. *I see I've passed some mysterious dragon test.*

Lord Egri chuckled. *It's of no importance, Supplicant Queen.*

I made that wish because I didn't want any future Supplicant to fall pawn to the priesthood as I had. Sureya rubbed her brow. *But it isn't difficult to imagine a time when the sisters and nuns behave as manipulatively as the priests and Brothers do now.*

"Maybe the Supplicant should be independent of any government, any people," King Kalief said.

Sureya looked at him in shock. She'd thought—well, she'd thought he wanted her for his own.

Go on, Egri urged King Kalief. *What do you have in mind?*

"I've been wrong, Sureya." Kalief stood. "But for the right reasons."

Sureya looked at him, not knowing what to say.

"I've wanted you all to myself, it's true, but not for the reasons you think. I didn't want you for the power. I want you for your heart." He walked toward her and said, "I want you for *my* heart."

She looked at him, drank in the fine shape of his lips, the planes of his face, and she said, "I can never be faithful to you, King Kalief. This land requires my body." She swallowed. "It requires my cunt," she said, using that word for the first time in her life.

And that's not something a king can share, Egri added. *Especially a king who has no heirs.*

"Her wish is a good one," Kalief insisted.

Part of Sureya rejoiced. He saw the value in her work, her power. But she wanted to cry. Kalief was abdicating any tie to her.

"I see only one problem, Sureya," he said in a voice that seemed for her ears only. His tone was loaded with intention, vibrating with emotion.

"And what's that, Kalief?"

We don't think you'll find it unpleasant, Etol answered, her black eyes locked on the Supplicant. *The Penetrator must repenetrate you.*

Repenetra—she began.

But Kalief was already walking toward her, that intent look burning his nearly black eyes.

When his hot fingertips brushed hers, reality evaporated. Sureya looked around, but an opaque fog had shrouded them. The indigo fog pulsed around them, smoldering, almost like . . . dragonglow.

Sureya understood—this was dragon magic.

"Kalief?" she asked.

"Where are we?" she heard.

She stepped toward his voice, then looked down in surprise. Her feet were strapped into the most amazing shoes. The black heels were so high she walked on tiptoes, and black leather straps were woven from her ankles to her knees. Her toenails had been painted a deep magenta, which stood out shockingly against her pale feet.

"Sureya?" Kalief asked. "I seem to be tangled here. Would you help me, please?"

"Yes, my lord." As she walked toward him, her heels clacked against the floor, making an authoritarian sound. She liked it.

When she bumped into the bed, the indigo smoke cleared slightly, and she saw Kalief. He was tied—each hand to the headboard post above him, each ankle to the footboard post. He wore nothing.

"I don't think you're tangled, exactly, my lord," she said.

"Sureya, don't 'my lord' me. Just untie me, please." Then he blinked and looked at her. "What is that you're wearing?"

Suddenly realizing she had a riding crop in her hand, she looked down at her clothing.

A black leather bra pushed her breasts high, but the center of each cup was missing so that her gold piercings were exposed. Her nipples had been painted a deep magenta that matched her toenails.

Scant webbing ran over her hips, over her waist.

"By the Above," Kalief said, craning his neck to see. "Turn around so I can see the back of that."

"You're in no position to give orders," Sureya said, smacking the crop into her palm with a small smile on her face. His cock was throbbing and engorged. And he was all hers. "You need to beg."

"A king does not beg, Sureya."

"You can call me 'Supplicant Queen,'" she replied. "And a king does beg when he's tied as you are." She strode toward him. "Now, what was it you wanted of me? Did you want to see the back?" She took her free hand and ran it over her ass. "There seems to be a thin strap that runs the length of my back, over the curve of my—"

"Turn around," he demanded. "Please!"

"That didn't sound like a plea to me." Sureya's voice was husky, and he could see the telltale glisten of her gold ring between her thighs. She was as excited as he was.

He realized in a heartbeat that he'd taken exactly the wrong tone with her—he hadn't begged. He'd ordered.

And she was in no mood to show him mercy. He couldn't blame her. He'd spent a year both wanting her and resenting every heartbeat she spent in someone else's bed. He was King of Marotiri. He shouldn't have to share anything with anyone, especially his wife.

But that sounded petulant, like his father and grandfather. The truth was, as rumors of her accomplishments had come to his ears from across the lands, as the barbarian incursions had stopped, he'd known the needs of the world outweighed his personal desires.

He knew it in his heart, but he'd been too proud to talk to her.

Here she was, and discussion didn't seem to be on her mind. Sureya leaned over him, running the fat tip of the crop along his inner thigh, then around the base of his cock. The promise, the threat . . . She was driving him wild.

"Maybe you don't want to see the back view," she suggested. "Maybe what you see in front of you is enough." Her tone was arch, even playful, as she ran the rough texture of the crop over her nipples, which hardened further.

This wasn't a side of her with which he was familiar, but . . . he liked it. It didn't matter that someone else had given her this education. He could live with it.

She pressed the crop hard against her breasts, rolling it over her nipples while one spiked heel rested on the bed. He could see exactly how wet she was, how much she wanted him.

"Which is it?" she asked.

"The front is—" he swallowed. "Mouthwatering."

She laughed. "It isn't your mouth I see lathered with moisture." Sureya leaned forward to run the tip of the crop over the fat drop of liquid gathered at the tip of his cock. His eyes rolled back in his head as she traced the head of his cock with the crop. Then she pressed the crop hard against his cock, smacking him enough to get his full attention.

The promise. The threat. He ached for her.

"Beg, Kalief," she demanded. "You know you want it."

He had no choice. He would've laid down his life for her. "Please," he croaked, his voice thick with desire.

"Please, what?"

"Please let me touch you, lick you."

She smiled. "I like how you ask." She leaned forward so that one of her nipples danced just before his lips. He strained toward her, desire clear in his pulsing cock, his hardened nipples.

She let him capture her nipple ring, but it wasn't what he wanted. He wanted her hot flesh beneath him, in his mouth and in his arms, under his chest and under his lips.

Stifling his animal urge to grab what he wanted, he tugged

gently, not wanting to hurt her. Then he flicked his tongue over her pebbled nipple, fast.

And she groaned in pleasure.

He'd won some quarter, he knew, when she moved closer to him, letting him suck her. First she allowed him to tease just her nipple, but as desire grabbed her by the throat, she gave him more. And he cherished each bit. The tip of his tongue, the flat of it, memorized the texture of her areola. She pushed her breast toward him, begging in her own way.

"I like how you ask, but you didn't address me properly." He felt the smack of the crop sting his thigh, but she didn't need a weapon like that to have him at her mercy.

"Queen Sureya," he said, surprised at the thickness of his voice. "My queen."

She graced him then with her lips. He longed to cup her face in his hands, to run his fingers over her cheeks. But as his lips captured hers, as her tongue danced over his, tangling with his, Kalief decided that he could live on her terms. He would take what she offered, and he would be grateful.

Because she made him the luckiest man in the world.

"Sureya," he said, the words muffled in her mouth.

"Hmm?" Her tongue glided over his, sending lighting flashes of pleasure through his balls right to his cock.

"I love you, Sureya."

Her eyes flashed open, maybe in surprise, maybe to read his expression. Whatever she saw there, she believed. The crop fell from her hands, and she spread herself over him. Crushing her breasts against his side, she moved her hands across the contours of his chest and stomach. Her fingers slid lightly over his cock, over his balls.

With his arms and legs still bound, he felt a helpless inability to show her his burning desire, the truth that lay in his heart.

"Untie me, Sureya, please." He shifted his hips toward her,

craving the weight of her body, the heat of her cunt. "Let me love you."

"Not so fast," she said. "The dragonlords put you at my mercy for a reason." A wicked smile lit her face. "And I plan on enjoying it."

With that she gripped his cock in one hand, and straddled him. In one swift move, he was embedded deep inside of her.

Bending forward, she grabbed his shoulders. "You're going to fuck me so well that I forget a whole year of heartache."

He leaned forward as far as the binds permitted and licked a nipple, then pulled a ring. He felt her throb around his cock.

Never before had he felt so hard, so hungry for any woman. So hungry for her.

"By the Above," he gasped. "You feel so fucking good." He grunted as he buried himself deep inside her. He would have stayed there, savoring her wet heat, but she was moving in short, quick bursts. Her head was thrown back in pleasure, and he knew she was close to coming.

She thrust again, and he met her there. That's all it took.

He felt every muscle in her body start to quiver. She vibrated above him. A hot, boiling ball of ecstasy erupted deep inside of him, radiating into his cock, into his balls. Sureya cried out as he felt her orgasm roil through her. He'd never felt anything like it: his head spun and blue, blinding light flashed behind his eyes.

Only it wasn't behind his eyes. The electric blue light filled the room, as it had on their wedding night in the forest glade.

A heartbeat later, he exploded, emptying himself inside of her. Her cunt tightened around him, wringing him dry with each contraction.

And the blue tendrils curled around her face. The magic between them was thick in the air around them.

The One God, or maybe all the celestial beings, were well pleased.

Gasping for air, Sureya collapsed onto him. As they lay there, their breathing labored, sweat trickling over their bodies to mingle on the bed beneath them, she said, "I love you, too, Kalief."

"I've loved you since the first moment I saw you, so wide-eyed with my cousin," he answered, longing to hold her. "When you insisted on saving that family, even after you knew they'd drugged you, your loyalty amazed me."

"I thought you were a brute," she laughed.

"And you were right."

She bit his nipple playfully. Then she lay her face against his chest so that he couldn't read her expression. He felt her stomach muscles tighten, sensed the tension in her shoulders. "Can you share me, Kalief?" she asked. "Can I fulfill my role as Supplicant to the land and be your queen?" She propped herself up to look at him and asked, "Can you live with that?"

"I cannot live without you, Sureya, and the land cannot live without its Supplicant."

"Will you love me after I've taken the peasant to my bed? After your enemy has made me howl in pleasure? Are you strong enough for that, Kalief? Because I don't think many men are."

"Untie me, my queen, and I will show you."

"Then I'm still your queen?"

"You'll always be my queen."

Sureya expected the indigo haze of the room to dissipate when he fell to his knees and made his heartfelt supplication under dragonspell. She thought they'd immediately find themselves back in the chamber with the Council of Dragons now that their task was completed.

But that's not what happened.

The bed remained, complete with its amethyst coverlet. The

outrageous shoes stayed on her feet, and the leather bra pushed up and presented her breasts.

Kalief flopped back onto the bed and said, "You never did let me see the back of that outfit."

Sureya shifted to her stomach so that he could see the black strap that ran down her spine and over her tailbone. He pounced on her, like he was some jungle cat and she was a prey. "By the Above, I'd love to be that piece of leather," he said.

"I'm sure you could make that supplication," Sureya teased.

"I have something better in mind," he growled.

He licked the backs of her thighs, the curves of her muscled flesh. She breathed in a ragged breath when he sank his teeth into the sensitive flesh right below one buttock. His tongue traveled right under the strap, following the path to the valley of her cheeks.

"What are you doing?"

"Do you trust me?"

He'd asked that before. And she had answered. He'd been a man of his word then. He'd saved her.

"I trust you," she said.

Kalief brought his hands up and massaged her cheeks, spreading them apart until the black leather pressed against that most private part of her.

And then he trailed his tongue down. And down. And he lapped her. He touched her where she'd never been touched. She wanted to run. She wanted more.

She wanted more.

Flipping onto her back, she squirmed and bucked underneath him, urging him to go deeper. To slake the passionate sensations with his pounding cock. Hot flames of desire scorched her, licking at her like flashfire.

He stopped, tearing a small mewling sound from her lips. "Do you love me, Sureya?" She could feel his hot breath against her cheek.

"I do."

"If a Supplicant could bear children, would you bear mine?"

Sureya heard the catbird's call, even as his question shocked her heart. She turned to her back and looked at him. "What are you asking?"

Kalief buried his face between her thighs. His tongue slid over her pearl. She couldn't help herself. She opened her thighs wider for him, bucking her hips toward him.

But again he stopped. When he looked up at her, his eyes were black with desire. "It occurs to me that I'm in a great position to make a wish for myself. Should I wish to hold our child in nine-months' time?"

"Yes," she answered in a catbird's voice, as cherry blossoms fell from her lips. But when he parted her sex with his thumbs and slid his fingers deep inside her, her moan of pleasure sounded exactly like a woman's.

With a sigh, Sureya closed her eyes as Kalief stroked her pearl, traced the contours of the ring. His fingers languidly dipped inside, then over her nub.

She started to quiver, nearing that point, and he sensed it. He straddled her and slid his cock as far as it would go, filling her, filling her completely.

When she met his gaze, she saw love, pure and simple. And she melted into him, pressing her hips toward his. He began to move faster, and she wanted, needed, more of him. Tilting her hips, she urged him for more. She wanted him buried in her.

Together they moved faster still, and then his hand snaked back, sliding over her anus, sliding his fingers down to where her entrances joined.

With a slow, careful movement, his slid one finger into her. The shock it gave her was unadulterated pleasure. He couldn't fill her any more. She couldn't give any more of herself to him.

But she was wrong about that.

As he pounded her with his cock and filled her with his fin-

ger, his free hand stroked her pearl, tugged the ring. With unrelenting pressure he stroked her pearl hard, and it was all she
needed.

Huge waves of ecstasy surged through her veins. Every
muscle in her body quivered with delight, starting deep inside
her belly and reaching her fingertips, her toes, her eyebrows. A
heartbeat later, Kalief joined her in the orgasm. He emptied
himself inside her.

Twined around each other like snakes in autumn, Sureya savored his scent, the weight of his body draping hers.

"My love?" he asked. "Do you see that?"

Sureya opened her eyes and looked.

A cherry tree, filled with fat, ripe fruit, had sprung from the
head of their bed.

Sink your teeth into BLOOD ROSE!
Coming in August 2007
from Aphrodisia . . .

1

---

*L*ondon, *October 18, 1818*

Sex. She wanted sex. But she wanted this anticipation, too.
Serena Lark stirred sensually on the bed, enjoying the feel of
silky sheets beneath her bare skin.

A candle lit the room—it could only be one, for the light
was weak and the candle must be close to guttering. Golden
light wavered on the wall and danced with the reflections of silvery blue moonlight.

Serena's hands skimmed her tummy and touched—boldly
stroked—her cunny, which ached in delightful agony.

Shadows swept over her. She saw the sudden darkness cross
her belly and she looked up. Her heart hammered but she
smiled a greeting at the two masked men who strolled arro-
gantly into her bedchamber. Lord Sommersby and Drake Swift—
the Royal Society's two most famous and daring vampire hunters.
Both men were dressed for the hunt, though masked, and they
swept off their greatcoats as they crossed her threshold.

A gold mask framed Swift's glittering green eyes and a deep

royal purple mask clung to Lord Sommersby's face. Swift threw his hat aside, revealing his unfashionably long white-blond hair. He dropped a crossbow on the floor, followed by a sharpened wooden stake. He lifted a heavy silver cross from around his neck, letting the chain pool on the floor and the cross fall with a clunk.

As dark as Swift was fair, his lordship gave a courtly bow and doffed his hat. Thick, glossy, and dark brown, his hair tumbled over his brow. Her breath caught at the heat in his eyes—the dark, delicious brown of chocolate.

Serena crooked her finger and both men came to her, tugging their cravats loose as they prowled to her bed. They tore at their waistcoats and shirts, and stripped to the waist. She could barely breathe as she drank in the sight of two wide chests. Swift's skin was bronzed to a scandalous shade, which brought the gold curls on his sculpted muscles into stark relief. The earl was massive, possessing a barrel chest and biceps as big as her thighs. He looked like a giant, one with a body honed by battle with the strongest creatures on Earth.

She was dreaming. Even lost in it, she knew somehow. And in this dream, Serena had no idea what to say—what did one say when two men came to one's bed for the first time? Everything seemed inane. She was most terribly shy. And as a governess, she'd been well trained to be a silent servant. But she gave a welcoming moan—the prettiest, most feminine one she could muster.

Tension ratcheted in her. Desire flared as the men approached. They would touch her. Her heart tightened with each long, slow step they took. *Yes. Yes!*

Laudanum. Even here, in her dream, she remembered the laudanum. A few swallows in her cup of tea because she couldn't sleep.

Mr. Swift paused to yank off his trousers, and he flung them aside as he stalked toward her, his ridged abdomen rippling. He wore no small clothes. His magnificent legs were formed of powerful muscle, lean and hard.

And his cock. Serena looked at it and couldn't turn away. It curved toward his navel, thick and erect and surrounded by white-blond curls. She knew it would fill her completely, stretch her impossibly, and she knew it would be perfect inside.

Mr. Swift reached the bed first. He smiled, his teeth a white gleam in the darkened room. His hand reached—she followed the arc of his fingers with breath held—and he touched her bare leg. *Oh!*

"Miss Lark." He dropped to one knee. "Let us dispense with the pleasantries and begin with the delights." And with that he parted her thighs and dove to her wet cunny.

Candlelight played over his broad, tanned shoulders and the large muscles of his arms. His tongue snaked out and slicked over her. Serena arched her head back to scream to the ceiling.

So good!

Boot soles sharply rapped on the floor. Leather-clad knuckles gently brushed her cheek. Lord Sommersby. She flicked her eyelids open as Mr. Swift splayed his hands over her bottom, lifted her to his face, and slid his tongue in to taste her intimate honey.

Lord Sommersby looked so serious, and he never smiled. He required encouragement, so she held out her hand to him, but her smile vanished in a cry of shock and delight as Mr. Swift nudged her thighs wider, until her muscles tugged, and feasted on her. His lips touched her clit, the lightest brush, and pleasure arced through her. She tore the sheets with her fisted hands, heard silken seams rip.

Then, she squealed in frustration as Lord Sommersby lay his strong hand on his partner's shoulder and wrenched Drake Swift from his work.

"She is a woman beyond your ken, Swift. A woman to be both pleasured and treasured."

Pleasured and treasured. Serena could not believe she'd heard those words from the cool, autocratic Earl of Sommersby's lips. He thoroughly disapproved of everything about her, didn't he?

And then the earl was gloriously nude. The hair on his chest was lush and dark, and the curls arrowed down his stomach into a thick black nest between his thighs. His cock was straight and hard and remarkably fat, and it pointed downward, as though too heavy to stand upright. It swayed as he walked.

A sweep of his lordship's arm and his rich purple mask flew aside, revealing dark brown eyes narrowed with lust and a predatory determination in his expression that made his fine features harsh. "Out of my way, Swift."

"I think the lady wants *me* to finish, Sommersby." With an insolent grin, Swift rolled back onto his lean stomach and lowered to her sex once more. She lost all her breath in a whoosh.

To have two such beautiful, naked men argue over which would lick her to ecstasy . . .

It was almost too much to bear.

Lord Sommersby bent and licked her nipples. Of course this was a dream, for she lifted her breasts saucily to the earl and spread her legs wider for Mr. Swift. His lordship sucked her nipple at the exact instant devilish Mr. Swift slid fingers in her cunny and—dear heaven—her rump.

Her heart pounded; her nerves were as taut as a harp's strings. "I will let you bed me," she gasped, "If you let me hunt with you."

Drake Swift laughed, and thrust *two* fingers in her quim and ass. "You were made for this, lass. For naughty fucking. Not for hunting vampires."

How illicit and wonderful it was to be filled, to feel invaded with each thrust of his fingers. Serena looked to Lord Sommersby. "I would never risk your life."

"But you know it is what I want most of all," she whispered.

"Is it?" Drake gave a roguish wink that set her heart spiraling in her chest.

In the blink of her dreaming imagination, both men were kneeling on the bed at her sides, looking down on her, their smiles hot and wild.

How had—?

Mr. Swift's cock approached her mouth from the right, his lordship's from the left. The two huge, engorged heads met in the middle, touching right over her mouth.

Serena had never seen anything so erotic. So wildly arousing that she forgot about decorum, about bargaining, about hunting vampires.

What would if feel like to run her tongue around and between the two heads?

Their fluid was leaking together, making them deliciously wet and shiny—

What on earth was she doing? This was scandalous!

Her mouth opened to protest.

They moved to push their cocks in, parrying for position. Serena lost herself to the moment and stuck out her tongue . . .